"The Bloom family will absolutely have your heart. Ada Bloom
is a sweet, precocious girl traversing that strange territory on the
edge of childhood. Her sister Tilly and brother Ben are testing
the waters of adulthood, each in their own way. Their parents,
Martha and Mike, are both tempted by people in their lives, old
and new, in disastrous ways. Readers will be spellbound by this
honest and tender accounting of each Bloom family member,
told in a chorus of voices, revealing an intimate and flawed family portrait that leaves you feeling connected to everyone around
you. Martine Murray's stunning debut is a true delight."

—**JULIA FIERRO**, *The Gypsy Moth Summer*

"Murray's beautiful gift for language and keen eye for nuanced
human behavior shine in this story of a long, hot summer that
shatters the innocence of young Ada and unravels her family. I
felt this wonderful story as much as read it."

—**SUSAN CRANDALL**, *The Myth of Perpetual Summer*

"In this story of a young Australian family whose concealed decep-
tions are driving them apart, Murray writes with sensual tenderness about the buried yearnings that threaten and sustain our most
cherished relationships, as well as our perverse human tendency to
constantly test their strength."

—**COURTNEY MAUM**, *Costalegre*

Published by Tin House Books, Portland, Oregon

Distributed by W. W. Norton & Company

Library of Congress Cataloging-in-Publication Data

Names: Murray, Martine, author.
Title: The last summer of Ada Bloom / Martine Murray.
Description: Portland, Oregon : Tin House Books, [2020]
Identifiers: LCCN 2019042692 | ISBN 9781947793613 (paperback) | ISBN 9781947793620 (ebook)
Classification: LCC PR9619.4.M872 L37 2020 | DDC 823/.92--dc23
LC record available at https://lccn.loc.gov/2019042692

First US Edition 2020
Printed in the USA
Interior design by Diane Chonette

www.tinhouse.com

THE
LAST SUMMER
OF
ADA
BLOOM

MARTINE MURRAY

TIN HOUSE BOOKS / Portland, Oregon

For Mannie

1

Ada found a forgotten windmill. She was walking with PJ in the patch of bush between her house and Toby Layton's. She was already nine and still wearing her jumper back to front. PJ was old and broad as a wombat, with three legs that worked, so he waddled along and Ada often had to stop and wait for him. She swished a stick, absentmindedly whacking at the tea tree and singing over and over again, "Did you ever come to meet me, Farmer Joe, Farmer Joe?" She couldn't remember the next line. She wasn't sure the words were right, but because she was alone, and because it was her traveling-along song, she sang as loudly and confidently as a trumpet. The bush was unaffected by her song. This was the great consolation trees provided—they heard her without commenting.

It was early enough that the air was cool and there was a damp, silvery gleam and rustle to the leaves. The song ribboned ahead, as if escaping, drawing her through the thin trees and pale sky as if she belonged to the landscape—as if she were not the child Ada Bloom with a bunk bed and a green bike and words to speak and homework to do, but a creature whose soul could rise with the trees and enter by the breath of song.

Ada followed her song deeper into the bush, until the wind-mill loomed up before her. Its tin blades creaked and flapped like startled elbows, causing Ada to swallow her song whole. She gathered herself with some indignation. She had never seen this windmill or the little clearing it presided over. Was it right that it should be here, hiding away in her own patch of forest? Its stature made it seem important but also forbidding, like the headmaster at school, whose appearance caused in Ada the same sort of dis-obedient urge she was feeling now. And if Mr. Gray had been a windmill instead of an old headmaster, this was exactly the sort of windmill he would be: stern as a judge, with a ghostly clanging air and rotting on the inside.

The windmill was cross, Ada could tell, because it had been forgotten. It was terrible to be forgotten. As if it were a curse to think it, Ada dropped to her knees and scratched her name into the dirt with her stick. *Ada is here.*

But the windmill didn't care. It was bitter and stricken, so haunted with olden times and so neglected by current ones that its struts were as rutted and splintering as old people's bones. From its damp wooden skeleton came the stink of rot. Ada never wanted to become an old person. The old windmill was secretly forlorn about it and probably dying. Yet it wasn't this aspect of death that scared Ada, but more the sense that the old windmill was possessed of a life and that, with the remaining shreds of it, it rattled and stood, guarding its last tenure with mad gusts of faltering pride. Ada moved forward to touch it, half hoping for a nasty great-aunt shriek. Instead, and in a malevolent silence, it revealed a great never-ending hole, which it straddled, and from which came a chill breath of buried darkness. Ada stepped back.

PJ gave the hole a wary sniff. This hole definitely had some intent; it was square and lined with wood. Fixed to one side was a wooden ladder whose first rungs had almost rotted away.

The ladder went farther into the hole than Ada could see. She dropped her stick in and watched the hole swallow it. She didn't hear it land.

Her mind began to dance. What lay at the bottom of the hole? Did the hole even have a bottom, or did it go right through the earth? What would happen to her if she dropped into the hole? A pleasant tremor of danger passed through her; she squatted next to PJ for comfort. Then she stood up and pushed some dried leaves and twigs into the hole with her foot and leaned over to watch them fall. The sight made her vision almost black with dizziness and she ran back through the bush, as if something were chasing her, even if it was just the thought of climbing down into that hole.

She ran home to get the others. There was no point in climbing into the hole if nobody saw her do it.

Tilly was at the window, reading. She uncurled her legs and frowned disbelievingly. "Don't tell Mum or we won't be allowed to go there." She sighed, as if weary of the hole before she had seen it.

Let her be bored. Tilly was already seventeen and had taken on grown-up airs. But after Ada had rounded up the littles, and Raff Cavallo and Ben, Tilly decided she would come, after all.

Ada led them through the bush to the old windmill. She was planning to show Raff her trees. Especially William Blake, who was the largest, a blue gum. Ada had found names for the trees on the spines of her mother's books. In her mind, Emily Dickinson, who was a black-tailed wallaby, was standing nearby, marveling at Ada's courage.

But Emily Dickinson wasn't there, and Ada didn't tell Raff anything about William Blake. Instead, as they all followed her through the bush, she bloated up with a shy sort of importance, so that she marched irreverently, like a grown-up, ignoring the trees.

When Tilly saw the endless hole, she pretended it wasn't anything. She said it was a mineshaft left over from the gold rush. She walked back through the bush without even dropping a stone into the hole. Ada watched her disappear into the tea tree and fumed. Tilly had ruined the hole's mystery. Tilly had named it, though it was too full of gloom and portent to be gathered up into a name.

Raff watched her go too. He watched her intently for ages, and he jerked his head away as if he'd been stung. He picked up a stone and flung it at the windmill blades, which it hit and ricocheted off. None of the others cared though. It was clear that the most thrilling way to use the hole was to dare to climb down the ladder and to see how far it went.

"I'll go first, since I am the one who discovered it," Ada declared. If she went first, before the big boys, everyone would know Ada Bloom was someone.

The hardest part was that the first rungs were rotting. If her foot slipped or a rung gave way, she would fall down the hole like that stick. She went as fast as she could, so as to not leave her weight anywhere for too long. Tilly was wrong—the hole was alive, swarming with secret blackness and doom. Ada could feel it. Hidden there were the earth's insides: the unseen, long-silenced, rattling bones of life's endings. And it reached up and around her with a cold-tongue quiet. She drew herself into a tight fist of concentration and went deeper. Down into elsewhere, while the world faded and the bush sounds hushed, and the daylight shrunk itself into a heartbeat of brightness above her.

Ben was shouting at her. The panic in his voice came chasing her down the hole.

Her stomach unfurled. If she didn't get up right away, she would fall. She raced against the old windmill, against its endless, obliterating hole. A monstrous, unholy death had her within its grasp.

She reached the top and wriggled out, blinking in the light and gasping with relief.

Ben glared at her. "You shouldn't have done that, Ada," he said.

But Ada was elated. She had gone so close to death and escaped it. She gazed up triumphantly at Raff Cavallo. For one glorious moment their grins burst together in a conspiratorial fire, but in the same instant Raff trampled it all with a snort of laughter. "Crazy kid," he said. "You could have died."

2

Ada didn't need Martha to walk her to the bus, but Martha wanted to. It was one of the simple rituals of motherhood still available to her. PJ needed the walk too. It was the right distance for a three-legged dog. The walk took twenty minutes. She could give her whole attention to it. And Ada and PJ were the easiest beings to walk with: Ada's little hand nestled in hers, and PJ's lopsided waddle accompanied Ada's birdlike chatter. The world felt as if it had been dreamed into existence.

Someone had told Martha that listening to birdsong was good for one's health. So there was that too. Health was important. And to watch the morning take hold was worthwhile, to be borne up by the unfolding motion of it, as if she too were just a tree shaking its branches in the growing light.

Afterward, with just PJ, she felt a slight downturn in mood, as if through a crack in the atmosphere, her simple, timeless morning was losing air. Was it that the bus had taken away Ada and Martha's task? That PJ panted and plodded—an incontrovertible sign of old age, inevitable and looming? Soon she would be the one to plod and pant or hobble inelegantly along. And now that the walk was almost over, she would be home again, and life would surge in with all its vague dissatisfactions and petty irritations: the kitchen would be a mess, the day would be too hot, the garden would need to be watered. Even worse was the sense that none of this mattered. Whatever did matter eluded her.

Today at least was swim club. Today she'd meet Susie at the pool. She could never talk herself into exercise; she had to arrange to meet Susie there or she wouldn't go. Even then she was reluctant. She didn't like swimming—she liked having swum. She liked moaning with Susie afterward in the sauna. It was possibly more therapeutic to moan than to swim. Martha only swam for her arthritic toe. When she first got the pain and the doctor had said the word *arthritis*, her heart dived and hid. The diagnosis was the first sign, a harbinger of the degradations of age. She had arrived on that other side of life where bodies start to undo.

Of course, it wasn't exactly like that. Life was fluid; she had been undoing for a long time, and every now and then something had the bad taste to make a stark announcement. The woman at the pool didn't have arthritis yet, it had to be said. She wore cornflower-blue eye shadow and a sun visor. She was cheerful and always said, "Enjoy your swim." The pool had recently been subjected to a renovation. What satisfaction it must have given that cheerful lady to set that potted palm in the reception area, endowing it with a hint of hotel-lobby pizzazz.

But Martha missed the old pool. Or maybe she just missed the man at the desk who used to call her "mate" as he leaned on one oversize arm. "Mate, it's bloody hot, isn't it?" Always sunstruck or slightly hungover or just so lazy his voice dropped out as if by mistake. He had once surprised her by mentioning the difficulty of getting his double bass into the car. How had he mustered the energy to learn an instrument when he could barely be bothered to talk? Another time he told her the pool was closed on certain Fridays for nude swimming. She couldn't tell if he was joking or not. He was one of those men. Dry, large, laconic. She loved how devoid of ambition or drive he was. He was another country to her.

Then one day he was gone. No one knew what happened. He just skipped town. So he was a scoundrel, really. Martha was glad to have known a scoundrel. The pool was closed for months. And she hadn't realized till then that the man at the desk, the scoundrel whose name she didn't know, had been part of her life. Now it didn't feel the same to go swimming. The pool was bright, as if someone had just turned the lights on and cleaned out all the shadows.

Susie was all for the new brightness. She was in the changing room, already humming, one foot on the wooden bench, stuffing her hair under her rubber cap, ignoring Sheila who was head down, drying her hair with the hand dryer, her showered body pink and gleaming like a pig. Sheila was older and doing pottery and waiting for grandchildren to appear. At that end of life. Brimming with observations, Sheila guffawed a lot and said things like "what rubbish, what utter rot," and since these disparagements issued from the authority of a naked body, they seemed to Martha irrefutable, even if she disagreed. Even Sheila's flat sloping breasts were not obliged to be otherwise. There was some dignity in this. Sheila's body was as comfortable as an old tracksuit. Martha's body was a site of fault lines, from which she averted her own gaze with an anxious sense of failure.

Sheila paused to give forth on her lover Peter—why did Martha always imagine him in striped pajamas?—whose house had recently flooded and who bored her in most ways, but she put up with him for the sex. Martha blushed inwardly, but outwardly she laughed like a compatriot. As if she too would take a boring man as a lover just for the sex.

Martha undressed quickly. Then she swam as fast as she could. She always did it this way. The idea of exercise made it tiring. She was tired of feeling there was something she should have done, arrived at, vanquished. She gave it all she had and collapsed. Susie paced herself, went steady the whole way.

Susie had first approached Martha at the kids' school, wearing lipstick and a tube skirt and showing straightaway that she had an animal nature. Since Tilly had made friends with her daughter, Alice, Susie thought she and Martha should have a cup of coffee. Martha didn't drink coffee—her system was too fragile—but she said yes anyway, as she was ashamed of her fragility and the caution it required, and she sometimes staged minor, fleeting rebellions, which she later regretted. Susie instantly consulted a diary. Martha thought they could never be friends, but later in Susie's kitchen, Susie had laughed avidly and given Martha the sense that there was something else to be got at in life, something Martha had not yet uncovered. She spoke of everything as if it were still alive with possibility. At their first meeting, Susie had peered over her mug of coffee and said, "Well, my dear husband, Joe, kindest man alive, but he has some trouble, you know . . ."

Martha didn't know. She waited.

Susie put her hand to her mouth as if sheltering the admission, though no one was there except Martha. "Getting it up," she said.

Martha had met Joe already. He was a big, kind, weary man with a slight paunch. Martha felt for him. He looked like someone whose will had been stamped on early in life and who had given in to his own diminishment. Not like Mike. Mike strutted from one posture to the next, a real rooster. He was always ready for action.

"Oh, my husband has the opposite problem—of keeping it down." Martha shocked herself by saying such a thing. She had meant it to be funny—though it was true.

But Susie didn't laugh; she slid luxuriously forward across her peach laminate bench. "Honey, in my book, that is not a problem."

Martha laughed to cover up a sudden feeling of inadequacy. She felt so unwomanly, so lacking in carnal impulse. Yet it was thrilling to be in the midst of such a conversation and she wanted it to keep going. No one had ever before spoken to her about the deep and personal intricacies of relationships. Maybe she and Susie would be friends after all.

Over the years, Martha had been surprised at how much she was able to divulge, how Susie's candor had led her out of herself, and how it was a relief to say it: to admit she was bored; her husband was tiresome; he only thought about one thing, no two things—sex and tennis.

That wasn't true, of course. Though the possibility that it could be true had shocked Martha, once she had said it. She tried to think of what she loved in Mike. His jaw, for instance, when he leaned in to kiss her. His good humor and steadiness. His reliability. If he said he would do something, he would. That was something, after all. Mike had nice hands too; when he irritated her, she would look at his hands to see if they might strike in her that little flare of love.

Martha summoned another burst of energy and plunged into her laps again. She tried to keep her head down and watch the painted line beneath her and not think so much. When she fatigued, she thought of her big toe and pushed on. If she stopped for too long, the ache in her toe joint would get the better of her. There was another woman who swam for her arthritis, an English woman with buck teeth, who told Martha that when she was a young mother in England she had been so poor she had eaten chips from a rubbish bin. Martha couldn't offer anything that would compare. She wanted to have lived beyond the bounds of her own small existence. She wanted to be a loudmouth, to have skipped town, played the double bass, driven trucks across deserts, got drunk in dive bars and been dirt poor, lost in the wilderness or jailed for protesting. The things she hadn't done seemed more character building than those she had, and she suspected that those sorts of experiences were what she was lacking. She hadn't transgressed. She had simply kept going. What had made her so careful?

After the pool, she and Susie steamed themselves in the sauna. Susie leaned back, lifted her feet and circled her ankles. "What's on today?" she said.

"Dishes, chickens, dog, children—my exciting life." Martha didn't mention Arnold Buch. He was coming for tea and she was trying not to think about him.

Susie rolled her eyes.

Martha went on. "I dreamed I came home and everything in my house had been stolen. It was empty. I started to tell someone what I needed, what I would miss, and I couldn't remember—I couldn't remember what was even in the house."

"You want me to analyze?"

"I don't know."

"Okay, you're sad about some loss, but you don't know what that loss is?"

Youth, Martha thought, but she didn't say it, because this was obvious and dull. She had fallen to thinking about how there was nothing in the house after all, nothing she would need to take with her, nothing she could count in the big tally at the end of it all.

"Joe is depressed," Susie said. "He was reading about John Lennon today. It's two years since he was shot. Joe's got such a tender heart. He despairs about a world in which John Lennon can get assassinated."

Martha felt a pang of love for Joe. It made sense that Joe loved John Lennon. John Lennon had been the guiding star of her burst of youth. He'd stood against the tide of opinion and Martha had admired that.

"Apparently the man who shot him was reading *The Catcher in the Rye*. Have you read it? I was in love with Holden Caulfield when I was young," Susie said.

Martha had read it. She wasn't sure she would like it now. She felt old and despairing. It was as if in failing to escape a steadily advancing orthodoxy, she had been flattened by it. It crushed the peace movement and John Lennon, and it turned the ear away from birdsong.

And, on top of all that, Arnold Buch was coming to tea.

3

Tilly didn't see why she had to be there. Ben had got out of it because he had cricket practice. Usually she was just a disappointment. Martha always berated her afterward. *Why didn't you use their names? Please look at someone when you speak to them. Stand up straight, you're always hunching, you don't want bad posture.*

When Mr. Buch arrived, Tilly stood up straight and said, "Hello, Mr. Buch."

Mr. Buch said, "Call me Arnold. No one calls me Mr. Buch."

But she couldn't call him Arnold. She didn't call any adults by their real names. She would have to avoid calling him anything and her mother would be annoyed.

Mr. Buch crossed his legs as he settled into the living room chair. He was a tall gray-haired man, elegantly dressed but awkward in the chair, as if his limbs were not amenable to folding. He reached into his jacket and pulled out a packet of cigarettes. Martha told Ada to get an ashtray. Ada was staring at him, wide-eyed. Because he was unknown and had arrived from their parents' past—that exotic place that seemed to have happened in black and white on beaches and outside motels with names like Time and Tide Motor Inn. Arnold Buch looked like history, like someone you might meet on an overnight train. Tilly suspected he was an intellectual, because of his style, which was dignified and seemed impervious to trend, though his expression was similar to a baby's, gazing about in wonder. How could her parents fit with this man? They were so unremarkable, so normal, so humdrum. What exoticness had her parents' lives once touched?

Her mother had gone to a lot of trouble. She had vacuumed the house, puffed the couch cushions, and made cake with the blood plums. She'd put on a dress with a panel of black lace, which made her look like she had borrowed someone else's glamour. She was wearing lipstick. Even this seemed extravagant.

"Tilly plays the piano," Mike said to Mr. Buch.

"No, I don't," said Tilly, appalled. She'd never had a lesson. What she did on the piano was like finger painting.

"Yes, you do," said Mike. "She doesn't learn; she makes things up." Her father was doing his best to impress Mr. Buch. "Arnold is a great pianist," Mike explained, crossing his feet. He didn't know where to look. Martha blushed. Tilly began to crumple inwardly.

"I can play chopsticks," Ada jumped in.

Mr. Buch nodded, but he didn't say anything to Ada. He looked at Tilly.

It was surprising he didn't indulge Ada like adults usually did. Obviously he had no experience with kids. He leaned forward, as if about to tell Tilly something important.

"Would you like a drink, Arnold?" Martha interrupted. "I've made a plum cake for dessert. I never make cakes, so be warned."

Mr. Buch stared at Martha as if he had never seen her before. For a moment he didn't answer her. He smiled and slipped his cigarette packet back into his coat.

"So, what do you do now, Arnold? Do you have a family?" Mike drew Ada onto his knee. Ada was curious enough about Mr. Buch to oblige and stay.

"Yes, I have a dog. Beefheart. A fine family we are. We often go out walking. Over the hills."

"Where do you live?"

"In a small village in England, near Bath. I spend a lot of time walking in the woods, so to speak. Occasionally I come back here to see my mother and sister. I lead a fairly itinerant life, but that way I can cause as much trouble as I like: I'm always about to leave."

"What's itinerant?" said Ada, wriggling.

"That just means he is always on the move," said Mike.

"What sort of trouble do you cause?" said Martha, arriving with a gin and tonic.

"Oh, just the usual. Highway robbery. That sort of thing."

"But what's your line of work?" pressed Mike.

Arthur Buch's eyes showed a sort of faint amusement. He glanced at the ice in his drink and swirled it around, as if he had found in the drink whatever it was he was looking for.

"Well, I'm a futurist. Which means I look at what could happen in the future and, in some cases, what should happen in the future, in order to prevent what might otherwise happen in the more distant future."

There was a silence. Martha frowned. She looked as if she were not listening to Arnold Buch, though she was staring right at him. Ada jumped off Mike's lap and helped herself to cheese and a biscuit. Tilly watched her mother.

"Jesus, Arnold, that sounds complicated," said Mike.

"Not really. It's like being the weatherman."

Martha smoothed her dress over her knees.

"What do you see, then, for the future, Arnold?"

"Dark times, mainly."

"What do you mean?"

"I mean as long as we continue to believe that prosperity depends on economic growth . . . I mean, we pollute the ocean, the sky, the earth."

The way he said this, with his eyes faintly closed, like a priest, as if this were a religion, were magic. Tilly stared at him. What he said had to be true.

"That's a bit dramatic," Mike said.

"Have you forgotten too, Arnold?" said Martha. Her voice was cold.

Arnold Buch faltered. "No," he said. "I don't think so." It was the first time he seemed uncertain. Tilly liked him better then. As if he felt it, he turned to her. "How old are you, Tilly? Do you like the ocean?"

Tilly startled. It wasn't that it was an odd question, but it was odd coming from Mr. Buch—he looked as if he knew what she was thinking, as if he and she both knew something that no one else would understand.

"I'm seventeen. I like the sea. But we never go there."

Mr. Buch didn't reply. He didn't seem to take much interest in the answer. Perhaps she wasn't any different from anyone else, after all.

"We have a son, too. He's fifteen, but he's playing cricket right now. He's very athletic. Like Mike," said Martha. She glanced at Mike.

Mr. Buch smiled. He turned to Ada. "And what about you?"

Ada frowned as she considered this. "I just make things up to play."

"Oh, that's the best way to play, I think," said Mr. Buch.

It was always Ada that people liked the best, thought Tilly. She didn't care. She took a biscuit and left the room.

4

Mike knew they would have to talk about it. Martha would ask him. She always dragged everything through such unnecessary scrutiny. He had already begun to prepare his thoughts. He envied Arnold, who would be sitting on a train, alone. There would be no one countering him, prodding him. What did Martha need to discuss, anyway? They had performed their lives for Arnold as well as they could.

Of course, Arnold was never going to be impressed by anything as conventional as their lives. But Mike had inadvertently managed to impress himself. He and Arnold had stepped from the tidy living room into the garden, with its sun-singed lawn, strewn with relics of family life: a rusty swing set, totem tennis, the homemade tree swing that Ada had painted sky blue, PJ panting in the shade of the elm. This wasn't just his life's backdrop; it was inscribed with his existence. It proved him. His children's lives were worn into this patch of earth. His bones knew this place. The house's atmosphere was alive in him. He had a life worth holding on to. His gaze roved so possessively over the garden that he was almost oblivious to Arnold, and the quiet rapture that came from the perceived sense of his own life entirely absorbed him.

But later, Mike had clapped Arnold on the back as he got on the train, more with a sense of relief than triumph. He realized he no longer needed Arnold's approval. At one point in his life, to prove something to Arnold Buch had been everything.

Martha was already doing the dishes when he got back from dropping Arnold at the station. She was wearing an old dress.

"You've changed," he said. The dress had been for Arnold, not for him. She hardly ever dressed up for him.

"Yes," she sighed. "I didn't want to get it dirty."

He knew that sigh, that tone of voice. Like a north wind it came, full of hot, silent reproach. For what this time? Had he said the wrong thing? Maybe he shouldn't have boasted about Tilly playing the piano. Had he embarrassed Martha by revealing their little failures as parents? Martha was difficult. His family, the warm little rosy unit he had just folded into his heart, was already dissipating. He leaned against the bench, folded his arms. Could he be bothered trying to rally her? He could put his arms around her. She would probably prefer he get the tea towel.

"Where are the girls?" he said, doing neither.

"I don't know. Tilly is probably in her room. She's obsessed with her John Lennon record. She's playing it over and over." Martha didn't turn from the sink.

"Have you got a headache?"

"No, I'm all right." At last she turned. She looked at him while wiping her hair off her face with her forearm, her hands deep in yellow rubber gloves.

"Arnold seemed well," he offered. One of them had to say something. Arnold Buch had always been a silence between them. Mike had expected her to prod, to push against that silence. But that night was so distant and sealed off, like a tomb inside him, that anything she said would falter against it. He could feel his own resistance to even thinking about it. Now that Arnold had come and gone without incident, he could relax again.

"I guess so." She leaned her back against the sink. "It was a shock seeing him as a middle-aged man. We must have looked old to him too. Old and boring."

So that was it. She felt the opposite of what he had felt. He had wanted to come home, to the room with his family in it, his lovely wife who made cake, his daughters who had accomplishments, and his son who was athletic like him. But Martha had changed into an old dress, had got herself in a sour mood, and his children were nowhere to be seen.

"Honey, you still look young," he said. He wasn't lying, though he felt as if he were. He had got so accustomed to lies, sometimes the truth felt more awkward.

"No, it's not that, it's what I feel . . . I feel like I . . . failed . . . I don't know . . ."

At least she wasn't questioning him about Arnold Buch. At least she was, as usual, thinking about herself. She pulled the yellow gloves off and came toward him. She leaned into him and began to cry.

"What is it?" he said. He did love her after all. He did. He held her head as if it were a precious thing.

She turned her face to the side, resting it against his chest as she hugged him close.

5

A foreboding had gotten inside Ada and she couldn't get it out again. Something felt threatening and inevitable. The sun had shrunk the whole town, turned it brittle as a pip and sucked the creeks dry. The cherry tree had died, though Ada had emptied the cold kettle water under it every day. No wonder the people of the town were tired; if the sun didn't stop drying everything to a cinder, their hearts would turn as black and hard as coal. They all needed to sit still and pant. Or lie on their backs in the shade. But they carried on, just like the flies that buzzed and thudded like fools against the kitchen windowpane.

"These flies drive me crazy," said Ada.

When Tilly didn't reply, Ada let out a loud sigh and added, "The way they carry on!" She leaned over the stool and hung her arms as if they had just died. The flies weren't really to blame, but it was relieving to blame something: something small enough to do battle with, something other than the scorched summer days that arrived, one after the other without stopping, emblazoned and glaring and wiped of detail. The density and darkness and edge of life was all gone.

Tilly was smoking a cigarette and wearing a nice dress. She had turned on the fan above the stove and was standing near the window, so their mother wouldn't know. "There's a fire at Mount Macedon. It's burnt the whole north side of the mountain already. Because of the drought. That lemon tart shop has probably already burnt down," she said.

Bushfires didn't scare Ada. There were enough people afraid of them; she wasn't joining that queue. She had her very own fear and it belonged to her and she preferred it that way. The heat and Ada had their own private struggle, but the heat was winning.

"I heard about this woman," Tilly continued, fanning the smoke with her hand. "I heard her talking on the radio because she got burnt so badly by a ball of fire that her skin was black, and she nearly died. Well, she would have died if the neighbor didn't put her in the pool. And she lay in the pool nearly dying and watched her blackened skin float around her. And when she was in the hospital, every breath she took was so painful the nurse couldn't bear to watch it, and she thought she would die for sure. But she had two little girls who she had saved from the fireball by putting a blanket over them. She wanted to live for them. And she believed in God too. It always helps people survive if they think God is going to lend a hand."

Tilly said this with a little sniff, and Ada knew what it meant. She didn't like it when Tilly besmirched God. Ada believed in him. That ghost man who watched from the sky and looked like Gregory Peck and made your wishes come true if you were helpful to your mother.

"Mum wouldn't have done that," Tilly said. She squished her cigarette into the gold-rimmed china saucer and ran water over it.

"Wouldn't have done what?" asked Ada.

"You know." She leaned on the kitchen bench and sighed, pulling at her dark fringe to smooth it.

Ada got off the stool and turned it upside down and tried to stand inside the upturned legs.

"She would have for Ben, though," Tilly continued airily. "She'd put Ben under the blanket first."

Ada gripped the legs of the stool and began to rock it. She could ride it. She could ride it right out the door and keep going.

"You'll break it, Ada, or you'll hurt yourself." Tilly's sigh spread like a damp cloud over everything.

Ada stopped rocking. She squinted at Tilly suspiciously. If she looked hard enough, she might see past the new Tilly through to the old one. The new Tilly was hard to understand. Even the way she stood promised something and hid it too. What it promised Ada didn't know, but she did know it wasn't a direct thing—it was smoky and silent and sideways. Tilly wasn't a child anymore, and she wasn't grown up either. She was seventeen and no one was grown up till they were eighteen, but Tilly was trying to be eighteen, and Ada thought it gave her an unnatural sort of poise. It wasn't only because she was wearing lipstick and her hair was brushed, it was the sense of her being purposeful and sly. Tilly pulled at her shining dark fringe as if it might curtain her off from the world.

"Where are you going?" asked Ada.

"I'm not going anywhere, yet. I'm looking after you, remember, till Dad gets back." Tilly spoke with a slow whisper. She lowered her gaze, as if it had been too heavy to hold. The flies buzzed at the window. Ada poked at a half-eaten piece of watermelon on a plate.

"Why are you dressed up then?" Ada stood the stool back up the right way and sat on it straight and tall. She was uncomfortable again. The summer strain was mixed up with Tilly becoming different and she couldn't quite separate the two feelings. There should be a way that this could be worked out and got right.

"Well, I'm just ready for the party." Tilly had turned her head away and was staring into the hot still air. What was she thinking?

"Whose party? Will there be boys there? Raff Cavallo?" Ada sang his name. Raff had divorced parents around whom Ada sensed an enticing whiff of scandal. He was in the gang that included her brother, Ben, and Will Rand. Will Rand's mother smoked marijuana and let her three children do whatever they wanted, but their father was strict, and all the children were frightened of him. Raff, who was in Tilly's class at school, was the most interesting in Ada's opinion because his mother was rumored to have been a musical star when she was young. She still dressed quite flamboyantly. Even better, she had never baked a cake for the school fete, let alone attended it, all because she preferred to play piano.

Both Ada and Tilly had heard the talk about these two women, and while it spiked Ada's interest it had the opposite effect on Tilly, who looked at Raff as if he were a criminal.

"Of course, there'll be boys," Tilly said. "It's Gwendolyn Bell's party."

Tilly was not explaining things properly.

"Who is Gwendolyn Bell?" Such a name. Ada pictured her with windswept hair and a silver goblet in her hand.

Tilly made a tiny frown. "You always want to know everything. Gwendolyn Bell—there's nothing particular about her, she's just having a party. I hardly know her. She's finished school; it's her twenty-first. They've got a horse in their paddock."

"Then why are you going to her party if you don't know her?"

Tilly gave Ada a withering look. She sighed to show that the conversation had become tiresome, as if she had more important thoughts to attend to. Ada rolled her eyes to make a matching or even more bored expression, but she realized she still wanted to know the answer.

"Oh, Snug, it's just that everyone's going. It's that kind of party. You'll see one day. It's not like a kid's birthday party. I don't know if I truly want to go. I'm not sure I like those sorts of girls with those sorts of bedrooms, you know, where things match and there are standards." Tilly paused, and her hands drummed at the bench. "It's too hot to think. I'm going to ring Alice. You'll have to play on your own for a while."

Ada didn't get a chance to ask what standards. Tilly heaved herself up from the bench and with this one movement was gone from the kitchen. All that was left was a waft of cigarette smoke.

Ada watched the late-afternoon light stream in the window. It was golden and velvety, and caught the hovering motes of dust so that they sparkled as they turned slowly in the air. She drifted into a tender, sad mood because of the way the light and dust slowed time to a halt and opened up a soft hole of memory, and she had the sense that something had happened and would never happen again. She tried to think what it could be. It was the dying light that made her sad, because time died over and over again. Each day threw out its last lone note of beauty like a plaintive howl, and then it was finished. Dead forever. Passed over. She sank onto the stool with a quiet thud. The clock ticked loudly and wickedly, the vine leaves on the veranda drooped and the enamel water jug gleamed on the bench as if basking in its own splendor. For a moment life was so deep and still that Ada felt she had dissolved all her Ada-ness and had become part of everything. She was a golden mote of spinning dust.

Ada had not forgotten the small pain of Tilly's party. She resented it and she resented Gwendolyn Bell. The party was what was changing Tilly. Tilly composed herself carefully with her mind shined to a point, and she no longer crawled in the garden and she shunned the tire swing and the wild, stumbling, searching beat of how things used to be. Tilly had just finished school, and in the lead-up to her final exams, she had begun to do homework instead of lying about outside by the trampoline. Either that or she played the piano. Ada had never seen any determination in Tilly before and she felt excluded by it. Tilly had become sharper, arrow-like, and perhaps she had become thinner too, slipping quietly through doors, as if she were deliberately fading herself out.

Ada's heart flung itself into the gap between how things used to be and how they were becoming and strained to drag everything to one place. Soon there would be a breaking or a snapping or an ending. What would end she didn't know.

She stood up and pressed her face to the window. The grass outside bristled beneath the weight of another day of scorching heat. The sun had squashed the lawn down to a pale straw color. The cherry tree stood dead and stiff and as bare as a skeleton, with its branches reaching up as if it longed to wrench itself out of the ground and fly up to the heavens. Ada didn't want to look at it all the time and think about how it had died. What was it like for a tree to die? Ben was supposed to cut it down.

Ada could still smell Tilly's cigarette. If their mother smelled it Tilly would cop it. But their mother was in Melbourne visiting their granny and her friend Glenda who had a sadness disease. Glenda wore long black dresses and had small round glasses and was given to staring mournfully into the distance and eating Tim Tams on the sly. Whenever Glenda got the sad sickness, Martha went to stay with her, and she often came home with something new: a book or new clothes for herself. Ada was glad her mother wasn't home, sniffing for clues. Old Sherlock, they called her. Ada could take all the fruit she wanted and not get told off for being greedy.

She leaned over the fruit bowl to see what she'd eat next. But there were only apples left and they were floury, and some had patches of brown rot. She should go and see what Louis and May were doing next door, see if they were watching television. But she remembered that she hated Louis and she had told everyone that he was the meanest person in the world because he had punched her. Tilly said Ada had probably done something first to upset Louis. She always stuck up for everyone else.

Ada flung open the flywire door and let it bang shut. She went straight to the cherry tree and put her hands on it. Perhaps there was still a trickle of life in it, a little hum going up and down the trunk. Ada listened; she listened so hard, her face turned red.

Ben was never going to get around to digging it up. It would stand there dead the whole summer.

6

It was almost dark, and their father was still not home. Ada sat at the kitchen table sorting her rock collection. She was hungry. Every now and then she glanced up at the sunset: a luminous smear of silvery pink sinking behind the dead cherry tree. She felt obliged to watch. If she ignored a show like that, if she didn't watch things that were splendid and final, she would adjust to magnificence as if it were nothing. She didn't want to watch it. If only it would be done with, so she could concentrate on her rocks. The flies had stopped buzzing and the heat was a thick dullness that seemed to have enclosed everything.

Tilly appeared again, wearing their mother's best shoes: high-heeled silver ones with a strap round the ankle.

"Mum will really kill you if she finds out," said Ada.

"She won't find out." Tilly stood staring at the shoes, willing them to not be found out, the bones in her shoulders hunching up under the straps of the dress. Louis's and May's voices sang out from next door. May shouted crossly. Louis had thrown a plum at her. A sprinkler hissed. The garden sighed beneath the twilight sky. It was going to be a stinker of a night, and Tilly was making everything worse by wearing those shoes.

Their father came in and slumped onto a kitchen stool, making a show of his hard day. He tugged at his green tie and wriggled his neck out of the shirt collar. He specialized in life insurance and had to wear a suit nearly every day, so he was sometimes dissatisfied with life and plainly sick of death. Ada knew, too, that he was once a handsome man. That was what her mother said when she told the story of why she married him in the first place. Her mother always said, "And what a fool was I," and smiled with her teeth, to show it was a joke.

Mike glanced up at Tilly, who sat on the other stool in her shimmery blue dress, doodling with a pen on the electricity bill. She was showing off the high-heeled shoes, with her ankles crossed.

"Are you going out?"

"I already told you I am." She sat waiting, her head tilting to examine her drawing.

"Okay, okay. Where's Ben?"

"He's not home," said Ada, pleased that Ben could be in trouble. "He's probably at cricket training." Ada was sorting her rocks into piles: piles of ones she liked the most and ones she didn't like as much, and ones that she would give away to other people if they wanted one, and ones that didn't belong anywhere. For these unbelonging ones she had some sympathy.

Their father squinted as he sorted through the information. He rubbed at his face, glanced at his watch, and bounced up out of the chair.

"Well, I need a shower."

"What about dinner?" Ada burst out. She was holding a pinkish piece of quartz and couldn't think to put it in any pile now, though it was a piece she had always had strong feelings about. She was too hungry and too tired to reason with either the rock or her father.

"Dinner?" Mike looked at Tilly helplessly.

But Tilly wasn't going to help him. She was going out. She sailed her gaze out the window again to show it, and Mike sank back onto the stool and began to frown and rub again at his head. Even his hair didn't sit straight, and his leg bounced up and down, one hand tapping at his knee. He looked as if he'd arrived in someone else's life. "Well, I forgot about dinner," he finally admitted.

"Can't we get fish-and-chips?" Ada dropped her pink rock and rushed forward, hopping on one leg in front of him. All was not lost. They never got to have fish-and-chips. If their mother were home, it would be hard-boiled eggs, but their father couldn't boil an egg.

"I suppose so, if it's still open." He fished his wallet out of his pocket. Ada thought he was going to say he didn't have any money, but he looked inside it and nodded at her. "Come on, then."

At the door he turned to Tilly—Tilly, with her mermaid legs, lost in her own promise of adventure. He frowned. He had to win something back, whatever it was he had lost. "And you need to be home before twelve," he said with an uncharacteristic sternness.

Tilly grinned as if she didn't care what he said.

Ada wished Tilly would care more. Their father would feel special. And Martha wouldn't be at everyone about everything, and Ben wouldn't be the only one, the only one who—Ada couldn't remember what. She was tying her shoelaces and getting ready to go. If only Tilly behaved better. If only everyone was like the nice people in the Gregory Peck movies. Instead, life was unsteady, sometimes prickly, but slow and dreary too. She could never be sure whether it really was what you thought it was or if it were a theater show, all slipping behind the curtain of pretending.

"Wait, can I get a lift?" Tilly erupted, dropping her pen. "To Farnsworth Street."

"Did you hear me? Home by midnight." Mike was insistent.

"I heard you." Tilly hardly looked at him when she spoke.

Mike looked as if he wanted to get angry but couldn't be bothered. He plunged out the door, and all Ada could do was scamper after him.

Tilly's heels tapped along the path. That was the fine-chiseled sound of sophistication, and one day it would be Ada clicking down the path on her way to a party. The party had made the night different from other plain old nights—now it shimmered like Tilly's dress. It was hot and nearly dark, and the air was heavy and lurking with feelings of mystery and promise. She would get to see where the party was, see its glittering guests, and hear its bright, muffled sounds. She would stick her head out the car window. Tilly's good time would become hers as well. Ada wriggled close to Tilly in the back seat of the car. Tilly's perfume smelled as false as a pink lolly.

Ada watched the streets pass by. The shops all looked different: emptied and lonely, unimportant. But the pubs were lit up; the footpaths outside them glowed under the awnings. Windows were squares of inviting gold light. The movie theater looked the best; everyone sat outside at tables, slumping in or leaning back, probably laughing and talking about parties.

Above them was a dotted line of globes lit up like stars hung on a clothesline. The theater rose up all rickety and regal. It was not only a theater; it was also a place for music and dancing. All this was a world closed off to Ada, thrilling to the heart and forbidden. And it had caught Tilly. Her head was turned to the other window, her fingers stroked at her own bare neck. Tilly was as sly as the night.

"You shouldn't have worn those shoes of Mum's," Ada said. She wanted to be taken seriously. "If you get them dirty, then she'll know. Old Sherlock."

Tilly didn't turn to reply, but she grabbed Ada's hand as she pressed her other hand to the window. "There's Ben, look! Ben's at the theater." As soon as she said it, her hand flew to her mouth. But their father heard, and he pulled the car over.

"Oh, for God's sake!" he said, and he sat there for a moment before he opened the door and got out.

Ada craned her neck to see past Tilly. Ben was slouched at a table, with a beer in one hand. Next to him was a girl with red beads and a white dress. She sat up straight, like a little animal who had just popped out of its hole. She also had a drink and she was talking and talking without stopping.

"Don't tell Ben I dobbed him in," Tilly said.

Ben was tall enough you might think he was eighteen, but he wasn't. He was fifteen, and fifteen-year-olds weren't allowed to drink beer. When he came loping after their father, his hands were in his pockets and his shoulders were hooped up in a shrug as if he were responsible for nothing. He got in the front seat, smelling of beer and cigarettes.

"You stink!" Ada said.

"Yep." He let out a little laugh and turned and grinned at them both. Ben had a winning smile. "Going out, Till? You're all spiffed up."

"She's going to a party," said Ada. "Were you drinking beer?"

"Don't ask," Tilly murmured, giving Ada a shove. Tilly didn't want to aggravate their father. He was stiff and silent and hunched, just a mound of darkness in the front seat.

Tilly leaned forward. "Dad, you can just drop me at the top of the street."

Later, Ada thought Tilly had done that just to spite her for saying something about the shoes. But Ben said it was because no one wants their entire family dropping them at a party. Either way, the feeling of the night was ruined; the mood tightened. Everyone was silently straining and none of the glitter of darkness could get in. And when Tilly slammed the door, it gave a deadening thud and the inside of the car seemed tomb-like and forever cut off from the night's mysteries. Ada watched Tilly walking through a pool of streetlight straight into the swallowing mouth of blackness. She felt a tiny stab of terror. All that was left was the empty pool of light and the fading sound of Tilly's steps.

7

At home fish-and-chips were only ever good for a minute. Ben's tongue was greasy and his insides too. Ada was always happy to scoop up the rest. Ada or PJ, they were both Labradors. Another beer would cut through the grease and ease him into the night, but there was no chance of that. Beer was not something he wanted to mention to his dad. Best not remind him. In fact, he'd try to keep Ada around as long as possible to avoid any grilling about the theater. Though once the chips were gone, Ada would scoot off.

"Your mother would be really annoyed if she knew you had been drinking." His father was going for it anyway, Ada or not.

"Was Ben drinking beer?" Ada was kneeling up on her chair to get better access to the pile of chips.

"It was only one. Everyone was."

"I don't care what everyone was doing. I care about what you were doing. If everyone jumps off a bridge—"

"Yeah, yeah," said Ben. They trotted that line out every time.

His father sighed. "I don't think we should mention it to your mum."

"No," Ben said, trying to show a remorse he didn't feel. He was grateful to his dad for keeping the lid on it, as long as Ada didn't blab. It made him feel sort of chummy with his dad—they could share a secret together. The beer secret.

"We're playing the Old Blacks tomorrow." He intended to capitalize on their new complicity.

His father nodded. He was still stiff, but he was bending.

"You opening?" he asked.

"Yep, with Sam." He was opening batsman—that should square the deal. Ben wasn't someone who sweated under pressure. He felt good after that beer. He could handle anything. He had been handling it all, even Kitty Vickers in the white dress.

"Tilly saw you outside the theater," said Ada. "She saw you first."

He knew Ada wanted to bring it all back to there, so that there would be more trouble for him. Little beast. She was a vulture at the roadside of his accident. He could play that game too. He wasn't opening batsman for nothing.

"You're going to make yourself sick if you keep shoveling chips in like that."

"No, I'm not."

"Hey, that's enough," Mike said.

Enough what? Enough chips for Ada? Enough arguing? He didn't care which. Ada had ruined his chance to get in with his dad. If she hadn't been there, they would have been men together sharing cricket experiences. Now he was being told off as if he were a kid.

He stood up. "I've got homework," he said.

"You never do homework," said Ada. She was right.

"You wouldn't know," said Ben. "Anyway, I'm going outside."

His room was the bungalow out the back. He had convinced Martha to let him have it. Tilly had been mad and jealous. But it was his idea, and Tilly wouldn't have coped. It was cold out there in winter. She'd be scared too. She acted as if she was hard done by, when he was the only one who could manage that room. He loved being out there on his own. He lay on his bed, the night at his window, the slice of moon, the shiver of branches. PJ was allowed inside. And Ben's mates.

"Okay," said his dad. "Mrs. Layton is coming over later to go over some insurance stuff."

Ben nodded. What did he care about Mrs. Layton's insurance policy? It was his dad's way of signaling his unavailability tonight, just in case Ben had thought that since Martha was away, they might drink a beer together. Ben smiled to himself. As if he would have thought that, as if he would even have tried. He'd rather go to his room and roll a joint. He would lie on his bed and make some plans.

8

Ada couldn't sleep. It was too hot. She threw off her sheet and clapped at a whining mosquito. Maybe she had slept and hadn't noticed since the night was quiet, except for the fluttering of the curtain and the occasional eruption of small lonely sounds that lived outside and tugged dreams out of sleep before they had properly unknotted. Her thoughts were tight and beating against her head, because of the heat and the pale, moon-bleached sky or the empty bed beside her. Tilly wasn't home; the bedcovers were ghostly still.

Ada lay and watched the room. The moonlight had crept in and bathed everything in eerie shining tones. Everything that looked so familiar during the day was hiding its true self in a cloak of shadow. Something monstrous lurked in that sort of stillness. It was getting ready. Ada didn't like it.

Her old wicker pram, which she didn't play with anymore, was parked with its nose indignantly in a corner; Big Baby probably lay abandoned inside it. Ada ran her eye along the top of the bookshelf, which was covered with indistinct shadowy things like the matching porcelain rabbits in blue jackets that were dust covered and so haunted with Ada's own long ago that they belonged to an elsewhere that time had closed off. Though it was satisfying and right to be so much older than she had been, Ada sensed in their merry frozen faces the remains of a magic that had been spent.

And in the corner was the special stained-glass lamp that Ada had accidentally broken one day, and their mother said she would never buy them anything beautiful ever again, because Ada and Tilly had no respect for the quality of things. Her mother was wrong about that. Ada felt fiercely that she knew the beauty of things. It wasn't just the sunsets, which everyone knew about, but also the coiled patterns of snail shells and the sliding of raindrops down windows and the fine veins in leaves, the glass balls of dew on nasturtium leaves. Tilly used to notice things, but now she forgot to look.

Tilly's jar of buttons sat next to the broken lamp. Ada got out of bed and took it down. She squatted on the floor and emptied the buttons. They splattered on the floorboards, shiny, hard, and colorless. She picked one up and held it close to her eye. It was a button, a button and nothing else. There was nothing lurking in it.

Ada straightened up. She wished she hadn't tipped the buttons out because she'd have to pick them up. She left them there and opened her door. Later she wondered what had made her go down the hall. It wasn't that she needed to go to the toilet; it was just that she wanted to go away from the buttons—and that she'd heard something.

The sound came from a person, but the person wasn't talking. The lamp was on in the living room. Its glow spilled down the hall and with it crept the sound of the breathy voice, as if it had rushed away from itself and come seeking her. Ada was frightened. Should she run back and hide from it in her room? Should she go and find her father? She was motionless for a second as the breaths came toward her with an urgent sound, as if something were about to break. The note of pain frightened her, but she was trapped by her own curiosity, which drew her forward.

What she saw, she saw for an instant, but it etched itself vividly and permanently on her mind. Her dad and Mrs. Layton had no clothes on, though her father, who lay on his back, wore one black ribbed sock. Mrs. Layton was sitting on top of him, leaning forward, her arms straight and holding her up, her back arched while her head tipped forward and her hair fell across her face. Ada could tell it was Mrs. Layton. Toby Layton was in her class at school. Toby Layton was one of her friends, and it was from his mother that the breathing sound came, and it went along with her movements, upward and down again. Ada's father's eyes were open, and he was watching Mrs. Layton. His hands were reached up, catching her large breasts. He had a look in his eye that Ada had never seen before. It was a half-lidded, pained look and it made him seem not like her father at all, but someone she didn't know.

Ada drew back into the dark hallway and ran back to her room. She grabbed Big Baby out of the pram and climbed into Tilly's bed. She would wait for Tilly to come home. She closed her eyes but as soon as she did, the scene in the living room replayed in her mind. She turned on the lamp and stared out the long window into the moonlit garden where the tree branches struck out across the night sky. Should she run outside to Ben's room and tell him? He might know what to do. Should someone stop them? Ada's mind was in a commotion. Mrs. Layton on her father, her father so consumed, he didn't see Ada even though she'd looked straight into his eyes.

Ada shook her head and clutched at Big Baby. Big Baby wore an ice-blue crocheted bonnet. Her eyes were closed, and her mouth was open. Her padded arms were flung up, and she looked as if nothing bad had ever happened. Ada held the baby doll and curled up on her side. Poor Big Baby; she wasn't real. Nothing was the same as it used to be. What she had seen had gotten inside her and Ada knew it would never sink into the pleasant, jumbled obscurity of other memories.

She felt serious and old, and she pushed Big Baby away. She was too old for dolls.

9

Tilly had gone to the party even though she didn't really want to. She had worried about it all day. She hadn't really been invited. Not by Gwendolyn Bell who was having the party. It was Alice who had told her to come: "You *have* to come," Alice said, as though it were Tilly's duty to be there alongside her.

Alice was going with her boyfriend, Simon Marsh, who was picking her up in his car. Tilly had to go on her own.

Alice had taken her by the arm and stroked her soothingly. "Please come, please, you'll have a nice time," she'd said, and Tilly had felt cross and obliged all at once—obliged to go and obliged to have a nice time. It was Alice who would have a nice time. She always did. The thing with Alice was that she had a way of organizing life so that people and circumstances agreed with her. Alice had organized to arrive in a shark-gray Holden with Simon Marsh, who was twenty-two, while Tilly had to arrive on her own, uninvited, to be there in case Alice needed her. What an expert manager Alice was. No matter what Tilly did, there was a mess about it. Nothing could be worked out neatly, and her mind ached with the failed effort of it. She had always sat gingerly on

Alice's bedspread, careful of creasing it and wary also of a little inward duplicity, because sitting so pertly was pretending, and the room was as unreal as a stage set. Tilly sometimes felt like an actor in Alice Layton's version of life.

She didn't know what Alice was aiming for, but it seemed she would get it. The inevitability of this always struck Tilly as similar to the inevitability that Tilly would fail.

Still, it was annoying that Alice expected her to arrive on her own. Would Alice have done that? Very unlikely. It would be much more cozy to just stay at home and let Alice cope without her, and yet . . . Alice knew how to have a good time. Alice laughed and beamed her white teeth, while Tilly was quiet and inwardish. It was an effort to fight her way out. But Alice knew it was like that. She tugged Tilly forward. Alice, after all, was Tilly's best friend, and it was true, wasn't it, that Alice cared about her more than anyone else did, apart from Ada. Wasn't this something to cherish, to care for and keep alive, even with its failures?

When Tilly got to the party, she stood and listened to the muffled hum of voices and clouds of laughter that burst against the door. What an intruder she was.

It was a white door and the knocker was like an ugly silver tooth. She stood heavily and stared out into the distant bush that blanketed the hills. Something might appear. An animal in trouble. Something she could attend to instead of going inside. Or Ada would turn up and call her home. But there were no animals in trouble, and Ada had gone. There was nothing except her and the still night air that hung over the row of somber weatherboard houses. Amidst them Gwendolyn Bell's house hammered and thronged and glowed like a lit-up beating heart.

The longer Tilly stood there, the louder her silver shoes glittered and mocked. And she began to blame them for showing off and for being untrue. Ada had known all along. Ada knew things without being able to say what it was she knew; she had a sense for things, just like Ben had an inclination for trouble. The shoes were trying too hard and they didn't match her at all, and if her mother found out she would be in big trouble. And she would find out—Martha had eyes of steel. Tilly shouldn't have come.

As she turned to scuttle away, a boy opened the door and stood like a puppy in front of her. He raised a bottle of beer for a swig. "I'm Frank," he said, wiping his mouth with his arm. "You coming or going?"

Put like that, so straight and simple, Tilly buckled. His bluntness nicely bludgeoned the delicacy out of the whole matter. "Coming," she said.

Frank looked at her with a singular sort of enthusiasm before he turned and marched inside, swaying a bit. Tilly slid along in his wake like a little fish. She squeezed past the people crowded in the hallway and lost Frank somewhere along the way, landing beside a table laden with bowls of chips and half-empty bottles of wine. She poured herself a plastic cup of wine.

Suddenly she had a place at the party. It was thrilling. The excitement gave her some weight and some lightness too. She jiggled with anticipation. Alice wouldn't know what that was like. Alice would just saunter in, cool and blond, with her boyfriend. But Alice wasn't anywhere yet. Tilly loitered for a while by the table, pretending she was hungry and not entirely an impostor. She looked up and tried to imagine that the light shade on the ceiling was her God of all things and that she and it could work it all out. But there she was, perched on a rickety wooden stool, acting as if this party mattered.

Two girls were dancing together. One was round and loud and she wore a tight silver dress. She was proud of herself, oozing there in her fleshy resilience, like a big, rich field mushroom. The other girl was more sober and plain and trying hard to be lively, but it was clear she was as steadfast and reliable as a donkey. Both of them had one eye out into the crowd and one on each other. This was how it was at parties, one eye in and one eye out and a lot of disingenuous chatter in between. Talking at parties was hard work—you had to wear your party self, that pretend sort of lively shining self, and the effort to conjure it showed through like a dirty mark on a pale dress. Sometimes it was all Tilly could think about, and the more she fixated on the dirty mark of truth, the bigger it got, until the conjured liveliness was absorbed by the real her, the one she tried to keep hidden. She would trudge home with the feeling that she had let herself out and ruined everything.

She finished her wine in one gulp and leaned back on her small stool with her legs straight out. She admired her legs in the silver shoes. What a faker she was. Where was Alice? Tilly got off her rickety stool and looked into the sea of people; perhaps there was someone else she might know. A man with a handlebar mustache arrived by her side and leaned across to reach for the dolmades. He said *ahem* and struck up a conversation, told her about his "charming abode" and his "humanist tendencies," both of which would make anyone uneasy. He said *abode* instead of *house*. And what was humanism? He must have thought she was older than she was. It was a party of older people, after all. Tilly poured herself some more wine, which seemed to relieve her of the need to care about humanism and whatever other beliefs she had or didn't have. Sometimes the worst was not having beliefs. As for people, she told the humanist, searching for a position on humanism, she loved some of them, though they annoyed her too sometimes and other times they just frightened her and they were terribly disappointing too, but so far no one had disappointed her as much as she had disappointed herself.

The humanist rubbed his moustache. Either he hadn't understood or he had tired of the dolmades, as he excused himself and moved toward a more promising cluster of people. What a great pity to be so disappointing. Either improve, or lighten up about not improving, she said to herself. But all this improving was tiring and lonely, especially if Alice didn't show up.

But there was Frank, leaning ungracefully against a wall. The little flame in his eye was bleary as his gaze roamed around the room. She could imagine him with horns, reddish ones. It was easy to tell he didn't put a lot of time into gathering beliefs. But he seemed puzzled, and she could feel close to puzzled people, even if they had horns. He saw her, grinned, and came lumbering over.

As Frank moved from his post at the wall, Tilly saw Raff Cavallo sitting on a couch, one arm over the back of it, and probably around the girl who sat next to him. Tilly had never seen him out of the normal context, with Ben and Will—they were all on the footy team together and often ended up at her house after a game. Together they were coarse and gang-like, but if you separated one from the others, you would see that while Will was as sturdy as a loaf of bread, Raff was the sort to steer clear of, unless trouble was your game. Maybe it was for her.

It was always hard to tell what Raff Cavallo had fixed his mind on. He never attached himself to anything but seemed like a torrential rain, full and sudden and then gone.

He was listening to the girl beside him. He was smiling too. What was she saying that made him turn so tenderly toward her? But Tilly couldn't hear, and now Frank was there, slouching in his camel corduroys.

"You never told me your name," he said.

"You never asked." She offered him a chip.

He shook his head and sucked at his beer.

"Want to dance?" she said. It would be too dull to just stand and talk—she could tell that already.

Frank was reluctant, even slightly appalled. He leaned against the table, shaking his head slowly. "I warn you. I don't dance."

"I'm not expecting pirouettes." She moved toward the middle of the room, assuming he would follow, but he lurched forward and grabbed her arm to stop her.

"What do you do?"

"I'm a humanist," she said. Frank didn't get the joke. It didn't seem to matter to him what she was. He didn't reply, but he followed her dutifully to the dance floor, looking at her with distant bemusement. He hadn't lied; he was a terrible dancer, thick and heavy and heaving like a ship. The more he wavered there, as drunk as a Viking, the more it was possible to merge with the party, and for this Tilly was grateful. She floated as easily as the smoke-filled air. She had found the right mood, an invisible, reckless mood. The silver shoes dazzled. Frank lurched his hands toward her. He leaned in and pushed a hot gush of breath at her ear. He wanted her to come with him into the garden.

It was dark there and quiet. They sat on a cold stone bench and Frank asked if he could kiss her. Why didn't he just go ahead and kiss her without asking? Especially as the kiss, when it came, was violent. He might have called it passionate, but it went against the quiet of the garden, its shaking leaves and faraway sky and the muffled music snaking out the door. All this, and still he lunged heavily and thrust his tongue right into her mouth as if he were invading a small foreign country. She had wanted some disarming tenderness, a great, hidden, unfathomable depth.

She unraveled herself from his arms, shook off her disappointment, and walked inside. She had been kissed. She had earned her place at the party and now she could stop trying. She had finally gotten rid of herself. She would dance. She closed her eyes.

Someone took her hand. It wasn't Frank. It was Raff Cavallo. He had a cigarette in one hand and he was laughing.

"Tilly Bloom, you're drunk."

"So?" She would have taken her hand back, but he pulled her in and swung her out again, spun her under his arm like an expert.

It was so surprising, she frowned. "Who taught you how to dance?"

"Why do you care?" he said, dropping her hand. His green eyes were looking at the rest of the partygoers. If only he would leave her to enjoy her glorious mood. Instead, he swept them both back into a dance as if she were just something he'd carelessly reached out and caught. He had timing, she had to admit, and he knew how to dance her along with him, in to him and out again. So typical of Raff to show up with hidden talents.

The lamp's dim glow mingled with a haze of smoke and heat. No one was themselves anymore—they had slid their party selves into the atmosphere, as if their bodies were made of air. People were kissing. Tilly didn't know where to look. What was swaying? Everything? Her little heart too. Waves of Raff Cavallo washed over her. She could feel the warmth coming off his body. The dance had drawn her closer and set loose a current between them. It snaked up through her spine. The night had taken hold of her too. She didn't care. Her soul had turned over and the shiny side was up. It was like being drawn out to sea, when she'd aimed for the shore.

Then, just as stealthily as he'd arrived, Raff let her go. He didn't speak, just turned and walked out of the room.

It was as if she were falling.

"You're here!"

It was Alice. She had landed in front of her. Tilly stared out to wherever Raff Cavallo had gone, as if lost in his wake.

Tilly grabbed Alice happily. "Listen to this," she said. "The strangest thing just happened. I danced with Raff Cavallo. I didn't mean to. But he was here. He can actually, really dance."

"Raff?" Alice laughed. "I wonder who invited him." She frowned and, struck by another thought, she shrugged. "He's strange. I can't work him out."

Before Tilly could plunge into any further thoughts about Raff, Alice passed her a bottle. "Here, drink some of this. It's ace. I'm as high as a kite."

10

Ada woke up as Tilly slipped into bed. "What time is it?" she asked.

"Move over. Don't you want to hear? About the party."

"Yes," said Ada, solemnly. It was her duty. She sat up and blinked. The moonlight had gone and she could see the black branches outside and hear their rooster, Captain George, crowing. That meant it was almost dawn. Oh, Captain George, she thought, because he was always there calling out in the morning.

"It's funny, at the beginning I almost ran away and came home. I didn't want to go in," said Tilly with a little laugh.

Ada remembered how she had felt afraid to see Tilly being swallowed by the mouth of blackness and she realized why she'd had the fear. It was a premonition of her naked father on the couch with one sock on and Mrs. Layton on top of him. In comparison to that terrible thing in the living room, which had filled Ada with an unnameable horror, Tilly seemed so exactly like the Tilly she knew and could count on that she began to hope the world would be returned to how it had always been. Tilly's story would take over; it would sweep away everything that had happened in the living room.

"But you did go in, didn't you?" Ada said.

"Of course I did. A guy came to the door and I went in behind him. Later he kissed me. He was a terrible dancer and a terrible kisser too. He was drunk enough to like me, I could tell."

Ada snuggled into the bed, relieved. She would close her eyes and just listen.

Tilly lay on her back stiff with excitement and her feet danced a little. "Here's some advice, Snug, for when you're older. If a boy can't dance, he probably can't kiss either, because it shows he doesn't know tenderness and listening."

Ada made a mental note of this. Tenderness and listening. In the morning she would write those words in her diary. Even though she had no interest in boys. Or kissing. But dancing was important. Everyone wants to dance.

Tilly yawned. She told Ada about the humanist with the charming abode and how she had gotten cross with herself because she didn't know how to be interesting, and how she was scared of something and it could have been the shoes or it could have been just the feeling that she couldn't be true.

Ada couldn't see how Tilly could not be true, but she remembered that Tilly had become sly. If only she would go back to how she used to be.

"That's silly," mumbled Ada. But she couldn't muster the right authority. Tilly ignored her anyway and went on. "You still awake? I haven't got to the main bit."

Ada's eyes were closed. She nodded. "Keep going."

"Well, I got it in the end. I found the right mood—the wine helped. And I didn't care at all, about anything. And someone took me by my hand while I was dancing. Open your eyes, Snug, this is the good part. Who do you think it was?"

Ada obeyed. Tilly had a wide smile, which she shone up at the ceiling as if she were seeing God himself up there. Ada stuck her finger through one of Tilly's black curls, which were spilled out on the pillow.

"Raff Cavallo." Tilly gave a little laugh and forced into it a condescending note, which Ada didn't like, and although Tilly had turned expectantly toward her, waiting for Ada to share her scorn, Ada frowned and turned on her side, with her back to Tilly.

"Why is that so funny?" she whispered. She felt grave. Romantic figures shouldn't be laughed at. Ada didn't like it. She had not forgiven herself for what had happened at the windmill. She had failed to impress Raff. Had Tilly impressed him without even meaning to? That would be too unfair.

Tilly didn't answer.

Ada lay quite still for a moment. The filtering of morning light had begun to restore the room to its ordinariness. Things were distinctly things again. Their outlines came back with the same old exactness. Ada could no longer blend things into a sense of endless possibility. Tilly's night with all its glittering grown-up mystery was over. Life was plain old life again, with its list of things to do, and Raff Cavallo was still Ada's secret hero.

Tilly turned over, cuddling Ada to her. "You be little spoon," she whispered.

For a moment all was quiet except for the 5:00 a.m. train hurtling through the dawn and the first uttering of birdsong.

Ada listened to Tilly's breath getting deeper. She was sinking into sleep. "Tilly?" Ada said in a panic.

"Hmmm."

Mrs. Layton had not gone away. Ada had to tell Tilly before the night was over, before the day really began, when Ada would get up and see her father and not know how to look at him or what to say.

"I saw something. Something bad. It was Dad . . ." Ada stopped. If she said it out loud it would become something, it would become a fact, it would push its way in alongside all the other things that happened—breakfast, birthdays, holidays, illnesses—with all its ugliness lit up like a shop sign. It wouldn't belong to Ada anymore, it would belong to the great span of life, delivered into existence by Ada's voice. But Tilly had to know. Ada couldn't hold it all alone.

"What was he doing?" said Tilly, waking up.

"He was with Mrs. Layton," Ada declared. "On the couch, in the middle of the night." And just to make sure Tilly understood, she added, "With no clothes on."

11

Martha caught the 9:20 train home on Saturday morning. It was already hot. Summer was too bright; she was always having to hide from it beneath wide-brimmed hats and dark sunglasses. She put her hat on her knees and stared out the window. A man sat opposite her. He could have sat somewhere else. There were empty seats after all. Martha preferred to have no one sitting opposite her. More room to dream. But here he was. She would be compelled to watch him from behind her dark glasses, and she would imagine something about him. That was what she did. She shouldn't do it. She would try to decide who he was, even though she could never know. She would construct his life and she would wander through that life as if she were that man, in his shirt, on the train, as if she were no longer herself. She was always losing herself in other lives, while her real life waited there, like an empty seat without a window view.

The man opened a large textbook on his lap. A suit coat, a wristwatch, black hair with gray streaks, unshaven lined face, similar age to her. He was probably married. She peered closely enough to read the book's title. *The Competition Market*

Challenge. She leaned back, instantly disappointed. Would he be just as tedious as his book? If he had been reading Thoreau, that would have been nicely surprising, and she would have wanted to find out more. But there was nothing to be interested in.

She might be wrong. People were always more than what you thought they were, but not always in an interesting way. And all those houses the train rushed past, like new false teeth. She shouldn't dislike them either. But she did.

Susie had tried to talk her into staying away and doing an aerobics class. Martha didn't like aerobics. She did it once, and it was exhausting. "No, I have to come home." She didn't explain properly. She was too tired. She didn't even know why.

Home. She was constantly heading for home. Not because it was that cozy place with the dog, but because if she kept hurrying toward something, she would rush right past the hollowness. Bypass whatever it was that made her uncomfortable. Envy or regret, or even just longing—deep, aimless, habitual longing.

"Are you sure? Would be good for you," Susie had said. "You'll need a bit of time after visiting your mother." Susie always pushed. Always knew what was good for Martha. And it was true; she did. But what was one aerobics session against the great onslaught of life? She had had enough of the city. It made her want things she didn't need. She had bought Tilly a record, *Revolver.* It had been one of her favorites. She would listen to it with Tilly and together they would sing "Good Day Sunshine." It was so hard to share anything with Tilly now that she had shut herself off. But Tilly would love the record.

Martha had also bought shoes. She didn't need those shoes. No one needs yellow shoes. She had hidden them from her mother, who would have thought Martha was wasting hard-earned money on fripperies. Martha just wanted to feel the rush that extravagance gave her. It was like buying a different life, in which she was someone who had an important role, with shoes to match and more than one handbag. Martha wasn't that person, and she'd hate the shoes before long for their false allure and their evaporating joys. Already she wanted to go home and lock them in her cupboard. But she didn't like being at home. The house jammed her in. The chicken poo on the veranda defeated her, as did the broken lawnmower, the pine needles in the gutters, the singed lawn, the dust, the struggling roses, and the dying trees too with their branches as leafless as bones. Those big trees, the magnificent silent creatures, were dying from the outside in. Her garden was almost a graveyard; she felt responsible. And in the face of that, she had bought yellow shoes.

If only she had stayed in the city, or—even better—if she had traveled, found a job and got an apartment in a real city like London, had the life of a single girl, done something affecting, important. Her friend Fiona Dark had gone off to London and never come home, and Fiona's friends were the type of people who funded film festivals in Transylvania and owned old mansions on private beaches in Italy. Martha imagined them with wind in their hair, belting down country roads in convertibles.

Martha fixed her gaze on the last sprawl of brick suburbs. The uniformity of them intrigued her and depressed her, and in some way terrified her. The sprawling homogeneity. It would overtake them all. She was running from it, but was she just running into a different version of the same thing?

What had happened to her life that there was no place for a frivolous, unreasonable shoe? She didn't want a completely sensible life, which was why her heart had pounded with a confused sort of trepidation as she paid for them, just as it had when, as a child, she once stole a cream bun. Just as it still did whenever she visited her mother. It was a feeling all pummeled with hope and childish longing, and wariness too.

But Martha was visiting Glenda this time. Glenda's oasis of cool white space was admirable and painstaking and elegant. There were no tennis balls or socks on the floor at Glenda's. There was nothing but vases and "pieces," primitive statues carved in black stone. Martha felt judged by so much good taste. And yet she admired it and sometimes hoped to find things that imitated Glenda's "pieces," and if she did find a vase in the op shop that just might be good, she would try to picture it in Glenda's house to see if it fit. But this was demeaning. She was always behind Glenda and in deference to her, but Martha had her way of making up for it. The pale-blue silk dress with the black lace panels, for instance. Glenda had admired it, but she couldn't have it, because Glenda was fat and wore full-length black dresses. Martha had not yet gone that way. Her hair was not yet gray and she wasn't fat and she could escape into that dress, like men sped off in their sports cars. That dress or those shoes or that vase, they all refused the drab, repetitive, frugal, appropriate life that threatened her. Or did she just believe they did? Had Arnold Buch seen through it instantly? Was that why her head ached?

Martha was already forty-one, and there were signs: sunspots, lines, sagginess, but nothing—she struggled to reassure herself—that couldn't be hidden or overlooked, forgiven. And while Glenda's face benefitted from her plumpness, Glenda hid her gluttony just as Martha avoided the close scrutiny of her own skin. Martha came to Glenda when Glenda felt low. She listened and talked to Glenda in all earnestness and made Glenda feel attended to, and they gently soothed each other's hidden shame and private failures. Yet Martha always came away feeling discontent. Perhaps it was that the unspoken underlying comparison undermined all her good intentions toward Glenda. She'd gorged on something without being nourished by it. She'd left Glenda's house feeling inadequate and inelegant, and now she strained to go home and redeem herself by being at least in some way a good mother and wife. If she couldn't be sophisticated, she could at least be wholesome. She would plant broccoli in the vegetable garden and hide away all evidence of her city binge.

Martha shifted in her seat to avoid the sun's glare and brushed eyes with the man opposite. He looked up as she moved. He put down his fluoro marker and closed the book. He leaned back in the seat and folded his arms.

Should she talk to him? She could tell him how tedious his book looked. That would start a conversation. She noticed with some relief that he had a potbelly. She would easily forgive it. But what was the point? They weren't teenagers. There was neither a future nor freedom. What sort of wife waited at home for him? Was she happier with him than Martha was with Mike? Did his wife love his little paunch? Did she care if he flirted on trains? He stood up and reached for his bag. The train was stopping. It was all about to be over. She took off her glasses and smiled at him, if only to fend off the gloom. He smiled back and said goodbye.

Once off the train, he walked past her window and waved. She waved back. His smile was purposeful, well aimed. A perfectly timed collision. Her whole body leapt toward it. Something sprang to life inside her, which she knew at once had nothing to do with that man, but which he had caused. The train pulled out and he was gone.

Martha closed her eyes. It was sometimes terribly dull to be married. And yet she couldn't imagine life without Mike. It was her fault, really. She didn't make enough effort. Love was an effort. She would cook him something fiddly like lasagna, buy a bottle of wine and stay up.

When she arrived home it was midday. The old weatherboard house slumped quietly under the blaze of sun. She found Ada in the garden, lying under the trampoline with Louis and May and PJ. Martha squatted to see them. May was wearing nothing, as usual, though Ada and Louis wore bathers. They all had wet hair, and drops of water still wobbled on their shining skin. They were lying on their tummies looking at Ada's Endangered Australian Animals cards. Ada was playing teacher. There was something about the three of them with their small suntanned bodies lying in a row in their hiding place that gave Martha an instant rush of maternal warmth and a stab of regret that she was not privy to these moments of childhood for her youngest child. She was too busy, too swamped with chores and obligations. And yet it wasn't that; it was something else. She had rushed through all of her children's lives, because she just always rushed forward, rushed away from where she was.

Her tenderness rushed out to claim them, and so claimed her too. She had never known love to move like a flood as it did then.

Who was here looking after them? Her heart jolted angrily. Had Mike left Ada by herself?

"Hello, monkey," she said.

"Mama!" Ada slammed her cards in the grass so she could scramble out. "Mama, Tilly is still in bed!" Ada looked as if she expected this to be terrible news, as if she were frightened for Tilly. She whispered carefully, "Because she went to a party and didn't get home till nearly morning."

"I see," said Martha, stiffening. Ada was right. This did irritate her. She had never liked anyone to sleep in. It was slovenly, a waste of the day. And Tilly should have been up to look after Ada. "Well, where's Dad?" she asked.

Ada frowned. "He's taken Ben to footy."

"Why didn't you all go? Didn't he tell Tilly that she should be looking after you and not sleeping in?"

Ada shrugged. She twisted away from this interrogation. Louis and May watched wide-eyed from under the trampoline. PJ heaved himself up and limped out to say hello. Martha gave him a pat and sighed and kissed Ada and, remembering her gush of maternal feeling, she asked Ada if she'd put sunscreen on and if they had remembered to use the groundwater sprinkler and not the tap water. Had they eaten fruit? Did they want her to make them some cheese-and-tomato toasties? May piped up. "Not with tomato. Just cheese." Louis nodded silently. Ada wanted olives in hers. Martha went inside.

She went straight to her bedroom and took the shoes out of the shoebox. Things were always more affecting when they weren't hers, and these already seemed to be simply another pair of shoes. She pushed them to the back of the wardrobe. She put the record in there too. She would give it to Tilly when she wasn't feeling so full of resentment. She changed out of her good clothes.

She stuffed the shoebox in the bin and started on the toasties. She moved quickly. She always did. No one had cleaned up the breakfast dishes and she soon came across the greasy fish-and-chips paper in the bin. Her irritation flared again. Why hadn't Mike made them some dinner? Why were the dishes always left for her? He should have gotten Tilly up. Mike was hopeless. How had she managed to marry a country boy who couldn't use a hammer or fix a lawn mower, let alone boil an egg? Susie Layton's husband could fix anything; he could build a whole house if he wanted to. Whereas Mike was like a prince, a sensual sort of athlete who had ended up in a suit and tie. He called himself a country boy, yet he'd grown up in the suburbs of Bendigo.

Martha had been drawn to Mike because his smile suggested waywardness, which she had interpreted as individuality and adventurousness. It was the night after Mary Galmotte's party. They were at the beach in the early evening, and she had sat on the ground and lit a cigarette, balancing the matches on her knees, while he picked up a stick and swung it like a golf club, his whole body flinging itself, exploding in a simple, unquestioning upward arc. Her desire flared, so startling her that she assumed it was love. What was it? A conflation of honeyed light and a man's body: assured, intelligent, caught in an action that gave the moment a deceptive fervor, an exaltation of what was simply physical. And in that moment she had decided.

"Mama, are the toasties ready?" The flywire door banged as Ada appeared in the kitchen. "Can we have icy poles?"

Ada leaned on the bench, her little brown arms propping up her face. Ada had Mike's sensuality. She loved food. She was the one at the birthday party left eating the cake while the other children ran off and played. She was the one who checked through her lunchbox and made sure there was enough. She was the one who demanded cuddles, who wanted her back tickled and would not go to sleep without this touch. Martha had resorted to placing baby Ada in bed with Tilly to get her to sleep, and Ada still climbed in with Tilly.

"Yes, you can have icy poles, after the toasties." Martha was determined to be popular.

"And, Mama, you won't get cross at Tilly, will you? Or Dad?"

Martha cut the toasties in half and shoved them on a plate. "Your father can look after himself. And don't worry about Tilly. Here, take these outside and share them out." It always annoyed her that Ada sought to protect Tilly. As if Tilly needed protection. Tilly was selfish enough as it was, and she had turned Ada into her minion.

Martha smiled. "Go on," she said. Ada was examining her; she could feel it, and she could feel that Ada didn't believe her. She turned away. Why did she worry about Ada? Was it because she was the youngest and her last? Or was it because Ada didn't have her older sister's prettiness? Martha looked at Ada's frowning face. It wasn't that Ada wasn't sweet. As a toddler she had been like a little brown-skinned pudding with round, startled eyes and a declaring little voice, and everyone was instantly charmed by her. She still had such a wide-open face and an endearing way about her. She looked as if she had tumbled out of a Dickens novel: orphan-like, hair askew with a sleep-nest of knots at the back, mismatched clothes, often back-to-front or piled on in layers—a summer dress over a woolly jumper—a hairclip as a deliberate but awkward attempt to adorn, which added to her ragged charm. When Martha did try to polish her up, Ada looked straitjacketed, pinched in, like a child who had been dressed up for a family portrait. And she became instantly gloomy, as if the real Ada had been harshly rubbed off with soap. But there were her strange sensitivities and her unearthly scrutiny—they made people uneasy. Martha lowered her head and began to wipe the bench. Ada sniffed the wafts of buttered toast and ran outside, eager to share her bounty.

Martha marched to Tilly's closed door. She paused before opening it, gathering up her accusations in a hot intake of breath. Tilly lay with her back to the door, her ink-black curls spilled behind her on the pillow. Martha scanned the room first and, finding nothing other than the mess of carelessly peeled-off clothes, she stood above Tilly and whispered her name.

"Tilly."

Tilly had hardly stirred. She had always been a good sleeper, unlike Martha, who woke at the slightest sound.

"Tilly, wake up."

Tilly groaned and rolled over. She saw her mother and closed her eyes for a moment. She sat up and sighed, awaiting judgment.

Martha launched into her speech with an equally disgruntled sigh. "You realize that you are meant to be looking after Ada. What are you doing in bed? It's past one o'clock."

"I slept in." Tilly was sullen.

Martha pursed her lips. "And what about Ben? Weren't you meant to be watching him play?"

"Mum," Tilly simpered, "Ben doesn't care. Why do I always have to go and watch him play?"

"Well, I don't see why you don't want to. He's your brother. He'd come and watch you if you did anything apart from going to parties."

Tilly didn't reply.

Martha felt terrible. Why did she say that?

Tilly started to get up. Martha's voice rose, as if scrambling up after her. "And the kitchen was left in a mess, again. I really think it's time you became more responsible and stopped just thinking about yourself. No one ever thinks to help me. I shouldn't have to come home to a dirty kitchen." She placed her hand on her heart, as if to protect it from this mistreatment. Tilly was old enough to be more thoughtful. She had to be told.

Tilly sat on the edge of the bed. She picked up the clothes that lay on the floor. "If the kitchen is in a mess, it's Dad and Ben who left it. It was tidy last night. Don't blame me."

But Martha did blame her. Tilly was slippery. She slid behind things like a shadow. Martha always had to catch hold of her and haul her into the light. Show her how to behave, how to be responsible.

Tilly stepped into a short sundress and reached behind her to zip it up.

Martha eyed her warily. She was like a just-opened flower, still soft, dewy, and quivering in fragility, on the brink of something. It plunged Martha into a sudden tumult of yearning for her own youth and the familiar tang of regret that she had lost it. She had missed it, or messed it up. Tilly had drained it out of her and taken it all for herself.

Tilly pinned her gaze to the floor. Her shoulders hunched against the weight of Martha's disapproval. The more Tilly brooded, the angrier Martha grew. Was it possible that she simply didn't like Tilly? Tilly pulled shadows around her like a coat and shrank beneath them. Martha had told her right from the start to stand up properly. But Tilly wouldn't listen, or she wouldn't learn. She was furtive and unassured, moving always in awkward bursts, like a tree in a gust of wind. And her personality was indistinct; as if she had purposefully blurred her own edges. No matter how much Martha wanted Tilly to do better, Tilly refused to improve. Martha's anger pulsed at her throat. It had been like this from the start with Tilly. She had been a difficult child. Not like Ben. He had gurgled and smiled and slept like a plump and cheerful Buddha.

Martha tightened herself inward. She stared coldly at Tilly, and as she spun around to leave the room, her voice shook. "All I can say is that you can be difficult to love."

12

Tilly waited to find her father on his own. He and Ben had come home from the cricket match jocular and sweaty, bristling with an exclusive and masculine chumminess. Her father slapped Ben on the back, beaming. "He played well. Really well," he said with a sort of proprietary satisfaction.

Martha, who was preparing their lunch, rolled her eyes. She wasn't impressed with Mike's vainglorious adoption of their son's talents.

"Do you want some help?" said Tilly. It was a grim sort of offer and she knew Martha could tell.

"If you want to do something, put some plates on the table." Martha sliced rapidly at the tomato, as if in a rush because there was so much to do and no one to help. Martha liked to play the martyr. Tilly's parents were performing their favorite roles to each other and neither was watching.

Martha's whole life was a performance, with men as the audience. Everyone else, especially Tilly, was backstage and failing her. Martha gazed at Ben as she always did, as if he was her only hope. He was her shining star.

"Did you win, darling? You must be starving." She spoke in her sweet tones. One voice for Ben and another one for Tilly.

Mike answered. "They didn't win, but Ben was best on field. His team let him down."

Ada danced over to the kitchen bench and nabbed a piece of cheese. "Did you hit any sixers?"

Ben ignored Ada. He sawed himself a piece of bread. "What about Brunner? He played a cracker game. Cavallo let us down by not showing up. If he'd been there, we might have had a chance."

Tilly blushed, but no one noticed. The sudden burst in her heart surprised her. She tried to unravel the Raff Cavallo who'd danced with her from the one who only showed up when it suited him. He was probably still sleeping, flat out across the bed, a sheet wound around him. She blushed again and pushed the whole thought of him away, in case Ben noticed.

Ben wasn't watching her, though. He was leaning back on a kitchen chair, like a king, waiting for the world to come to him. And it would come. Martha would bring it on a plate. His game would be admired as it always was. And he accepted his adeptness as if it were just the skin he'd grown in. There was talk at the matches about Ben and his way of "reading the play" and how he had a "sense of the ball," which anyone who knew him like Tilly did would know was just an adaptation of his inclination for trouble. He sniffed around for any possibility of transgression, grinning while he did, and escaping any consequences as well. He'd once been caught driving Martha's car without a license, and he and his partner in crime, Jimmy Grigson, had also been found lying drunk on the crash mats in the gymnasium after nicking a bottle of wine from the staff room at school. But these were the only two incidents he had been punished for, and since he was a sporting hero, these misdemeanors just added to his reputation as a charming rascal.

Both he and Ada were blessed with their father's olive skin and animal grace. Whereas Tilly came from Martha: she was circling above the ground, pale and filled with ether rather than flesh. She didn't care for sport and she wasn't entranced by lunch. She'd never learned piano, because Martha didn't believe in extra lessons—school was enough for a child, she always said. Alice had lessons, though. She had showed Tilly the major and minor scales, in both hands, and Tilly was off, rough as a child pounding at playdough and just as intent.

She lingered on the piano while they all had lunch. Martha was often irritated by her playing, since Martha thought she was the one with an ear for music, and she was always sighing and saying Tilly never played a tune through. But now, while Martha was absorbed in Ben's glories on the field, Tilly could play without anyone bothering her. Playing the piano always soothed her, just as eating honey toast soothed Ada.

After lunch, her father had a shower, which was unusual for him. He showered punctually every morning, straight after his alarm went off. He rarely broke routine. But it was a hot day and he didn't like to sweat. Tilly waited till he went to dress in his room and followed him. He was standing on the other side of the bed with a towel around his waist, reaching into the cupboard.

"Dad," she said.

He swiveled around, a folded shirt in his hands.

"Dad, Ada saw you last night." This was the best way to say it. She had considered not saying anything, but that would have left it too unattended in her head, and in Ada's too. And it wasn't to defend their mother that she confronted him, but to bring the transgression to light, to show him that they knew about it. This was something her father had done to her and to Ada. He had damaged his role as father, and he had to repair it. She wanted to believe he could fix this, he could explain it or make her feel it wasn't as wrong as it looked. Maybe it hadn't happened, and Ada had been dreaming.

His head dropped, and he picked up a corner of the top sheet, as if it had just occurred to him that he ought to make the bed. The shirt he was holding unraveled. For an instant nothing happened at all. When she spoke, he shook the sheet and let it float down like a leaf falling.

"Ada saw what?" His voice was petulant, accusatory. He wriggled into a collared T-shirt as if it were some protection from the accusation.

"She saw you . . . with Mrs. Layton." She realized she didn't know exactly how to say it. It was ugly, after all. She did not want to speak of sex to her father. But it needed to be clear. "On the couch, Dad. Ada knows Toby Layton." Tilly's voice rose. Did she need to elaborate? He knew Alice Layton was her friend. Her best friend. The Laytons were family friends. They all knew each other. It was not only wrong, it was a mess.

He rose too, with her voice, as if her words had drawn them both upward. He leaned forward. His body pitched as if he were about to charge. He pointed his finger at her, flicking it as he spoke.

"Look, Tilly, Mrs. Layton came to discuss insurance matters.

I don't want to hear another word about it. And I certainly don't want you talking to anyone about this, including your mother. You understand?"

His face was rigid, glowering.

Tilly backed away. "Why would I tell Mum?" she said. "I just want you to be truthful."

He didn't speak. He slammed himself shut. He turned his back on her and began searching in the cupboard.

Tilly ran to her room. She lay on her bed. Ada hadn't been dreaming, and her father hadn't been truthful. If he weren't truthful, then what was he? What sort of parent? And he hadn't defended it or tried to fix it; he'd just blasted the whole thing out of existence, as if it could be forced out, annihilated.

It was still imprisoned inside Tilly's mind, and Ada's too, a stalking, hideous waft of something that would lurk behind everything her father did, everything he said. What else was not true? She shut her eyes and tried to think of something else. But she couldn't find a way to steady herself.

Ada woke her sometime later by climbing onto the bed. Tilly was curled on her side and didn't turn to look at her.

"Tilly," Ada said, stroking Tilly's hair.

Tilly moaned. "Snug, you woke me up."

"Have you got a sore head?"

Tilly gave the semblance of a nod.

"Did you kiss Raff Cavallo?"

"Of course not." She stirred agreeably at the thought of him. And then frowned. Raff Cavallo.

There was quiet. Ada was making her own appraisal. Tilly closed her eyes. But Ada started up again. "I took Captain George and Bolshie for a walk in the wheelbarrow. Louis said I was bossy. But I wasn't bossy. I was just trying to help. He can't even read yet. I was reading out the instructions."

"For what?" Tilly gave up trying to go back to sleep.

"For how to set up the badminton net."

"That's not bossy. Louis is just frustrated that he can't read yet, so he gets cross at you."

"I don't like him, anyway."

"You always say that, and then you forgive him again."

"Well, I won't this time."

"Snug, you took those silver shoes back to Mum's room this morning, while I was sleeping, didn't you?"

"When I woke up. In case Mum came home early. Did you get in trouble?" she whispered, proud of her stealth.

"Not really. I owe you one."

Ada was quiet for a moment, as if considering her options.

"Can you buy me an ice cream at the theater?"

"Sure."

"Rainbow flavor?"

"Whichever you choose."

Ada was pleased. She began to trace a shape with her finger on Tilly's back. "Guess what I'm drawing?" she said.

"A butterfly."

"How did you know?"

"You always draw butterflies."

"Yes, but this butterfly can't fly because it's too hot, so it's sitting on a little dog. See." Ada was drawing the dog.

"Not PJ?"

"No, not PJ. Elmer. The little blind dog."

It was quiet again. Tilly couldn't remember who the little blind dog was.

"Did you say anything to Dad?" Ada whispered.

Tilly hadn't yet worked out what she would deliver back to Ada. She sighed and turned over. She took Ada's hand and held it. "Don't think about it anymore. I won't either. Deal?"

Ada pouted. She climbed off the bed and ran out.

Ada wouldn't forget it. And Tilly wouldn't either. It was there, like a hard bit of grit flung in Ada's eye. Nothing as insubstantial as a few words could change it. She had given Ada nothing but a blind, bald deal—the same one her dad had forced on her—the Old Maid card. Tilly stuck her hands over her eyes. Her head ached. She heaved herself up. It was a shame. Another sort of child might just forget it, but not Ada.

13

It was still hot when Mike Bloom undressed for bed. Martha took no notice. He unbuttoned his shirt and threw it, with an exaggerated flourish, on the chest of drawers, mostly to amuse himself. Martha's gaze didn't swerve from her book. She lay in the bed, on her back, under the white sheet, straight and small and clenched, holding the book close to her face. She frowned as she read, and Mike wondered if her reading were causing her a slight displeasure or whether she was frowning at the possibility that he might intrude and warding him off, should he try. Martha had many ways of warding him off. It was the same every night.

Whereas Susie was hungry for him. Susie would peel off his shirt as if unwrapping a delicacy. She took audible pleasure in touching his chest; her hands ran over his arms, she deposited kisses on his stomach; she sought him out and moaned. Her body was soft—a landscape of accommodating flesh that she willingly arched over him. She gave herself as if to be eaten.

"Did you get everyone fish-and-chips last night?" Martha looked at him, finally, as he pulled back the sheet to get in.

"Well, I got home late from work; I had to." It annoyed him the way she asked. It was just to show him that she knew and she disapproved and that he had failed. Why did he need to justify himself? They were his children too.

"What time did Tilly get home?"

Again the implied criticism. He frowned. How could it possibly be his fault that Tilly got home late? He sighed. He hadn't wanted it to go this way. He was tired and he wanted to sleep, but he also wanted to make love to his wife. His desire was more proprietary than carnal. He had to balance things out. But she was already pissing him off. He propped himself up on his elbow, looking at her.

"It's too hot tonight," she said.

Martha had always been coy. No matter how much Mike complimented her, she still tried to hide herself. He'd thought it was just a girlish habit that he would break with the force of her attraction to him. He'd pleaded with her to stand naked before him but no matter how much he adored her, she wouldn't do it. Susie Layton was not perfect, but her perfection was that she didn't care. She almost purred. In bed, she crawled over him, her breasts above his face.

Susie's voice was what had first drawn him to her; it was slow and she left sentences hanging. She made allusions to sex. She flirted with him and laughed or made throaty noises of appreciation. They had met on many "family occasions," at school fetes, sports days, and at the bottle shop, where she had confessed to him that whiskey made her horny. There had been a dinner at her house, with her husband, Joe. She had worn a silk shirt, undone enough to reveal significant cleavage, and a short skirt, though her thighs were large. She had licked her fingers, drunk too much, put on a fake moustache and posed for photos. Then there were the times when she was visiting Martha, caressing the teacup, leaning over the kitchen bench. Finally, she had rung him at work, drawling like Elizabeth Taylor. She wanted to come in and discuss her will. He felt her drawing him in, pulling him closer. And it excited him. He felt her desire for him in her voice, in the risks she took, the way she would return his gaze, say something coarse or something sweet. Vulgarities and tendernesses issued from her with the same sort of carnal intent.

"Tell me, Mike, what were you like as a child? I bet you were a scamp." Her voice was syrupy with suggestion.

The truth was, he hadn't been a scamp at all. He'd been a well-behaved battler who had wanted to win from the moment he knew what winning was. And as he'd grown up in a country town that still retained its gold-rush grandeur, he'd got a whiff of what winning was early on. The shine of it had caught at his soul. From their modest rented weatherboard home, his father left each morning to drive trams, and his mother cleaned houses and played bingo on the weekend. He and his brother had their weekly bath warmed by the old chip heater and spent afternoons aimlessly kicking a football on the vacant block. In winter they went to bed early to escape the cold and listened to the crackle of the radio serial, that faraway voice that whispered the stories of elsewhere, awakening in him the possibility of other possibilities. He was startled out of this somnolence by the much-touted arrival of the Ashmans' television set, which came in time for all the neighbors to crowd in and watch the Melbourne Olympics. Sometimes, after that, they went to the Ashmans' at 6:30 to watch *The Lone Ranger*. The television, with its Olympians and lone rangers, spurred Mike's vague ambitions, which later were realized in the singular glories he achieved on the football field.

Obviously, Susie was picturing a young rogue who ran barefoot through the paddocks. And Mike knew that when he called himself a country boy, it wasn't only to excuse any lack of urban sophistication, but also to lend himself a rugged hue that didn't belong to him. He'd never sat on his father's knee in the tractor; he'd never milked a cow or mended a fence or shot and skinned a rabbit. At Christmas when his dad brought home a chicken and they watched him chop its head off, Mike experienced an unmanly sort of horror, which he tried not to show, because it didn't do to be a girl about these things. Likewise, he didn't cry when he was strapped to the dentist's chair and choked with chloroform. Whatever courage he had he'd forced upon himself; it hadn't come naturally. His adolescence took place mostly on sporting ovals and riding around in the town center checking out girls.

The enviable pleasures the city offered were carefully stirred into Mike's boyish soul by Arnold Buch. Arnold's father was a Jewish barrister and, according to Arnold, a descendant of the Hungarian oligarchy. The family had left Hungary during the Soviet occupation. Arnold, whose pale, fine face was crowned with glossy dark curls, did in fact have a regal manner. Mike could still picture him sitting on the tram like a dark bird, with ankles flashing bottle-green socks, and a wry smile, which usually foretold a witty comment about whomever or whatever had just caught his eye. It was a mystery to Mike why he had been chosen by Arnold. Though this bestowed on him a sense of superiority, it also made him all the more aware of the lowliness of his origins. If it weren't for his athleticism, and the moments of transcendence it afforded him, he wouldn't have had the heart to strive for more. He had tasted glory, and it had awakened a hunger. He'd begun to look for something bigger when along came Arnold—delicately hewn, glowing and sardonic. His elegance was bold and his aim precise. Arnold had no interest in sport beyond that of making incisive and sometimes cruel comments on the strange culture that he, like an exotic plant in the wrong landscape, had found himself in. But he had an interest in Mike. Before school finished, Arnold had devised a plan for them to flee. Mike had used the anticipation of this plan to quell the usual gnawing of youth, so that when he launched his life, it would be with the force of a stone released from its catapult. And when he went, he took with him not a glimmer of canny knowledge or intention—just hunger, guts, his good looks, and his best mate, Arnold Buch.

Three years later he returned with Martha.

The instant of meeting her had swerved his whole life in a direction he hadn't been planning to take.

Mike wouldn't tell Susie any of this. Men should make their own plans. And he wouldn't speak of Arnold. Every time his mind arrived at Arnold Buch, it reared up, like a horse coming across a snake.

"Yeah, I was a bit of a scamp," he lied.

Mike wasn't ready to give Susie Layton up. Not yet. But Tilly had threatened everything. He was annoyed at her for this. He wasn't a man to drag his thoughts into the heart of things. He rarely wondered what other people might feel. It wasn't his business— just as this wasn't Tilly's. As for Susie's husband, he and Joe weren't proper mates—they hadn't played footy together; they just knew each other the way anyone who had been living here long enough did. It would be awkward were Joe to find out. He was a decent sort of bloke, well liked—Mike had nothing against him. But what he didn't know wouldn't hurt him. Who was Tilly to throw that high-pitched moral outrage at him? How could she chastise him as if she knew better than he, when she was too young to understand anything of marriage? She didn't know what it was like to be married to Martha. No one did. His anger started again. He turned away from Martha and closed his eyes.

But what if Martha did find out? He hadn't thought about this possibility until Tilly had stood there saying she knew. What would Martha do if Tilly told her? He didn't love Susie. He loved having sex with her. And did he even love that? It was more the whole affair that he loved, not as much for the physical pleasure it gave him as for the discovery of the erotic tension it had erupted from and gave life to. The affair with Susie Layton had thrown his life back into the headiness of his youth. It had unstitched the seams that had enclosed him within a home, a job, a family. It had undone the package he'd become and pulled him off the conveyer belt toward the looming inevitability of old age. Susie had done that as soon as she whispered in his ear a word that Martha would never have used. He hadn't known that a word could stir him up as it did—he hadn't known that this dirtiness could be thrilling. It had opened up in him a gaping hunger; the scent of something lay before him. His life was rushing into an alluring darkness. Distracting thoughts overcame him at work. He drove like a young man, already stirred up, to orange brick motels in the afternoon. It was sordid, alive, full of possibility and danger. Yet, he didn't want to leave Martha. It would never occur to him to not be with Martha, and if she left him, what would he do? The affair could not exist without Martha.

She had turned off the lamp. In the dark he could hear her breath and feel the warmth of her body. She lay apart from him, but his hand grazed hers and she didn't move it away. There was the familiar smell of her in the haze of heat that enclosed them. Or was it the interwoven smell of them, the two of them together? This was what he had lived within for twenty years. It was placid, familiar. And yet, Martha was still beautiful to him. He still watched her as she dressed in the morning. She always got up before him. Sometimes he ignored the whole scene; sometimes he pretended he was asleep. Sometimes it saddened him to watch her; it was better to dream.

On occasions Martha made an effort. She wore earrings, perfumed her wrists and made up her eyes. She didn't do it to please him; she did it to show him. She danced in the kitchen if the right song came on and although she didn't dance well, or because she didn't dance with any style, he was reminded with a pang of his attraction to her. In her graceless eruption of energy, there was a wild untethered girl. He'd imagined she would abandon herself, that together they would be animals in life. It had never happened. Martha still had a suggestive look about her sometimes, and she stomped her hoof as if she knew it, but she never gave in to the gallop. Instead she became stiff and clever. These days, if she drew his attention, it was only so she could throw it away again, or so it seemed to him.

And yet sometimes she crawled into his arms. When she was beaten. When she was tired or sad or defeated by her own frustrations. When she had argued with the school that art classes should not be removed from the curriculum with the funding cuts and failed. When she had cooked soup for a sick friend and dropped the whole pot. Then she came inside and crawled into his arms.

Mike wrapped his hand around hers. He encircled her small wrist; he had always loved her wrists.

14

Thunder cracked open the sky, but only a few fat drops of rain splattered on the tin roof. PJ woke Ada. He always did when there was a storm. He climbed onto her bed and shivered, pawing her and shuffling closer every time the thunder rolled. Ada waited for the floods of rain, but they never came. The sky withheld. She could feel it—as if the sky folded its great arms across itself. Only that sliver of breeze escaped and swayed the cardboard fish she had hung in the window. Had the terrible doom already happened? Was the affair, as she called it, since that was what Tilly had called it, the terrible doom? Since the mechanics of sex had been explained to her, Ada had been filled with dread for her future with boys, and now that sex had been presented, by Mrs. Layton and her father, with a close-up view, Ada thought of it as an urgent and frightening activity. Ada felt about it as she would feel about having an organ removed in an operation in a hospital.

But it was how you had babies.

Did that mean Mrs. Layton would have a baby? Ada would have to ask Tilly this, though Tilly had told her not to think about it anymore. Because the baby would be related to Ada, and

Ada had always wanted a younger sister. With these thoughts, Ada drifted back to sleep.

When she woke in the morning, and while Tilly and the others still slept, she ran outside with PJ and checked for signs of life in the cherry tree after the few fat drops of rain and the new coolness in the air. The sky was calm and gray, and the air smelled of grass and peppercorn. PJ almost galloped with relief. Ada broke a twig on the tree, but it still snapped, as brittle and gray as before. Not one blade of grass had sprung back up. Even so, there was a new feeling in the air, and it would take time for the world to know it and respond. Ada stared straight back at the dim blaze of sun to let it know it hadn't overpowered everything. She went to the coop to see if George and the chickens were pleased and would share her satisfaction. Esmeralda was in the nesting box. Peachie and Bolshie bustled at her legs. The Famous Friends and the Outsider, skittish as always, dashed straight past her. She gave them some clean water and threw some seed. She crept under the trampoline and lay still, closing her eyes and letting the cool seep into her so that she could keep it.

A fresh, overturned, beginning feeling filled the house, and her mother was suddenly happy again. Their father took them all to dinner at the Railway Hotel. Martha wore the Arnold Buch dress, which Ada touched to check how soft it was. Ben drank beer with Mike and played pool with some older boys. Ada had cheesecake for dessert. Only Tilly was quiet and withdrawn. Mike tried to draw her out by giving her hard pinches on her leg, and when this didn't work, by making jokes about how he didn't understand women's moods. Tilly forced a smile in return, which seemed to make her even quieter. She hardly ate her food. Martha said Tilly was ungrateful and ruining everyone else's good time. It was true that Tilly was ruining the night by being the only one not to have a good time, but though Ada knew what Tilly's reason was, Tilly had promised that nothing would change, and Ada was doing her best to make sure that nothing did. If she let the affair stop her enjoying her cheesecake, the affair would have won.

But deep down this disquiet of Tilly's ruffled Ada's faith in the calm, and for a while she resented Tilly for it. She wanted to believe that the thing that was going to break had broken and everything else would be fine, but Tilly had not returned to normal.

And then two things happened in that last week of the holidays that turned events toward the next hour of their lives. Only it was Tilly's and Ben's lives, not Ada's, and it compounded for her the sense that she was going to be left behind.

First Ben was caught smoking a bong in his bedroom with Jimmy Grigson. Ada ran outside to see the bong: it was a satisfyingly ugly and threatening object that had all the trappings of criminal activity, having been produced behind backs, with conniving, but also with know-how. It was made of old transparent hose that had yellowed and was folded over at the top. It had a stand made of a coat hanger and other smaller scientific bits, which Ada couldn't make out properly as Martha held it away from her (it ponged) and carried it directly to the outside bin. What Ben supplied to the making of the bong and the procuring of the marijuana, Ada wasn't told, though she did ask, but she suspected that it was considerable because of the fuss it seemed to cause. Tilly was always cross about Ben having his own bedroom, separate from the house. Ben got the room, but Tilly was the oldest. Martha had said it was because of Ada, who everyone knew still crept into Tilly's bed. Fortunately for Ada, Tilly didn't believe this was the reason.

"It's just because Ben is the favorite," she said to Ada on the side, because no one could accuse their mother of any wrong-doing or injustice without retribution. Their mother had a bad temper.

Now there was talk about whether Ben could be trusted to have the outside room, and for a dreadful moment Ada feared Tilly would be given the room after all. But instead Ben was put on probation. If he did it again, he would be returned to the house and grounded for a month. But it was clear to Ada that though their parents had desperately thrown threats at him, Ben would still slide out from under them, wriggle free and pad slyly away, hands in pockets, looking for the next thing. Martha must have felt this too, because she became irritable and snappy again and stayed in bed with a migraine for a whole day and night.

The other thing that happened was that Tilly received a gift. It came from Mr. Layton. She and Ada had gone to the Laytons' together. Tilly wanted to go alone, but when she told their mother she was going to Alice's house, Martha said, "Well at least take Ada with you. I've got a headache." Tilly complained, and Ada did a quick calculation of other options. She was still in her huff with Louis and she had decided he was too young and cowardly to play with, and the whole Maguire family, who were the neighbors on the other side, had gone to the beach for the weekend. But she didn't want to go to Toby Layton's, because she didn't know him well and she wasn't sure how to play with him since she didn't like games such as football or cowboys. But what was worse was that she was afraid of Mrs. Layton. She was embarrassed that she had seen Mrs. Layton in the nude and that her own father had touched Mrs. Layton's bare bosoms. She didn't know if she could hide that sort of embarrassment. Tilly told her not to say anything to Toby Layton about it, but Ada couldn't trust herself not to tell. She had no intention of playing with boys anyway. On the other hand, Alice and Tilly didn't play anymore. They just talked, and Ada knew they would want to talk on their own. She was exactly the wrong age for everything: too young to listen in and too old to play with boys just in case they thought of sex. Also, she knew things that Toby Layton wouldn't know. She knew, for example, what a bong looked like. She knew all the endangered Australian animals, she knew where there was a windmill and a deep hole, and she also knew about sex.

Alice lived on the other hill (the town was nestled in a valley and all the nicest houses were perched on the surrounding hills), and Ada would have usually gotten there by walking cross-country, through the bush tracks. But Tilly went on her bike, which was quicker, so Ada reluctantly followed on hers. The sky was bright and cloudless. It was a hard ride and the brightness of things hurt Ada's eyes. The heat seemed so locked within the ground, the sky, the fences and trees that everything was bone silent. The air was starved of breath and the birds were dead quiet. Ada felt she might just melt too. They went along the little path that ran between the tennis courts and the creek.

Evie was coming the other way with her little dog. Evie was old and sat in a wheelchair that went along like a little car. She wore a large white cricket hat and an orange nylon dress, which made her sweat and turn red in the face, like an umpire. Ada got off and stopped to say hello. Evie wanted to chat, of course.

"Hello, Ada."

"Hi, Evie."

"It's a hot day, isn't it? I just went to the shops for some bacon."

Evie had a bowl cut and eyes as wobbly as poached eggs. Her voice was as high and as eager as a kid in a cheerful mood. Her face arranged itself with an unnatural effort into a large beaming smile. Ada sometimes felt she was more grown up than Evie, which was why she liked talking to her. Evie was old and alone, apart from Elmer, her shaggy little dog, and she had to sit in that funny chair and couldn't walk. She could stand up, though, at home and make dinner. Ada knew this because she had asked her. But what was worse was that Elmer had had one of his eyes bitten out by another dog in a fight and the other eye got infected and had to be taken out by the vet, so now he had no eyes at all. But he still led the way, sometimes wandering off the path and bumping into the trees, so Evie had to call him back. Elmer still wanted to be a help to Evie and Evie let him believe he was the one leading the way, because she knew that would make him feel useful. It was a fumbling back-to-front kindness, which Ada appreciated.

Ada could see Tilly ahead of her, waiting. She had to pedal off before Tilly got grumpy. Ada called out to Tilly by way of an excuse, "But did you see Elmer, with no eyes?"

Tilly frowned. She stood still and watched Evie and Elmer in the distance. She looked confused and hot, but she didn't tell Ada off for holding her up after all.

Tilly got off the bike and pushed it. Ada was relieved. She didn't like to be the one to get tired or afraid first and hold people back. She began to push her bike too. She was sweating and thirsty.

Alice lived in a grand house with a front lawn that was always mowed and arranged with proper, squared-off flower beds that had no weeds in them. It had a sense of order about it that their house didn't have. Their house was tumbledown; the front fence showed straightaway how it was, with its missing fence palings, like the gaps in an old person's grin. In front of it were the sad, sizzled remnants of a lavender hedge. Over the path to the front door, there was an arch with a dogged old apricot rose that could hardly be bothered to flower. But since no one used the front door, the house was all round the wrong way—everyone came in through the kitchen at the back. The veranda, once you reached it, was an embarrassment to their mother. You could hardly walk down one side, it was so cluttered with junk: doors that had been replaced, boxes of hand-me-downs, Ben's old drum kit, a rain-ruined table-tennis table as warped as the sea but still okay to play on if you could find someone who would play with you. Mostly Ben and Tilly couldn't be bothered playing with Ada as she wasn't as good as they were. There were also hoses, some with holes that were meant to be fixed one day, spades, and a woodpile, which was dangerous because snakes like to sleep in woodpiles.

Alice's front porch had no junk on it at all, no snakes, just some potted plants and two matching chairs with a small table where Alice's parents probably rested their glasses of gin in the evenings. Mrs. Layton had nothing to be embarrassed about on her veranda. But Mrs. Layton had other things to be ashamed about.

When Alice opened the door, Tilly made a face. "Sorry, I had to bring Ada."

If Alice cared, she didn't show it. Alice was polite to everyone. She cheerfully pulled them both inside. Not only was the house in order but it was calm and cool, and once inside Ada forgot about the stifling heat outside.

"Ada," Alice said. "You can do whatever you want. We have loads of puzzles. You could watch a movie."

"I'll watch a movie," Ada said. She was too old for puzzles and felt insulted that Alice had suggested them, but a movie meant it wasn't going to be too bad after all. Alice was the only person Ada knew who had a video player.

Alice steered them both to the kitchen for cordial. Ada loved cordial. Martha didn't believe in cordial because it was just sugar and coloring and artificial flavoring. She made them drink water. Sometimes she would buy a big bottle of Harcourt apple juice, but she got cross if everyone drank it straightaway and there was none left. But how could you not drink it if it was there? Alice's father was at the kitchen table, which surprised Ada. Usually fathers were not home during the day, but she remembered it was Sunday and her father was only out because he was playing tennis. Alice's father was older than hers. His hair was already gray. He was reading the newspaper, but he looked up when they came in and stood up immediately. He was like Alice, very polite.

"Hello, Tilly. Is this your little sister?"

"This is Ada," Alice answered for Tilly because Tilly was shy. "She's going to watch a video."

Alice's father smiled. He understood, Ada could tell, that she was being shuffled out of the way by everyone today.

"A movie," he scoffed. "Why don't you have a swim? Toby will go for a swim with you." Ada was so alarmed at the prospect of swimming with Toby that she accidentally smiled.

"She doesn't want to play with Toby, Dad, she wants to watch a movie," said Alice.

"I see." He nodded and Ada felt he really did see, though what exactly he saw, she didn't know. He turned to Tilly.

"I'm glad you're here, Tilly. I've got something for you. Wait a minute. I'll get it."

Tilly looked alarmed, embarrassed.

"For me?" she questioned, as if it couldn't possibly be.

But it was. He returned with a white plastic shopping bag and handed it to Tilly, explaining that he had thought of her when he saw it. Tilly pulled a record out of the bag. Keith Jarrett, *The Köln Concert*. On the cover there was a black-and-white photo of a man with dark hair, his head hanging forward and his eyes closed, as if sleeping sitting up. Tilly stared at it apprehensively. She didn't know who Keith Jarrett was, and neither did Ada.

"He's a jazz pianist and this is a famous concert—it was all improvised," Alice's father explained. "I've heard you improvising here. Which is why I bought it for you. I thought it might be inspiring. But it's a waste of your gift, I think, if you don't have lessons. Tell your parents you should have lessons. Try Daisy Cavallo. She's good."

Gift? He had said Tilly had a gift. Ada had never thought of Tilly as being good at anything. Their mother had always said Tilly was hopeless, and Tilly seemed to agree. She wasn't top of the class, she wasn't a neat writer, she wasn't good at drawing, and she never remembered jokes.

It must have shocked Tilly when Mr. Layton said she had a gift, because she just stood there and didn't say a word. She stared at him and when her voice did finally come out (Ada was ashamed it took so long), she only said, "Thank you," and she went red and looked down at the floor instead of looking at Mr. Layton. But what Ada heard in Tilly's voice was the choking sound that Ada knew was the cramming down of tears. Why would Tilly cry when she had just gotten a present? She should have been happy, but Tilly behaved as if she had an internal pipe leak. Tilly wiped secretly at her eyes, while Alice tried to change the tone by saying that her dad was always getting presents for people, but he was right, Tilly should have lessons and Mr. and Mrs. Bloom should get their piano tuned properly.

Afterward, as they picked up their bikes, Ada asked Tilly about the record. Ada had watched *To Kill a Mockingbird*. She was feeling a bit sensitive and concerned, though she wasn't sure what she was concerned about. Tilly had pulled the record out of her bag and was examining it.

"Do you like your new record?" Ada asked.

"I don't know yet. I've never heard of it before."

"It was nice of Mr. Layton to give it to you, wasn't it? Poor Mr. Layton . . ." Ada didn't know how to continue. She didn't want to think of Mrs. Layton's embarrassment and how Mr. Layton would feel if he knew.

Tilly gave a crooked smile.

Ada persisted with a different thought. "Is the man who plays the piano a Negro?"

"*Negro*? I guess so, why?"

Ada didn't answer. In the movie, they put him in jail and killed him though he didn't hurt anybody. Ada couldn't talk about it because she didn't want to think about it.

Tilly stuffed the record back in her bag just as she stuffed her thoughts back in her head. Ada could tell when Tilly was clammed up with thoughts. Tilly kicked her bike stand up.

"Are you going to ask for piano lessons?" Ada was determined to get at Tilly's feelings, though Tilly was not in a forthcoming mood.

Tilly shrugged. "I don't know. They won't say yes. It will be too expensive."

"Ask Dad. He might."

"Dad . . ." Tilly rolled her eyes scathingly. She straddled her bike and showed with a little jerk of her head that she was ready to go.

But Ada hadn't quite got to where she wanted. "Why were you sad when you got the present?"

Tilly didn't look cross or surprised that Ada had noticed. She stared out over the town and sighed. "Oh, I don't know. I think . . . Just because he was kind. To think he went out and thought about something for me." Her lip wobbled. It sounded as if she might cry again, but instead she blew out a long breath and took off down the hill on her bike.

Ada paused before following her. Was this possible? Can you feel sad when someone is kind? She had felt a strange sort of sadness when the father of Scout in the movie (who was called Atticus but was really Gregory Peck) had sat on the porch with Scout, in a swinging chair, and tried to cheer her up. And when Scout had crawled into his arms, Ada's heart had lurched as if it were she who had crawled in and felt the radiating warmth of the truth and goodness of Atticus Finch's love and intention. And all at once she was so happy for Scout it made her want to cry and she had to jam her fists in her eyes to stop the tears from rolling down.

15

Martha's nerves were frayed. She wasn't sleeping well. She never did in the heat, but this was worse. Sometimes she lay awake for hours. Mike's breath came from the depths, while she twisted on the surface. Her back ached too, and she had other stabbing pains and tingling or numbness, which terrified her. Surely a deathly disease. The doctor told her it was her nerves. But what did a country G.P. know? She should see a specialist in Melbourne. And there were the migraines. Martha dreaded them the most; the fear of a migraine could be enough to bring one on. She had to stop thinking so much. She was becoming anxious about her own anxiety.

As soon as they had all left in the morning, she strained to make the most of her free time. She had to decide quickly what would be the best way to spend it so that she didn't fritter it away doing housework. She would ignore the fridge, which needed a cleanout. Instead, she would practice her relaxation exercises like the doctor told her to. She lay down grudgingly on the floor and bent her knees. She closed her eyes, wriggled her shoulders, and waited for calm, but she instantly felt agitated. Even relaxing felt like another chore, another thing that had to be done. She was annoyed at it, just as she was annoyed at the fridge for getting messed up again, for being in the way of what she wanted to do: that unaccountable thing. She wanted to do something that would add up to more than a clean fridge, something inspired and consuming, something that was hers and that would count. It was always like this. Always, the creeping fear that a part of her was unlived, uninhabited, and that life's grand tide had swept her far away from her true self. And that self she'd never tried on was snagged back in her past—a frayed and shrunken old skin that would no longer fit her even if she did find it. Should she waste her time looking? How would she find anything as lost to her as that in just an hour or two? The flies were making it impossible to relax. The heat too. The whole house was stuffy and as dark as a hole. She would pull up a blind at least.

Martha stood up and began searching for the flyswat; it was that time of year when the small, sticky flies arrived in swarms. Their buzzing addled her; she was constantly swiping them from her body. She couldn't hear herself think, let alone relax. She set herself upon the flies. Her neck hurt.

What had gone was the expanse of possibility, the space of unlived potential, the feeling of being hurled through endless days like a bird goes at the sky, unburdened, hungry, oblivious and free. And all that energy had collected its wild momentum and unrolled itself into the sedate, solid form of a weatherboard-enclosed family. She'd rushed to get here and now nothing more would happen; life would just plod on, achingly downward. More worrying, more cleaning, and more sleepless nights. A life inside a house. A small life.

She could live that small life, if she'd only taken something with her from her youth, something like what Daisy Cavallo had. She envied Daisy even though Daisy was divorced and had that wild boy to rear on her own and was as ill-fitting in this country town as a black horse on a city street. Susie scathingly referred to her as "the whore on the hill." She was convinced Joe fancied her. He probably did, but Joe would never act on any fancy; he was loyal, for one thing, but also too morally upright, and he would pale in Daisy's presence. Susie knew this, which was salt to the wound, and, perversely, she blamed Daisy for the infatuation. It wasn't just Susie; other women didn't like Daisy Cavallo either. "She's aloof." "She doesn't contribute to the school community." "She's a terrible mother to that poor boy." It seemed that Debbie Rand, around whom similarly scandalous conjecture gathered, was Daisy's only friend—the talk that followed them hovered above the Cavallos' house, where the barrage of opinion had hounded them into a friendship.

Martha doubted these opinions affected Daisy. Unlike Martha, Daisy had a passion that was unequivocally hers, and it lifted her above the sting of disapproval or made her impervious to it. Daisy had talent, a creative talent (Martha imagined her always singing), and no one could touch it; upon no less-than-perfect husband did it depend. Daisy Cavallo hadn't thrown all her eggs into the thinly woven basket that marriage had proved to be.

It was at once a terrible possibility and a strange comfort for Martha to wonder if she hadn't found her talent because she simply didn't have one to find. Her heart shrank. She dropped the flyswat and wiped her finger over the dust on the top of the piano.

But Daisy Cavallo was all alone; she should feel sorry for her. And think of Glenda, without a child to love. And there was Imogen. When they were children, Imogen had been everything to Martha. Imogen with her pale freckled face and blinking eyes, her large house and the older brothers making model boats on the back step. That was where Martha had been happy: studiously ignoring the taunts from the brothers, though she secretly marveled at the boats they made. She and Imogen had a club, which enclosed them in a world Martha's mother couldn't touch. Nor could the big brothers rubbish it, or their boat-building feats compete with it. There were special rites of entry into that world, secret ones. They were elaborate and always expanding: there were lines to avoid on the footpath and others to jump on. And the invisible creature who lived in a crack in a neighbor's wooden fence, acknowledged and worshipped with violet petals, cocoons, loquat pods. Words had to be uttered in all solemnity or whispered in code. A very particular magic illuminated and circumscribed it all.

What had become a vivid and enthralling game faded from their lives as they got older and turned to bottles of Lilydale cider and dance classes with rows of boys in buttoned-up shirts. As soon as they left school, Imogen was instantly married. Martha did up the long line of cream cloth buttons on the back of Imogen's wedding dress as they stood in her bedroom, the one they had grown up in, while Imogen giggled over a glass of champagne. Although it had once seemed impossible, their lives had gradually separated. Imogen had two children, one with partial deafness. There were all the operations to fix it, and later she divorced her husband. The children grew up and moved out, and Imogen went on a cruise, met a younger man, and moved for a while to Argentina. And while Martha knew the basic plot of Imogen Ashton's life— she'd seen a photo of Luis, the young boyfriend—whatever had been between them when they were at school had vanished. Martha's life with Imogen was only something she remembered every now and then, like a house, a holiday, a season. Martha had put the distance down to Imogen's lightheartedness, until her husband rang Martha and said Imogen was suicidal and had been hospitalized. Martha visited her, out of loyalty. Imogen had her own room. Her hair was pulled back and she sat in the bed in a pale-yellow nightgown as if she were ill, and Martha couldn't tell what was wrong and neither could Imogen. "Are you happy in your marriage?" Martha had asked. "It's okay," said Imogen blankly. Her voice droned as if it weren't her speaking but a recording of her. She didn't once smile, though Martha was there.

Martha wept afterward. Imogen never remembered the visit. She later laughed when Martha mentioned it. Imogen had invited her for afternoon tea and explained that they had zapped it all out of her and put her on medication and now she was happy again. She gave a hearty, brutal sort of laugh. Her eyes blinked happily, closing out any elaboration of thought. She had made a passion-fruit sponge for Martha's visit, but she wouldn't eat any of it, because she was dieting. Martha had panicked. She felt desperate to remind Imogen how alive they had been.

"But you remember sitting on my roof, don't you? When we stole the vanilla ice-cream tub out of the freezer and ate it with our fingers, clawing it like little cats? And the sky looked like a wave that was about to crush us. And we tried to watch the stars appear. And there was the sense that we weren't just girls sitting there, we were just as real as the stars and just as tiny and just as much a part of the universe. Don't you want that feeling again?"

Imogen gave a dead smile. They had zapped this desire out of her. Martha clung to the memory of that feeling, as if Imogen's loss of it imperiled everything, as if the root of all possible manifestations of that wholeness had been cut away—sizzled by Imogen's electric smoke.

Imogen said, "You know I hardly remember anything. I don't even read anymore. But Janie does. She is reading all the time. It's such a relief that she likes books. You always loved books, Martha. I remember that."

Martha didn't want to remember. This was the problem with relaxation—in marched all the thoughts she had done so well to keep at bay. Better she accomplish something, feel the simple satisfaction of having cleaned out the fridge, turn her mind away from that creeping yearning. She was Martha Bloom, wife, mother, housekeeper, and this was her life; she should step into it without resentment. She should clean out the fridge. No, she shouldn't. She should make a pot of chamomile tea and write to Fiona in London, write a nice poetic whinge, which only Fiona would appreciate.

But Martha didn't do that. There was a "yoo-hoo" at the kitchen door. Susie Layton poked her head in.

"Oh good, you're home. It looked so quiet I thought everyone was out."

Martha smiled wanly at Susie and struggled to swerve her energy toward graciousness. Susie looked as if she had dressed for an occasion. Was it her hair, had she done it differently?

"How funny. I sent Ada off with Tilly. They've gone to your house. I've got a bit of a headache." Martha rubbed at her temple for effect. It was unusual for Susie to drop over unannounced, especially lately. Martha had vaguely wondered if she had offended Susie in some way. Susie had canceled swimming twice. Martha would have to offer her a cup of tea; she would have to waste her precious Martha time chatting.

"Cup of tea?" she said. Susie looked agitated. She fiddled with the Indian bangles on her wrist. Her eyes—Martha realized what it was—were rimmed with eyeliner and her gaze roved distractedly from one corner of the room to the other.

"Oh, I don't want to interrupt? Especially if you've got a headache. I've just barged in . . ."

"No, no, it's lovely to see you," said Martha, improving her smile and silently bidding her hour goodbye as Susie wriggled onto the kitchen stool.

"So, where's Mike?" she said.

"Playing tennis." Martha rolled her eyes. She poured the tea. "It's Sunday, his one chance to do something with the kids, and instead he plays tennis."

"At least it keeps him fit, though it's wasted on you, darl. Joe, gawd, well you know, he's so flabby, he's past the point of no return, even if he did take up tennis, which I can't imagine. He's not the sporty type." Susie smiled and picked at her tooth.

Was Mike wasted on Martha? He was still physically attractive; it was just that he had turned out to be so self-centered, and small-minded too, that she had stopped admiring him long ago. Once the admiration had gone, everything about him had lost its shine. He had become ordinary, a man who took out the rubbish, who made irritating sucking sounds and didn't care to think about the drought or the Third World. And yet she was beset by feelings of obligation. Even if she could smother all that disregard and throw it out of the bedroom, his desire was always there, like an open mouth waiting, and she never had a chance to want him. Sex had become yet another wifely duty and the bed another battleground, so that she climbed heavily into it, her mind set like a fortress door against him, against what he wanted from her. Nothing he did could open her. The more he tried, the more pressure she felt and the harder she had to close. Yet in closing him out, she'd blocked her own access to desire too. This dismayed her. She wanted to feel it. She wanted to feel what Susie obviously felt. Every now and then, when he wasn't pressing her, when he was up a ladder and reaching to pull pine needles out of the gutter, his shirt lifted, revealing a place on his body that she liked without realizing it, and it caused a puzzling glimmer of attraction. Or was it just that for once he was doing something helpful, so he seemed capable?

"The holidays just do me in," she said. "I'm exhausted."

"Darl, you look exhausted. Why don't you go take a nap while the children are out? I've got to get going, anyway." Susie stood up to leave as suddenly as she had arrived, gathering her bag onto her shoulder.

Martha was surprised. "That was a short stay."

"Yes, it's . . ." Her hand flew to her mouth. "The heat, it tires you out and, you know, I should get home to Joe. I think he's still depressed. Everything makes him sad. It's so frustrating." She closed her eyes, as if to give a moment's respect.

"Oh, God," said Martha, rubbing her own brow as she searched her mind for the right words of solace. "Life . . ." This was hopeless. She couldn't explain what she meant.

Susie nodded as if she'd gleaned something from it. Was she welling up? This was so unlike Susie that Martha felt a sudden rush of sadness, as if she might cry, and she went quickly to the sink to stem the emotion.

"Anyway," Susie said shakily, waving her hand, bracelets jangling at her wrist. "What you need, honey, is a little trip away, just on your own. Promise me you'll think about it." She forced a grin and patted Martha on the arm before she swept herself out.

16

Tilly woke early. She had a plan. She'd listened to her new record as soon as she had got home yesterday. Ada had left the room once she realized the singing would never begin, singing to herself to make up for it. "Miss Mary Mac Mac Mac . . ."

Tilly wanted her own room. She was too old to share with Ada. She wanted somewhere to hide. The country was all space. It was sprawling and empty and hot—like the skin of something, and the vast distances were like bleached bone. It was all so inhospitable, so endless. The house was hot and old and full. She wanted a forest, a long, sheltering, dappled-dark forest.

The music was strange—probably glorious and exultant or something. Tilly had to find out about it. Especially because Mr. Layton had given it to her, she had to take the time to make sense of it, and to like it. If she didn't like it, would that mean Mr. Layton was wrong about her?

But the music wasn't songs with verses; it was just piano that went on and on, like thoughts themselves, pounding and mournful and as restless as an ocean, with that same sense of lamentable inevitability. She had better like it. Every now and then the man who was playing it moaned, and because of this, she could picture him trance-like at the piano. Imagine knowing the piano well enough that you could make it sound exactly how you felt. What if everyone spoke in piano, everyone's laugh a different melody, everyone's anger a stampede of black notes? If people spoke with sounds and not words, who would she be?

She put on the sundress she had bought herself at the Salvation Army shop and went out the front door. She didn't want to see Martha, the early riser, already out watering her vegetable garden before the morning sun struck it.

Tilly rode her bike, but soon got off and pushed it up the hill, so as not to arrive in a sweat. The hill led to the Cavallos' house. The house sat below the road, and to enter she went down a driveway and past the gaping mouth of an old garage. The garden was old and dark and the house as long and thin as a ship. There was something neglected and secretive about it. At the front of the house, there was a concrete patio with a round stone table. Tilly took off her hat and wiped the sweat off her forehead. She went around the back and knocked on the kitchen door.

Daisy Cavallo opened it. Tilly had never seen her up close. She was a similar age to Martha, but everything about her seemed smooth, as if beneath her skin she was alight. Her face was wide and her eyes seemed to hide a secret laughter. She had an apple in one hand, and she wiped at her mouth with the other. She laughed. "Oops, I shouldn't open the door when I have a mouthful."

She was like an elegant, grown-up child. Her dress came all the way to the ground. It was white, with a panel of green embroidered birds at the chest. Who else could wear a dress like that?

"I'm Tilly, Ben Bloom's sister."

"Oh," Daisy said, and she smiled, looking comfortably lost.

"I was at school with Raff. We were in the same class."

Daisy wasn't like a normal mother. She wasn't making an effort at all. It was strange. Time ebbed back and forth between them like liquid, so slow and hot, as if they were both as dazed as recently hit skittles.

"Oh," said Daisy again, and as if she had just realized what the etiquette was, "come in. That's nice. Are you visiting Raff?" She ushered Tilly inside. "It's too hot to stand out there. I'm so fed up with this heat. I'm sorry our house is hopeless against it, but come in and I'll get you a drink. I'm not sure where Raffie is. He might still be in bed. Would you like an apple?"

Daisy called out to Raff, and Tilly hurried to explain. "I didn't come to see Raff. I wanted to ask you about piano lessons."

But she hadn't worn her dress for Daisy, though she did want to make a particular impression. She wanted to appear to have nerve and independence of mind.

But there were the feelings that had snaked up inside her when Raff had danced with her, and later had barged in on her dreams, all steaming and elusive in that dream way. They were safely stowed—nothing could be worse than Raff suspecting her of having feelings for him.

"Piano lessons!" Daisy feigned disapproval, her hands landed on her hips. "You realize I'm a scandalous person, though?" Her voice dropped down instead of climbing up.

"I don't mind."

Daisy looked delighted. She folded her arms across her chest.

Tilly felt more and more certain that this was exactly what she wanted, because of Daisy standing there in the white dress unlike anyone she had ever known before.

"Do you play already? Read music?"

"I don't read music. I can only play what I play."

Daisy bit into her apple. "I like the way you say that. How about you show me what you know."

The kitchen was small, flooded with sun and crammed with brightly colored and randomly stacked crockery. Vases sat on top of the cupboards, and there was a bunch of proteas in a green jug on a table, along with a wooden bowl of lemons, and a novel, letters, a spanner, a ukulele, and a half-peeled banana. The bench was crammed with appliances: kettle, toaster, a bottle of vodka, orange plastic canisters. Dirty dishes were stacked beside the sink. A large, uncurtained window looked out over the garden.

Daisy pulled a pin out of her hair and stuck it in her mouth as she used both hands to rewind a stray lock and pin it back. "Sorry about the mess." She threw her hand toward the sink and rolled her eyes. "I'm a terrible wife—probably why I'm not married. Would you like a drink first? Coffee? Maybe you don't drink coffee?"

Tilly took a glass of water and followed Daisy down a long thin corridor lined with precarious towers of books and magazines and doors to other rooms, some open, some shut. One of these had to be Raff's room. If he came out, she would feel so childishly ashamed and astray.

Daisy opened a door onto a large room, apologizing again for the mess. "It's such an old house. It belonged to an uncle of mine, but I've given up on it. It's too much work, I can't do it."

The room was arranged around an impressive stone fireplace with a mantelpiece on which sat a bronze bust, candles, an empty wineglass, and books. It was faced by two shabby crimson armchairs and a well-worn Persian rug. Unframed oil paintings covered the walls. Some were vivid and abstract, others were somber landscapes, and one was a large modern portrait of a man holding a bird in his hand. At the other side of the room was an upright piano. There was a glass door, which led outside to the front patio, and another large window facing the garden.

"My uncle was a painter. These are some of his paintings, but some are by his friends, too. Here, this is my favorite." Daisy pointed to a small, unremarkable landscape. "It's not one of his, of course. Have you heard of Clarice Beckett? No? This is one of hers."

Tilly said the name in her mind to make sure she would not forget it. Clarice Beckett.

"She had to look after her parents who were ill, so she only went out and painted at dawn or dusk. All her paintings have this misty, smoky aura, which I love. Some silly man, another painter, claimed there had never been a great woman artist and there would never be, because women didn't have the capacity to be alone. Well, I never heard such rot; her paintings are much better than his. Look at this painting. It's all about being alone. Do you like it?"

Did she like it? Was this a test? Did truly artistic people like this painting? She peered in: an almost empty street or pathway, clumps of trees, a gray sky, two small figures, possibly old ladies, who looked as if they'd stopped briefly to say a few words as they passed each other on an empty country road. It was all indistinct and drizzly, misty like Daisy said. Tilly thought that the two old ladies' passing moment was a small, precarious comfort that was at risk of being swallowed up by the wash of grays.

"Yes, it's lonely," Tilly declared. She had made up her mind.

"Isn't it? She wasn't respected in her time. Critics found her work dreary. But they were all men. They didn't understand; it's way too quiet for them." Daisy's hand rose to her chin. Her head tilted, and she stared sadly into the painting, seeming to forget that Tilly was there. But then she continued dreamily, caught in some weary reminiscence, "What men don't understand they disparage, but you mustn't let them get away with it."

She swiveled and caught Tilly's eye, grinning. "Don't you think, Tilly, girls would change the world if they could only speak up? Or if they could only be heard?"

"Yes," Tilly stammered.

Did she mean that? There was no point speaking when no one listened anyway. How would that ever change? How would she change the world if she could? It was a confusing question, the way Daisy had put it. Daisy Cavallo was saying things that made her very uncomfortable. She didn't know any of this. She couldn't know it. She wasn't clever enough to know how to answer these kinds of questions and she had never once thought about changing the world. What did the world need changing from? And who was Tilly to it? No one. A pale speck of a person in a tiny dot of a town.

"But that's a silly question," Daisy continued. "When I was young I thought I could change the world. And then you don't change it, but at least you find your own place in it. And you can be generous to the unknown. Everything is so uncertain anyway. Fight even the smallest fight, I say. It still makes a difference. Do you like the abstracts?"

"I don't know," Tilly said. She felt a sudden thrill. It was as if the light of a new truth had just poured in through a crack. Still, she didn't want to admit she didn't know. It was shameful how little she knew. The unknown was where she faltered, moment by moment. But it was also what drew her forward.

"That's funny. Sometimes I do and sometimes I don't," said Daisy. "Now come here, to the piano." Daisy marched toward it, lifting the lid. "Sit!" she commanded. "And don't be shy, it doesn't matter what you play. Just show me what you know already, and we can work from there."

Tilly played badly. She couldn't play as she played at home, where no one listened. It was all coming out stiff and thumping, with such effort. "Sorry, sorry," she whispered. But the wrong notes kept chasing her.

Daisy shook her head. "Don't apologize. Think of it this way: there aren't any mistakes, just choices. The more you learn the more choices you have." Daisy sat down next to her. "For instance, you are playing only in C. Let's show you another key."

Raff appeared behind them.

There he was, after all. Tilly drew herself up, so she could hold in a little jolt of panic.

"Hey," he said. He wore only his pajama bottoms: bottle green with a black ribbon where they tied up. He looked so undressed Tilly blushed instantly. His body wasn't a boy's body. He looked back at her as he reached one elbow above his head, and rubbed the back of his neck, carelessly lengthened himself beneath her gaze.

"Ah, you're awake," Daisy pointed out, triumphantly. "He can sleep in this heat. It amazes me."

Tilly's eyes wanted to look at him but she tried not to. In the confusion—it had never been like this before—her hands dropped from the piano keys and found each other in her lap, wrapping and fluttering like birds.

"What's going on? A jam? Shall I get my trumpet?" Raff dropped his arm and slapped both hands on his thighs.

"It's a lesson," said Daisy. "Well, not really a lesson, we were working out if lessons would be a good idea. Where's Sigrid?"

"Getting dressed. I didn't know you played piano, Tilly Bloom."

It was nice how he called her Tilly Bloom. It made her feel that he held her name in his mind, that her name had a place. "I don't really," she said. "I decided I wanted to learn. And your mum was recommended to me."

"Recommended? By who?" Raff seemed skeptical.

Tilly reddened. "By Mr. Layton."

"Well," said Daisy, "isn't that nice of him? He's a music lover. He came to the concert I did once, during the festival, remember?"

She turned to Raff who was leaning against one of the crimson armchairs, watching them as if he were at the theater. A girl walked in. She was the same girl he had been talking to at the party. She swiveled toward Raff, uncertain. He delivered his explanation with a contrived formality. "This is Tilly. She's learning piano from Mum. Tilly, this is Sigrid."

Tilly jumped up straightaway. She said, "Nice to meet you." It was hard to pretend. She was silly to have ever thought of Raff Cavallo. No doubt her cheeks were red and everything was obvious. She needed to get home—because of Sigrid, who was dressed in a white shirt with a badge and a straight tight skirt. She had a proper job, she was older than Raff, and she must have been his girlfriend, as she had stayed the night. Tilly's insides were hot and taut and pounding. "I should get going," she said.

"Well, of course. It will be too hot to ride home soon," said Daisy. Her eyes flicked from one person to another. "When would you like to come back and begin? You have a good ear; I think we could work well. Are you leaving too, Sigrid, for work?"

Tilly had waded way out of her depth and was engulfed by the vast room of paintings and piano and fireplace, all remnants of a grandeur that seemed alive in Daisy and Raff, and even Sigrid, whose blond curls gave her an unusual Hollywood glamour. This and her apparent disregard for convention (older girls didn't usually consider younger boys, let alone sleep at their houses) made her either oddly sophisticated or willfully naïve, both of which fit this bohemian household way better than Tilly did. Not only that, Tilly had to approach the subject of money. She'd come without asking her parents, with only the intention of earning the money herself, and it would be awkward to have to explain this in front of Raff. Sigrid had nestled herself under Raff's arm and was clearly independent of her parents. Most of all, Tilly had to get out before this jumbled panic turned her red and speechless. She would arrange a time for a lesson and talk about the cost of the lesson then.

Tilly said goodbye and hurried out. She pushed her bike up the driveway. Raff's voice came after her.

"Tilly," he called. He had her hat in his hand and walked toward her, in bare feet and still half undressed. He stopped to flick a prickle from his foot and looked at her. "You forgot your hat." He passed it to her and smiled softly, as if everything that had been so hard and glamorous inside was no longer there, and there was the dappled sun on the driveway and the two of them beneath it.

17

When Ada woke up, she went looking for Tilly. Ben was the only one in the kitchen, hunched over a bowl, shoveling in mouthfuls of Weet-Bix.

"Slept in?" he asked.

Ada frowned. She didn't like sleeping in. She didn't like getting up and finding the world already under way. She stuck a finger in her ear, as if to unplug it properly from sleep.

"Where is everyone?" she demanded.

Ben eyed her over his cereal bowl.

"Dad's at work. Mum's watering. And I've got no idea where Tilly is. Gone on her bike somewhere."

Ada stood still, her mouth open, her gaze shifting slowly between Ben and the garden. Did she want food first or did she need to go outside and check everything? But what did she need to check? Something could have happened. She should go and see what it was. Because she had slept in, life had shifted without her being able to take account of it and there would now be a stumbling gap in time, which turned things dreamlike and baffling.

It was her job to let the chickens out—and they must think they'd been forgotten. She ran to the door and tumbled outside. The heat made the air heavy. The grass prickled. She skipped, in defiance of it, to the chicken pen and clambered up on the wood block to pull the catch.

Before the gate opened, Ada sensed that, just as she had suspected, something was different. It was the quietness. There was no clucking or rushing toward the gate. She slowly pushed it open.

Peachie was there, or what remained of her; her head was gone and instead there was a bloodied hole in the center of a collapsed puff of body. Ada's heart jumped; her eyes jammed shut and opened again. The fox had come. Peachie was squished right up against the corner of the gate. There was a whirlpool of feathers inside the coop. Bolshie was still standing, but with her head bent down. She didn't move at all. It was eerie and wrong. Usually Bolshie rushed toward her.

Ada burst into tears and ran to her mother in the vegetable garden. She yelled, "Mama, a fox, there's been a fox. Peachie's dead. The fox bit off her head."

Martha was at the tap, turning off the hose. She wore a man's shirt over her dress and a straw hat, which was how she always dressed for the garden. To Ada she looked like a scarecrow. "Are they all dead?" Martha asked. She began dragging off her gardening gloves.

"Bolshie is still alive, but she can't walk. Peachie has no head. I didn't see the others."

"Oh God, but how did it get in?" Martha gasped. She didn't cope well with these situations. It upset her to look at something that had died. Once Ada had been playing with Louis and May in the garden and they'd found a dead rat. Ada had held it by the tail and run inside with it, so they could laugh at Martha's reaction. She'd screamed and turned away and told Ada it wasn't funny.

"Ada, run and get Ben. I can't go in there. What about the Outsider? Can you see her?"

The Outsider had survived all the previous fox attacks. She was a small gray Araucana who laid blue eggs and was impossible to catch, even for Ada. She was also the last one to go in at night; for a while she'd been known as the Teenager. But a fox had never gotten inside the coop before.

Ada dashed to the house to get Ben. But Ben had left too.

There was no one but Ada and her mother.

Martha paced. She looked as if she were cornered and could not go past the chicken coop, as if she'd have to stay in the vegetable garden all day. Ada began to fret. She stood by the silverbeet, squinting into the sun.

"Ada," Martha pleaded, "can you go in and tell me? Is Bolshie the only one alive, is she bleeding?"

Ada crept back to have another look. Part of her was scared, but the other part wanted to see. Bolshie stood still, exactly as she was before, with her head unnaturally bent. There was the lifeless body of Esmeralda lying sideways, like a lady in a long dress who had fainted, but also without a head. The Outsider's gray feathers were everywhere and so were the Famous Friends', but there were no bodies. Ada didn't go close to Esmeralda, but she squatted down next to Bolshie and cooed at her, "It's all right."

Bolshie was their favorite chicken. She was an ISA Brown and she always came to the front doorstep when she was hungry. She laid her eggs in Ada and Tilly's washing basket, pecking at the window for them to let her in. For a chicken, she was happy in your arms. Now Ada was afraid to pick her up. She patted her on the back a few times and ran to deliver the news to her mother, who was still pacing in the vegetable garden. She felt proud to be the grown-up.

"Ada, I think I'm going to call the Laytons and see if Toby's dad is there, and ask him to come and deal with this."

"Why don't you ring Dad?" said Ada.

"Because he's half an hour's drive away." She rubbed at her head as if she were getting a headache.

Ada patted her, reassuringly. "Don't be sad," she said.

"Oh, but I am sad. Poor Bolshie, poor Peachie. I can't bear to think how it must have been for them."

Ada was puzzled. How had it been? She remembered how Peachie had been cornered against the gate. She shook this out of her mind. Why did her mother think about that? It made Ada feel awfully sad, too. She began to cry again.

Martha marched toward the coop; she put her hat in front of her eyes, so she couldn't see, and she bent her head to the ground and went straight past and into the house.

When Ada got inside, her mother was already on the phone. Ada wiped her tears. She hadn't had breakfast. But she didn't feel like eating—she kept seeing Peachie's bloodied neck. It was confusing, as she knew she would enjoy a piece of honey toast if only she could stop thinking about the hole where Peachie's head had been.

Mr. Layton arrived a few minutes later. Martha thanked him for coming. She told him she was too sensitive for this. He laughed. Ada had always liked Mr. Layton, because he had a gentle manner and once he'd bought her an ice cream at the pictures and another time had shown her a blue-tongued lizard lying in the sun by the step. That was when she was smaller.

Ada's mother had found a cardboard box, which she thrust toward Mr. Layton, asking him to put Bolshie in the box so she could take her to the vet. Mr. Layton smiled at her as if she were a child too. He didn't take the box.

"You know what we say in the country?"

"What?" said Martha. A note of desperation heightened her voice.

"A sick chicken is a dead chicken."

Martha shook her head. "Well, you know, Joe, I don't come from the country, and where I come from a sick animal goes to the vet. Please don't tell Mike, though. He'll think I'm wasting money." She pushed the box toward him and stood firm. Ada was glad for her mother's good instincts.

Mr. Layton smiled again. "All right, Martha. She's your chicken. But sounds to me like a broken neck."

"But Bolshie is still standing up!" Ada protested. "And she's our favorite chicken."

Mr. Layton nodded at her as he took the box under his arm. Ada followed him to the coop. He stood and surveyed what Ada would call the chicken massacre, and then picked Bolshie up and put her in the box, closing the lid slightly and telling Ada to take it to Martha while he dug a hole for the others.

Martha took Bolshie in the box straight to the car.

"Ada, do you want to come with me to the vet or would you rather stay here with Mr. Layton?" Her mother's voice was urgent. She was moving too quickly, sweeping everything up in a terrible hurricane around her. Ada wanted to go with Bolshie, but she wanted to see the burial too. She was perplexed; she couldn't move as quickly as her mother.

"I think you should stay here." Her mother decided for her. "Go and see what Louis and May are doing. And get dressed— you're still in your pajamas." She was already getting in the car. She slammed the door and leaned her head out the window. "You need to tidy that bedroom today, too."

Ada nodded but she had no intention of tidying her room, not after the chicken massacre. She turned back. The garden shimmered in front of her eyes, as if it were a pretend garden, a garden that had died and been painted on instead. The chickens should be pecking in a group together on the grass, or scratching the mulch from around the fruit trees. Usually this drove her mother mad. The garden looked unnaturally still. The thuds of the shovel rang out with a dogged, dull persistence. Ada crept closer. Mr. Layton's elbows jerked up and down. He was digging a hole beneath the old pine tree. Ada felt afraid of it all. Death. The bodies. The hole. Even Mr. Layton, because of what she knew about Mrs. Layton, which came back to her, as if it and all the other horrors had joined with the thudding shovel. She knelt down and crept into the speckled shade under the plum tree. She stabbed at the dry old ground with a stick. PJ lumbered over and Ada put her nose close to his ears and smelled the familiar smell of him.

"The fox killed the chickens, PJ. Didn't you hear it?" She knew PJ was too old to hear things anymore. But she felt he ought to know. He had failed the chickens too; it wasn't just her. This was the terrible thing that Ada was feeling. She hadn't protected the chickens properly from the fox. The chickens were so silly and helpless and dependent. Ada had failed them. Everything around her took on a grim, mournful air. Even the garden had succumbed to death. Hardly a leaf trembled in the windless air. Louis and May hadn't come out, Ben had disappeared and so had Tilly. Her mother had driven away, and the only one left was Mr. Layton, who was digging a hole, and who didn't know the awful thing his wife had done in the living room. Ada felt the familiar, stalking premonition of the trapped heat of summer, as if it had tightened its hold on her. She wrapped her arms around PJ and he plonked onto his bottom and let her hold on.

"What's going on, Snug?" Ada jumped. Tilly was leaning her bike against the fence. "Where is everyone?"

The appearance of Tilly broke the spell of doom, and Ada rushed to tell her. "A fox killed the chickens. Mum has taken Bolshie to the vet, and Mr. Layton is burying the others."

Tilly didn't like it either. Was she too sensitive, like their mother?

"All the others dead. Even the Outsider?" Tilly whispered.

Ada nodded. "Peachie had her head bitten off. I saw it."

Tilly winced. "Did Mum call Mr. Layton?"

"Yes."

Ada knew what Tilly was thinking, but Tilly said nothing. She looked toward Mr. Layton, who was transporting bodies on the end of the shovel. "Come on, let's get something to mark it with. Some sticks and flowers."

Why did it feel better when there was something to be done? Ada raced around but she only found some lavender and ruby saltbush, and Tilly found a smooth stone for writing *Rest in Peace:*

Captain George, Peachie, Esmeralda, The Outsider, and Famous Friends, though the last three couldn't be buried because they'd been eaten.

In the end it was just Ada and Mr. Layton at the burial. Ada placed the stone and the flowers on the dirt. Mr. Layton watched.

"It's nature, you know, Ada. Everything eats everything in nature. We eat chickens too. The fox was getting dinner for her family, probably," Mr. Layton said.

He was trying to be comforting. He put down the spade and squatted next to Ada.

"But why did the fox have to kill them all if it was for dinner? They couldn't eat them all for dinner."

"They kill them all so they can come back for more for the next dinner. It's tough, when you think about it, being born as a chicken," he said.

"Better to be a fox, then," said Ada. She knew what he meant.

"But as far as chickens go, yours had a pretty nice life. They walked around. They got to eat worms."

"Poor worms," said Ada.

Mr. Layton laughed. "Yes," he agreed. "Worse to be a worm. Worms can't even see."

"Some people can't see either. Or dogs. I know a dog that has no eyes." Ada felt sadder when she thought of Elmer.

"Well, I bet his ears are very good to compensate. I bet he can hear things other dogs can't hear."

Ada nodded. Mr. Layton didn't yet know what he'd have to endure either. She wanted to pat him on the back, but she didn't know him well enough, and anyway he had stood up again and was too tall.

Martha came home after Mr. Layton had left. She had been crying again. She said Mr. Layton was right; Bolshie had had to be put down.

Ada put more rocks over the top and rearranged the wilted flowers. She felt the fox watching her. She gazed into the dark folds of the cypress hedge that ran along their fence. She was sure it was in there, in the early evening shadows, lurking, like everything else, getting ready . . .

Ada aimed a deep and threatening frown at the hedge and ran inside for honey toast.

18

Ben Bloom arrived home after the chicken burial. He'd spied Ada still in the garden with PJ, Louis, and May, solemnly showing them the chicken grave. Ben went over and heard the grim news. He said, "Poor old chickens!"

Ada cocked her head at him, squinting queerly, as if checking that he spoke sincerely. He shook off her gaze and headed inside. He did feel a fleeting moment of pity for the chickens, but not enough for Ada. He wasn't going to let it darken his day. He'd snuck out earlier with twenty-five bucks in his back pocket and a handful of coins he'd nicked from Martha's purse and gone to Jimmy's house to score a gram of pot. Then he'd gone to the shop and bought some milk. He walked into the kitchen, planning to put the milk in the fridge in front of Martha so that not only would he have a cover for where he'd been, but she would thank him for being so thoughtful. But no one was in the kitchen to witness his good deed, and this was a shame. He'd have to explain it instead, which was trickier to pull off. It would have to slip out casually. He could hear voices coming from the bedroom, and he tiptoed down the hall to listen.

Martha was in there with Tilly. Tilly was copping it. Ben listened eagerly.

"Well, if you've got money to buy yourself a new dress," Martha was saying, "then you can start paying for your own shampoo too. It's about time you made a contribution and stopped just thinking about yourself. Where did you go, anyway? I've told you, you're not to leave the house without telling me where you're going."

Tilly didn't reply straightaway. There was a long sigh. "Mum, the dress cost two bucks. It's from the Salvos."

"Well, that's two dollars that could have gone into something else."

"Okay," Tilly shouted.

Again it was quiet. Ben began to tiptoe back, but Martha started again, her voice still tense. She hadn't finished yet. "Where were you this morning?"

Old Sherlock, thought Ben. Martha had to know everything.

"I went for a piano lesson, with Daisy Cavallo." Tilly didn't hesitate this time. She would have known this would upset Martha.

"Piano." Martha sounded disconcerted but made a quick comeback. "Well, how on earth are you going to pay for that? I hope you're not expecting us to pay?"

"No. I'm not."

"Well?"

"I work." Tilly's voice was full of accusation.

Ben chuckled to himself. There was a pause before Martha gathered herself again.

"Well, I didn't even know she taught piano."

"She does, and she says I've got a good ear."

"Of course she says that. She wants you to think that so you'll come for lessons. She wants the money. She would say that to any potential student." Martha said it as if she was trying to be kind, to save Tilly from humiliation. "You'll be wasting your hard-earned money, in my opinion. But you never listen to me anyway." She was angry again. But Ben could tell she was winding up. Self-pity was her favorite note to end on.

He crept back up the hall and approached the room, knocking as he entered.

"Hi." He breezed in. Tilly sat petulantly on her bed, with a notebook on her knees. She hardly returned his smile, but made a weary face at his entry. Ben examined the dress she was wearing. She looked nice in it. Why had Martha made such a fuss about it? It wasn't short.

Martha stood at the window. Her smile radiated back at him. "Hello, darling. Did Ada tell you about the chickens?"

"They were all killed," said Tilly flatly.

Martha looked at Ben. "A fox got into the coop last night. I've had an awful morning. It's been so upsetting. I took Bolshie to the vet but he had to put her down. Don't tell your father. He won't like me wasting the money."

"Where were you?" Tilly demanded.

"Just went down the shops for milk."

Martha's face broke into a smile.

Sometimes it was too easy. Ben rolled along without a creak. Poor Tilly always went in the wrong direction and slammed right up against Martha.

"Where's Bolshie? I'll bury her," he said, to add one final stroke to the image of perfection he'd created. Martha looked at him with such aching gratitude. Ben knew this pattern well.

Taking out the rubbish got him in the good books for a whole week, whereas Tilly could do the dishes every night and still not get close. Ben thanked himself for his own good luck. He felt sorry for Tilly sometimes. It was bad luck to be born a girl, really. But they made up for it. By holding out. That was how they got even. They wouldn't let themselves be touched unless you acted just like they wanted you to. You had to show an interest in their feelings. Tilly would do that to some guy one day. She would make him take out her rubbish and talk to her about love.

He went outside and buried Bolshie. He went back into Tilly's room. He was vaguely curious about Tilly's piano lessons with Raff's mum. He would wangle the full story out of her without letting on that he'd eavesdropped.

"So, where did you get to this morning?" he said.

Tilly scowled. "Why do you care?"

Ben was affronted. "Why are you so shitty? I didn't do anything."

This was true. He hadn't done anything to Tilly, but she always treated him as if he had.

"I don't feel like talking," she said. She was scribbling frenetically with her pen in a notebook. She was probably writing something secret in her diary. Ben wanted to find it out. He was bored.

"Mum said you're having piano lessons from Mrs. Cavallo," he said.

Tilly frowned. She stopped scribbling and let out a long sigh. "Mum thinks I'm wasting my money."

"Mum's just jealous." Ben hadn't formed this idea before, but it arrived exactly when he needed it. He silently congratulated himself. It was an insight, after all. Not only would Tilly appreciate him encouraging her, he was confident he had stumbled onto a real truth; women were like this.

Tilly looked at him properly for the first time that day, astonished.

"Me? Why would she be jealous of me?"

"Maybe she wishes she'd learned piano." Ben shrugged. He wasn't interested in examining the matter, but now that he had Tilly's attention he could go where he had wanted to in the first place. "Anyway, who was there at the Cavallos'? There's usually someone interesting hanging about. Did you see Raff? He missed the game on Saturday."

Tilly rolled her eyes. "Probably because he's got better things to do. He's got a girlfriend. She stayed the night."

This was what he was looking for. He had suspected something. It was his turn to feel envious. "Imagine Mum letting that happen," he said.

So Raff Cavallo had an older girlfriend. Anyone else who had an older girlfriend would be boasting about it. Raff neither hid things nor showed them. He talked a lot, but always about something else, an opinion he had about a song, a news item he'd heard on the radio. He didn't talk about himself. Now, not only did he have an older girlfriend, but she had stayed the night. Ben knew what this meant. It meant Raff was going the whole way with a girl. And he wasn't bragging about it. Ben hadn't yet had such luck, though he had gone further than Jimmy had, with Candy Newton, who had squeezed her legs tightly together but let him touch her everywhere else.

"His mum's pretty relaxed about all that stuff," he said, as if he were too.

"I like his mum," Tilly said. Her voice was clipped, and she'd returned her gaze to her diary, shutting Ben out again. He couldn't be bothered pressing any further. But as he turned to leave, he noticed that she was frowning and that there was a strange effort in the frown, as if a great wave of feeling could rush forward and break right through it. Was he meant to ask her if she was all right? He didn't want anything to break. Better to leave her alone. Girls were not meant to be understood, just as nature couldn't be beaten and Rubik's Cubes were not meant to be played with, unless you were a nerd.

19

Tilly was overwrought and not sure why. Alice would know. Alice loved laying her finger on such agonies.

She went to Alice's house without a word to Martha. Mr. Layton had not returned home. It was a relief to have missed him. She liked him, and it was exhausting to try to be liked back. If he were there, she would have to transform into the sort of girl he would approve of, and who knew what that was? Well turned out? Full of manners, standing up straight? Or the exact opposite: poetic and bewildered, a revolutionary? She could so easily disappoint him. But so far he seemed to like her without her having tried. And she couldn't be natural. She couldn't tell Alice. What would Alice think if she knew Tilly wanted Mr. Layton to love her like he loved Alice? Everyone knew this wouldn't ever happen, and that fathers didn't love other people's daughters, but that Keith Jarrett record had let a little hope spring that he would barrack for her.

What worried her more was the affair. She hadn't told Alice. It was too frightening to think of what could happen. If Alice knew, would she resent Tilly by association? Everything about Tilly—her home, her family, her lack of ambition—it all buckled into crumbling disorder when seen next to the good Layton family, and the sordidness of this affair would heap more weight onto the rubble. If Mr. Layton found out, would he see the infidelity committed by Tilly's father as a contagion that infected her too?

Tilly suggested Alice and she go for a walk. They didn't go far, just down the side of the hill toward the valley where a dry creek bed twisted through a huddle of poplars. They sat in the shade, slapping at the mosquitoes on their ankles.

Tilly lit a cigarette. "A fox got all our chickens. It killed them all. Poor Ada discovered them."

"Poor chickens," said Alice.

"Yes, poor little ladies," said Tilly. "And I nearly cried when your dad gave me that record."

"Yeah. I saw that." Alice picked at a scab on her knuckle. "You're such a baby."

That awful, telling rush of emotion had overtaken her before she could siphon it out some other way. It had showed her love not for Mr. Layton but for Mr. Layton's kindness, or his attention to her, which fell into the depths and landed on a tender spot.

"I was embarrassed. I'm not used to presents."

"What about on your birthday? Christmas?"

"Mum's in charge of presents. I told you she always forgets my birthday. Remember when I was nine? I was so upset that no one remembered, I ran away and built a cubby and ate a whole box of shortbread creams that I pinched from the cupboard. When I finally went home she had gone to the chemist and bought me a hairbrush." Tilly whistled with false enthusiasm.

"Are you serious?"

"And some lip balm," Tilly conceded.

"Lip balm?" Alice snorted. "What's wrong with your lips?"

"Nothing."

Alice put her hand though her hair and stretched. "That reminds me. My mum took me bra shopping," she said, popping her chest out. "We got one you'll love. It's got lace on it."

Tilly bit back her envy, which was not about the bra but that Alice's mum took her shopping. "Anyway, the record your dad gave me, it was pretty cool actually," she said. "And it did make me want to learn piano. I've been to Raff's house and asked his mum about piano lessons."

"Oh, so that's why the dress."

"What do you mean?" Why did Alice only just mention the dress now? Had she been too uncomfortable about it to bring it up earlier?

"I mean that's why you wore something special."

"Special? I got it at the op shop."

"Well, that was a good score. It's nice. You look good in it." Alice smiled to show her sincerity.

"Anyway"—now that it had come, Tilly swiped the compliment away—"I met Daisy. She's interesting and she's going to teach me piano. I'm excited. I mean, I'm sure I won't be any good, but I'm excited anyway. Can you tell your dad, and say thank you to him for me?"

"You will be good," Alice said, irritated. "You always say you're bad at things, but you're not."

But Tilly wasn't being falsely modest. She hung her head on her knees. This wasn't how she'd intended the conversation to go. "I don't mean to do that," she said.

"Well, you do. You act like no one would like you too, but all the boys like you—it's you who doesn't like them. They all think you think you're too good for them."

"Who thinks that?" said Tilly, aghast.

"Well, Blake Armstead, for one. He's nice. He's good-looking . . . Any other girl would be rapt if he asked her out. But he asks you out and you say no. Remember? And also Ted O'Brien. And Harvey what's-his-name, the brainy one who lives near the station. And Harry—remember, he wrote you love letters and you didn't even write back."

"I did write back, that's not true. I just didn't encourage him. You wouldn't have, either."

"But I have a boyfriend. You don't. You say you want one, but you never say yes."

Tilly tugged at the grass. She stared out at the creek bed, where the copse of thin, speckled trunks looked like pale, straining necks, strangled by the dark shade they cast. It wasn't that she thought herself too good; Alice knew that. It was more that she didn't seem to like anyone who liked her.

"I get an icky feeling. I told you that." It was a feeling that hovered somewhere between discomfort and repulsion and it came on when, for instance, Blake Armstead had tried to kiss her at the bus stop. Alice giggled and shook her head. "You'll grow out of that one day. I did." She blushed.

Tilly took the cue. "So, how are things with Simon?"

"Oh, my God. Amazing. Really, I'm like a lovebird." Alice

launched into a description of her evenings with Simon: what music he played, how he had bought her a ticket to see the Pretenders, what things he said about her, how much further he wanted her to go. Should she? What did Tilly think?

"I guess if you feel like it and you trust him."

"I do feel like it." Alice's voice was hushed, her face alight with mystery. She twirled a lock of hair.

This was terrifying. The time for sex had been approaching and now it was here, and Tilly was still stuck way back in the icky feelings. She had to catch up.

"There is someone I like," she said.

Alice looked doubtful. "Really? Who?"

"Don't laugh," Tilly said. "Raff Cavallo." She squeezed his name out as if it hurt to say it. Before Alice could respond, she added, "But he's got a girlfriend. She's older than him. And she stays the night. So it will never happen."

Alice didn't laugh. Her eyes opened wide. "Raff Cavallo! Because he danced with you?"

"No. Well, maybe that started it. Why, is it weird?" Tilly hugged her arms around her knees. Now that she'd said it, it seemed silly and childish. Alice might burst out laughing any minute, and they would both admit it was a terrible joke.

But Alice didn't laugh. She arched her eyebrows as if perplexed.

"It's not weird, Till. Well, it is weird, but good weird. I mean I can see why *you* might like him. Because he is hard to work out and he's got those romantic eyes. He's just . . . I can't imagine him having a girlfriend. I can't imagine him making that much effort."

Before Tilly could begin on her description of Sigrid, Alice flashed on the sudden insight. She lifted a finger and wiggled it. "No, I know why you like him. It's because he's got a girlfriend, which means he's not running after you. That's what you like."

Tilly stubbed out her cigarette in the grass and lay down on her back. She was as confused as she had been before. She'd said it out loud because she wanted to put it out in the air and see it. She'd wanted Alice to heave a sigh laden with the tones of *at last, you understand us, you feel something like we do*, we, the young-in-love-girls. This was what love was, feelings curling up and out of you, beautiful as flowers, blooming in joyous, secret skies.

But Alice had poked a hole through the whole notion. Tilly only liked him because he didn't like her. It wasn't a real feeling. It was a trick of Tilly's mind, a habitual, strangling twist.

But real feelings had erupted in her body while they had danced and when she had seen him again. And she hadn't stopped thinking about him. She could see his face clearly with her mind's eye, and she felt some magic had enabled it, and this had to be love's magic. Life, in that moment, was palpable, brilliant, and deep enough to cause rapture. There was a potential there that she hadn't noticed before.

And she couldn't tell if it was she who'd chosen Raff, or if the feeling had chosen her. Maybe it wasn't a boyfriend she wanted; maybe it was that everything conspired to make her think it was.

Alice felt her dismay; her eyes were bright with sympathy and in an appeasing gust of generosity she leaned over, put her hand on Tilly's. "Till, if you want him, I'm sure he will want you too. Boys always do."

Tilly pedaled home toward the trouble that she would cop from Martha for leaving again. She didn't care about that trouble; she was more interested in thinking about Raff and her feeling, about whether it was a true feeling or one she had summoned from the long afternoons of summer, because school was finished, because it was time—the time for sex was approaching.

20

When Mike arrived home he was met by Ada, who burst out of the kitchen door pointing at the garden and detailing the day's horrors, including PJ digging up the grave and the grim task ascribed to Mike of reburying the bodies. Mike blew out a sigh. He was already weighed down. Ada dutifully led him to where the lifeless chickens lay. He edged them one by one onto the shovel while Ada watched to make sure he was doing it with the right sense of gravitas.

"Aren't you sad, Daddy?" she said finally, squatting down to help heap dirt. She frowned up at him. She could tell he wasn't.

"Well, I didn't know the chickens like you did."

Ada's eyes were fixed on him, as if this wasn't quite acceptable.

"If PJ died, *then* would you be sad?" The question burst out indignantly. Her question pleaded as much as it accused. He stopped shoveling and wiped the dirt off his sock. He didn't want to meet Ada's questioning face. Those round, startled eyes unpeeled everything.

"Ada, of course I'd be sad if PJ died," he said.

She was still looking at him as if this had passed right through her—he had played a shot and she wasn't playing it back. She folded her arms across her chest, protecting herself from his ambivalence. Mike shrugged. He felt prickly and defensive and wanted to turn away. A mosquito landed on his forearm. He slapped it dead and wiped the small smear of blood with his thumb. Ada watched him and, letting her arms loose, she turned back to the grave and began patting down the earth.

Ada was like his grandmother, Ma Betty. In his memory she was a dark old woman who'd made him sit on her knee while she pretended to talk to the seagulls. Ma Betty had the same instinct for the arcane as Ada did. She made wafty pronouncements about people that embarrassed the family. Apparently she'd read the cards too. She died before Mike went to school, so it was hearsay, really, but he blamed Ada's penetrating gaze on Ma Betty and perhaps feared it for the same reason. Would he be sad if PJ died? He'd claimed he would without thinking about it. But he would. He was fond of PJ. He always gave PJ a passing pat.

"I would cry for weeks and weeks if PJ died." Ada's small voice sailed up from the grave she was assiduously attending. He knew it was true. She was crouched over, rearranging the flowers. She probably would cry for weeks when PJ died. But he could do nothing to match it. He had never understood this sort of emotion. It came out of women and seemed always dangerously imminent within them.

"Make sure you put some bricks on it so PJ doesn't dig them up again," he said, readying himself to leave. But the sight of her grubby little hands patting at the dirt, as if she were sending the chickens to sleep, caught at his heart. He swooped down next to her.

"Ada, PJ will die one day. He's old now," he said. It wasn't exactly comforting, but it was all he could think to say. Ada ignored him. She busied herself with the arrangement of flowers. She made a circle of flower heads and arranged the sticks so that they spelled out *peace*.

"Does this look magnificent?" she asked.

Mike nodded. It was no good counseling children about the future. The future didn't exist for them. He was useless at this sort of thing: talking, understanding, guiding children through the thorny moments. He didn't know how to do it. It was Martha's job. He stood up again and watched as Ada pressed patterns into the dirt.

"Daddy," she called out to him. She had stood up. From her hand dangled a limp, creamy rose. The hot falling sky was luminous behind her. She looked like a gypsy child—a pale lemon frock smudged with dirt, swaying over her shins while she stared at him with a dreadful aim.

"Have you finished?" he asked. He was flustered, tired of this burial.

"If Mummy died would you be sad?" She said it with an unnerving directness. She didn't accuse him, but she watched him intently, as if he were a prisoner about to attempt an escape. He wiped the sweat on his face. A magpie warbled above them. The weight of the world's truth heaved over him.

"You know I'd be sad if Mummy died." He was defeated as he said it. He stumbled over the words as they rose, hurrying to cover the image of Susie Layton astride him in the living room. Nothing he could say would change the act of his betrayal or the fact of love's fragility. He couldn't show her that love was a complicated work, that it wasn't always as simple, direct, shining, and pure as a star. That was how Ada wanted it to be—as simple as her own raw little love.

But she'd seen something else. She had seen how things tarnish, how people make it up to themselves when love fails. She would see it sooner or later anyway. Ada's first piece of love's shining star had broken, and it was too late to mend it. He frowned, rolled his mind over it. He squatted down next to Ada again and pulled her in close.

"That's a funny question. I'd cry for weeks and weeks if any of you died—Mummy, Tilly, Ben, or you. I promise. I would cry for years."

Ada relinquished a smile. Her arm wound around his neck. Her fingers danced over his ear. She stared thoughtfully into the distance and her face looked strangely peaceful. "Me too, only I'd cry forever," she said. She let him go and went back to the chickens' grave.

Forever. He remembered that feeling. Or he remembered the sort of innocence that built futures out of forever. Ada would never know how he had been so fresh and clean. How he had gone to his first formal party like a puppy trotting along at Arnold's heels. How he could still see Mary Galmotte's white house, sitting like a cake on a carpet of lawn with arcs of gold light that danced with the tree shadows on the white walls. Mike had felt it as a sort of ambient invitation. He had felt the mysteries too. That house was an apparition, from forever, from once upon a time, from heaven and Hollywood all at once. The evening had laid itself out for him. His heart had quickened walking down that long driveway leading him to another world, a tantalizing, out-of-reach world—a world to conquer. After all, he was brand new and heroic too. Just like Ada's, his moral universe had been intact.

There was a stairway in the entrance, the bottom step of which was occupied by a young man with a banjo and a cluster of girls in shining dresses. The room was ample, open, drizzled with the early evening light; alight with a hum of frivolity and opulence he hadn't ever felt before. Girls, as decorative as tulips, swayed on their high heels, their high voices mingling with those of the young men with combed hair. Arnold had given him a beer and ushered him over to the window seat. It was Arnold's way to sit back and hold court, but it was Mike's to go out and explore. Arnold patted his pocket and pulled out two cigars. Mike relented and sat down. They had a game, which they both knew well. Mike's good looks lured them in, and Arnold held them captive. Mike had barely begun on his beer when Martha appeared at the top of the staircase.

She advanced into that large room of honeyed light and silk and promise, a tiny dark-haired dart of a girl swathed in dark green, like a blot of ink. She inched forward so tentatively and stubbornly that she broke the spell of it all, as if until then everything had been made of glass, and there she was, so unable to smooth herself down that she tore the evening's murmuring surface. He rose instantly, as if she might need him. He stood in front of her and told her that he had thought she might fall. She had replied that she once saw someone fall down at a museum. The woman slipped down marble steps in front of a whole crowd of people and her skirt slid up and Martha couldn't stop herself from laughing, though she felt terrible about it. Ever after she thought she deserved to fall down some steps, as punishment for that laughter, so she was terrified, of course. Mike assured her that it didn't show, though it had.

He immediately regretted it. He should have told the truth, that her terror had been appealing because it cut through in a room of such glacial composure. She had failed to hold herself in. It showed in the heat on her cheeks as she gazed back at him, grateful, he hoped, for filling the space in front of her. She drew a finger across her hair and, breathing out, she gave a baffled shrug and asked if he ever laughed when he knew he shouldn't. She said that when she smothered her laugh, everything became much funnier. The more she held it in, the more it wanted to get out.

Mike had smiled. Here was the girl he had come for. He watched her shoulders rise up to fill the moment, determined and tentative all at once. The instant he knew she was the one, he became acutely aware that he might not succeed in getting her, and the accumulation of those two facts hit him with such a pang that he fell silent.

She didn't, though. She told him that it was similar with anger. It was so infuriating to pretend to be nice when you didn't feel nice that your anger leaked out in little fits of irritation. He remembered how much he'd liked her eyes as she spoke to him, how they looked into him, how worried they were, how odd it was that she should be worrying.

She said she supposed he didn't get angry much. She mustn't have meant to stare at him like that, as if uncovering him. He almost stepped backward. He'd never thought about it. Was he an angry person? Mostly he got angry with himself, when he missed a goal, when he didn't win something. If he had made a good impression on her, he was desperate to retain whatever it was she was projecting onto him, but he wasn't sure how to do it.

She asked him how he knew Mary. When he asked who Mary was, she seemed delighted that he didn't know, since it meant that he had stolen into the party. She was instantly more interested in him because of this transgression, which wasn't mitigated by the fact that his friend Arnold had brought him along. She asked if Mike was at university.

He had been in the beginning. He had enrolled in an arts degree. Only because of Arnold, who was doing law. Arnold told him to study history and art and literature in order to become interesting. English literature. Mike didn't read novels, not unless they were thrilling, and the ones in the English literature course were anything but. He had never read anything so convoluted as Henry James. By the time he came to the end of a sentence, he had forgotten the beginning. In the tutorials he floundered, but on the university football team he'd come into his own. And he got a job at a pub in Richmond. He had cash. He had work. Why persevere with Henry James and the French Revolution?

She replied that all she wanted to do was travel, to see other countries. Mike didn't want her to go. She would never come back. He suggested she come with him and meet Arnold. Arnold was European, after all.

Mike should have stayed there by the stairs and kept talking, but it was his habit to return to Arthur, and he escorted her there as if taking her home.

Arthur glowed. He asked Martha how Mike had captured her. "If it wasn't his handsome face it must have been his good manners, no doubt."

Martha smiled and began looking nervously in her bag for a cigarette. She said that Mike had offered to save her, should she fall. Arnold asked if Mike did save her, since he was a bloody good catch. She said he didn't have to. Not yet. She tapped the cigarette on her wrist, turning to Mike with a smile, and because the smile searched him for his approval, his heart had flared, and he had to stop himself moving closer to her. Mike had intended Arnold's wit to hold Martha's attention, and she and he could unwind, warm up as couples do, beneath the sun of Arnold's banter, and come to know each other.

Arnold expertly drove the conversation, Mike relaxed, Martha laughed, and they all drank more. But things changed before Mike could take account. Arnold twisted the night toward his own elaborate purpose. He lured them out of the party. They got in his car. He drove. None of them cared where. It had felt mad and free. Martha's hair had come undone and it blew across her face. Everything seemed empty, the road, the night, the future. They hurled themselves into it as if courting oblivion, as if pursuing something they never wanted to find. That was forever. Or it was as close he had come to it.

That night had chased him ever since. It had begun at Mary Galmotte's and spun out into a dissolute sprawl. Hours passed—they were drunk, exultant, tired, half asleep, wide awake and on fire. But what happened he'd never understood, except that something had been sacrificed and what remained was dark and turgid and sleeping. He and Martha never talked about that night, yet it was there, as he stood watching Ada while the day sank away. He felt the tension of that night rising in his throat. The game he played with Susie had the same rules, or lack of rules, as the game they had played that night. He wanted to believe he'd convinced Ada of his devotion, and yet he wasn't sure he had. Ada always looked into things too deeply. She was a child with the soul of an animal, a nose for anything that was off, for the emotional weather of a situation. He hadn't lied. It was everything to him, this family, if there was no forever. Most of the time he took it all for granted. Sometimes he felt burdened by it, but surely all men felt like that. It was normal. If losing some part of it wouldn't make him sad, nothing would. His own father had gone to work in the morning after Mike's mother died the night before, just as he always did.

He pumped himself with these reassurances so that his step regained its characteristic bounce. He could expertly dodge that niggling doubt, after all. He had been exhausted and he didn't know why. He'd blamed it on the heat and work and the way blame had collided with his excitement about Susie. Tilly's accusation had shaken his moral perspective. Bouts of guilt had been dragging at the thoughts that used to swerve so smoothly back and forth to the orange-brick motel. But now, hadn't Ada given it all back to him? His rightful place. He could still love his family, be a good father, bury the chickens. None of this had changed; none of it was compromised by what he had done. Ada saw that, she must have.

He braced himself to face Martha. She would be raw after the chickens' deaths. Anything would set her off. He would have to be careful not to get into any discussions. It always irritated her if they did discuss anything. Nothing he said was ever right. She found his opinions narrow-minded and chauvinistic and she told him so too. He tried not to let things veer that way, but they always did, because Martha provoked him, airing her contentious views as wantonly as Susie Layton revealed her flesh. She upset herself worrying about injustices that had nothing to do with her; she found the whole damn country small-minded and backward; she resented the government, criticized the school curriculum. If he didn't raise his objections, own his opinions, what sort of a man was he? A pushover?

Not he.

Still, tonight was not a night to stir things up. He had to try to be sensitive about the chickens. Perhaps he should offer to do something. Get takeaway? After all, it was Saturday. It seemed fitting, and Ada would love it. She could go with him. Just him and Ada. He would try to enjoy it. They could have a conversation in the car. He would listen to her properly. Usually he could let her chatter away, while still managing to steer his own thoughts over top of her voice. But in the car they could plan what dishes they would order. Ada always had the special fried rice. He could promise ice cream afterward and she might forgive him. And as for Tilly, he could secretly sling her twenty bucks; tell her to buy something special, a new dress or something. All his debts would be paid, and Martha wouldn't have to cook dinner. She might be grateful.

21

Mike took Ada to the theater to see *E.T.* Martha wasn't sure Ada should be seeing it, but Ada would have sulked if Martha had said no. And since Tilly was doing her supermarket shift and Ben had gone swimming with friends, Martha would have the house to herself.

After they had all left, she cleaned the kitchen and surveyed it with some satisfaction. For at least a few hours no one would mess it up and Martha could do whatever she pleased. But there were Ada's dirty little sneakers still sitting on the kitchen stool. Martha flinched as she caught sight of them. She'd told Ada so many times to take them to her room. She should throw them out the door and Ada would be sorry she'd left them there. She'd never learn otherwise. She could see Ada in her mind's eye, standing as if in a daze, singing to herself and forgetting or deliberately not hearing what Martha had asked her to do. Martha marched over and grabbed the sneakers, opened the kitchen door, and, emitting a little grunt, threw them overarm, one after the other, as far away from the house as she could. They landed with a satisfying thud on the sun-grizzled lawn. She closed the door against the wall of heat and sank down on the kitchen stool, slumping her arms onto the bench.

Ben was the only one who could keep his room tidy. He was the only one who ever helped her too. She sat up straight again. She would have to verify this by checking the girls' room, just to see how messy it was.

The house was so empty that it gave Martha the feeling that she had been left behind, forgotten like those dirty sneakers lying on the stool. It was because the garden was deserted now that the chickens weren't there. Life had been sucked out of everything, and in its wake was an unnatural stillness. Even PJ seemed ambivalent: too old to hobble down the hall after her as he used to, he merely opened one eye to watch her leave the kitchen. All their lives continued out there in the world—Mike's, the kids'. They were all steadily advancing, while she was left behind, guarding the crumbling fort with the old dog and the flagging garden. They would all return, knowing that when they returned the house would be ready for them, the kitchen cleaned, the garden watered. This was her life's work. It was hardly luminous, but sometimes, it had to be admitted, she didn't mind those dull, uneventful days with their slow, small non-accomplishments. When the chickens had run to her and gathered around her ankles as if they loved her, and PJ flopped at her feet as she resuscitated the tomatoes with the hose, yanked idly at the weeds, emptied the compost, allowing herself to be distracted by wrens chasing each other through the grapevine.

She ate a slice of apple and turned on the radio; the sound of it was like an old friend. She squatted down next to PJ and took his head in her hands and professed her love for him. She did this daily. He was so accommodating. Maybe this would all be enough—if it weren't for the certainty that there was something else, something that existed deeper within it. She almost wished she was religious, or had some other sort of faith, a belief that she could lose herself in.

She stiffened as she entered the girls' room. As she suspected, it was in a mess. Clothes were strewn everywhere, beds unmade. Martha examined the clothes: they were mostly Ada's. And it was probably Ada who had emptied the jar of buttons. The desk was piled with things. How could Tilly complain about not having her own room when she couldn't keep her desk clean? But it was Ada's things that covered the desk: feathers, balls of wool, rocks, a sun hat, and jars of colored pencils. Martha jerked open the drawer of the desk. Sticky tape, a cigarette lighter (so Tilly was smoking), Ada's diary with the lock. Martha had already looked in it—Ada only wrote lists of friend's birthdays and phone numbers. Ada's purse, too, which was filled with coins she rabbited away. Both beds were unmade. She lifted Tilly's pillow and caught sight of an unaddressed envelope that Tilly must have hidden there. Martha snatched it up as if it might evaporate before she'd had a chance to investigate. She hadn't expected to find anything; she was just doing her perfunctory checking. But this was possibly something. She sat on the bed and opened it. Inside was a small piece of paper folded over a twenty-dollar note. On the paper: *Buy yourself something special. Love, Dad.*

Martha almost crumpled it up, but she controlled herself. That would be childish. There were better ways to deal with this. She carefully folded up the note and slipped it back under the pillow. He had done this behind her back. And Tilly had accepted it, of course. Martha paced the room. But why would Mike give Tilly money? Was he helping her pay for piano lessons? Martha pushed at the spilled buttons with her foot. The piano lessons had already disturbed her. Tilly was always getting opportunities that she'd never had. No one had ever thought of giving Martha piano lessons, and Martha had an ear. Martha was musical. And Tilly was learning with Daisy Cavallo. This was too much. The woman who stood for everything Martha didn't have. Martha could hardly bear to think of it. And if Mike was giving her the money . . .

She looked out the window at the garden wilting in the bright midday sun. She grabbed her bag, keys, and sunglasses and got in the car.

Ten minutes later she arrived at Daisy Cavallo's house. From the street, which cut across the back of the hill, all Martha could see was the old gate and a driveway overhung with a large tree. She stepped out of the car and peered through the huddle of trees that shaded the back of the house. It was a narrow weatherboard wedged on the steep incline, as old and worn as her own house and almost disappointingly familiar. Despite the rumors of the house's sordid past, there was nothing sinister about it. (It had once belonged to a reclusive relative of Daisy's, an artist who had come to an unseemly death—a hanging, possibly?) She had expected to have to fortify herself to knock on the door. But this house only whispered a collapsing, domestic sigh of exhaustion.

Loquats fermented on the concrete driveway. Martha could see down to the front porch, a slated patio with a round table and potted plants. A bike leaned against the wall; there were green thongs outside, and some towels drying over a rail. A pleasant sense of life emanated from the house. It unnerved her. She forgot why she had even come. She had no idea what she would say. She should have at least planned something. The note from Mike had infuriated her and when she had fallen on the thought of the piano lessons, she felt so excluded that she had barged ahead. Mike probably wanted to meet Daisy himself, maybe flirt with her. It had all come to Martha in a torrent of indignation and it had occupied her so completely that she hadn't stopped to consider.

She took a breath and, stepping over the squashed loquats, she made her way down the steep driveway. There would probably be no one home anyway. And if there were, she would say she was making sure about the piano lessons.

But Daisy Cavallo was home, and she answered the door with a glass in one hand and a long dark lock of hair across her eye, which she tossed back in a way that made Martha think of a horse rearing. Yet Daisy looked at Martha invitingly, as if she were curious enough to indulge the ridiculous reason for the visit that Martha secretly and almost shamefully held closed.

"Aren't you Tilly's mother?" she said, her eyes girlishly peeping over the top of her glass.

Martha bit back her irritation. She had probably seduced Mike with this comely behavior. "Yes. I'm Martha."

Daisy smiled. Martha smiled. The morning's quiet wedged itself between them. Martha sniffed just to move the quiet away.

"Well, I just came about Tilly. She says you're giving her piano lessons. I'm just not sure that's the right path for her." She felt hot, uncomfortable. She rearranged her bag over her shoulder. The skin under the strap sweated.

Daisy widened her eyes in astonishment. "Why not? There's nothing wrong with the piano. Are you worried it will lead her astray?" She tossed her head again and let out a little laugh. "I mean, are you worried *I* will lead her astray. Is that the problem?"

Martha looked down. That wasn't what she had meant to imply. She wasn't a small-town snide. She wanted to be taken for a sophisticated, intelligent person who was above the petty-minded gossip that occupied smaller minds. What was becoming clear to her in the moment was that she wanted to feel a kinship with Daisy; she wanted Daisy to recognize in her something different and special. And now Daisy pitied her for her small-mindedness, for her inability to appreciate music, for her stiff disregard of the artistic personality, when all of this was exactly what Martha did hold in high regard.

She shook her head stiffly. "No, of course not. It's nothing like that. Look, it's more . . . It's that I'm not sure Tilly can afford it. She only works two shifts at the supermarket. And if she hasn't any talent for it, then I don't want her wasting her money."

Martha withered. It had come out with a false note. It sounded awkward; it sounded exactly as it was—an excuse. She was awful. She did want the best for Tilly. It was true she didn't want Tilly wasting her money. But actually, it was because of Arnold. When Tilly played, it made Martha think of Arnold. She was getting Arnold all mixed up with Tilly. All this nonsense about the piano was very wrong and of course Tilly should learn. She waved away a fly, while Daisy stood still, as if staring at the lie.

Martha suspected Daisy of something but also admired her for perhaps the same thing, and this curdled into a strange sort of attraction, which she fought off with one hand and reached toward with the other.

"Would you like to come in?" Daisy said, finally.

Martha nodded with a thudding certainty. Suddenly she wanted to explain everything to Daisy Cavallo.

22

Ben went with Raff Cavallo and Will Rand to Turpins Falls in Raff's mother's car. After years on the same football team, they had found a way of extending the competition beyond the field and into games of their own invention. There were no rules. They made opponents out of whatever they could find: the landscape, its rivers, boulders, paths, and caves. They played against death, to prove their invincibility. They rode motorbikes at full speed through the bush. They climbed onto the roof of the visitors' center at night, jumping from it to the pharmacy roof and scrambling down the back. They waited with their skateboards at traffic lights and grabbed hold of the backs of utes. They walked down the center of the train track and leapt off when a train came, at the last second. Now that Raff could drive they could look further afield. Others apparently had done the jump from Turpins Falls before—a girl, even. Though she had landed badly and broken a rib. In Ben's mind, it was a shame a girl had done it. It lessened the deed somehow. He was dubious because of it. But he swallowed all doubt once he saw the drop.

They all stood on the track leaning over the wire fence; the white water fell long and far over a sheer, jagged rock face. He gazed at the large dark pool of water below them. It made his body tighten with a familiar mix of fear and excitement. Even the girl couldn't take it away.

The three of them climbed over the fence without a word. They clambered, single file, toward the top of the ridge, each with a stubbie of beer in one hand. The sky was cloudless, the black pool of water as round as a gaping mouth. They stood gathering their nerves. Raff jumped first. The hairs on Ben's arms stood up. His skin tightened around him. He grinned. Here he was, alive. The sound of the water ran through him like a cheer. He wiped the beer from his mouth. He squatted, placing the beer on the rock ledge. His thighs tensed. He sprang out, opening his arms . . .

His forearms struck the water's surface as if hitting hard ground. The sting of it resounded through him as he plunged down. He fought against it, spread his aching arms. It was like falling to the earth's core, to hell or to death. He cheered inwardly. The falling slowed. He beat his arms and legs upward.

When he finally surfaced, he gasped, breathing in life again. He swam straight to the side, where Raff sat waiting.

"Good?"

"Yeah." Ben shook himself, paused to collect his breath, and examined the underside of his arms. "Killed my arms, though." It was the plunging down in that cold black water that had been frightening, not the jump. He stared up at Will, who was the last to jump. He was such a small figure up there on the cliff.

"A man died once. Had a heart attack when he hit the cold water. He couldn't swim back up. Christ, it was cold." Raff lay back on the warm rock, goosebumps on his thighs.

Ben nodded. "Fucking deep too. Thought I was never coming up." He kept his eyes on Will. They'd left their towels up there. They hadn't thought about the cold afterward, only the jump.

"Let's go to the Res," Ben said. It wasn't that the jump hadn't been thrilling. But it couldn't be conquered twice. He wanted to go to the Res, where there would be girls swimming. He was in the mood for it. He swung his arms. The veins throbbed. He thought happily of girls and their bodies.

Will Rand jumped, his body wriggling, trying to hold itself straight in the air. Ben cupped his hand to his mouth and shouted, "Hold your arms in." Will's flailing body looked so flimsy. When he hit the water and went beneath the surface, it was like watching life being taken. Ben waited, watching.

When Will burst through, with one eye shut, it was not as if he had triumphed, but as if the earth had relinquished him, given them all a second chance.

Compared to Turpins Falls, the Res was sleeping. It was a large flat body of water, flanked with reeds, with bush at one end and a group of pine trees leaning toward the water. The water was dark—a kid had drowned in it, snakes crossed it, kangaroos swam in it, and Ben had once seen a drunk man drive his car into it. Where it met the road, there was one large straggly blue gum, which looked over a sloping clay gap in the reeds. People sat there: towels spread on the clay, little kids wading in the shallows, older kids paddling out on Li-los. People perched on the large rocks, drank beers, flung sticks for dogs, stuck their kids in floaties and prodded them forward. An old lady in a bathing cap dog-paddled at the edge.

They stood watching this scene for a moment and Raff nodded toward the pines, a long way around. That was where they would find girls. Ben swung his towel over his shoulder and pulled on a cap. They followed the walking track that circled the reservoir.

Ben had seen a brown snake here last summer. He could tell them, but they wouldn't care. It had slithered across the path and Ben had stopped to watch it. Its power was elegant, efficient and final. Ben wanted to face the power and know it. A moment to seize and shake till it fizzed.

"Tilly's here," said Will, pointing. "With Alice. See?"

"Shit." Ben's triumph sagged. He didn't want Tilly there. She must have finished her shift early. Wherever Tilly was, he instantly became the younger brother. He didn't want to be young, and he particularly didn't like to be seen as younger. He didn't want to be linked to Tilly, or anyone. He intended to arrive undefined, unknown, ahead of the game.

How did Tilly get here? She wouldn't have ridden her bike all the way in this heat. Alice's boyfriend must have driven them. Ever since Simon Marsh had come on the scene, Alice and Tilly seemed to be sported around everywhere in his show-off car. Ben hardly knew Simon, but he didn't like him. Simon crowed and strutted. There he was, holding the rope swing with the knot between his legs, trying to draw an audience before he jumped out. Tilly and Alice sat together beneath the pines, in their bathers, bare legs stretched out in the sun. At least there were others here. Ben could probably avoid having much to do with Tilly's group, though he did like Alice's smooth brown body.

But Raff treacherously left Ben and Will, without a word, and walked directly over to Tilly and Alice. He stood in front of them, his towel hanging over his shoulder. A conversation began instantly, though Ben couldn't hear what they were saying. He considered joining them for a moment, to lure Raff back, but he decided it was better to stay away from Tilly. He would let Raff hang out with them; he probably wanted to perve at Alice and would tire of it soon. In the meantime, Ben would have made his own conquests.

He had spied Candy Newton already, and also Kitty Hatton, who reclined in her usual splendor amid a group of others. Kitty Hatton was icy and distant. She was indisputably the best catch in town, and she was said to look like Delvene Delaney. He decided the likelihood of getting anywhere with Kitty Hatton was so slim that he was better off taking his chances with Candy Newton, who wasn't as good-looking but would be much more likely to put out. He had already kissed Candy, so he had to be careful not to give her the wrong idea. He looked at Will, who stood beside him, arms folded, eyes fixed on Raff, or probably on Alice. Will would have to come along with him; he wouldn't be able to make his own way. Ben nodded at him. "Let's go sit with Candy. Come on."

"We should have brought more beer," complained Will. He glanced up to where Candy sat higher on the bank. She was there with her older sister and she looked embarrassed about it too. "I'm going on the rope swing," he said.

In the end, Ben was left alone with Candy. It wasn't exactly what he wanted but he settled for it. She was nervous and pulled her T-shirt over her thighs. She had a pimple on her chin. Her hair was wet. He would have kissed her, despite all this, if her older sister hadn't been close by. Instead, he would have to make conversation. This bored him immediately. He watched her thighs, the beads of water sitting on them. She had a nice body— rounded thighs, a soft small pouch of a stomach, breasts bigger than his hand could hold. He remembered touching them. She thought she was fat, because she wasn't skinny, because she didn't look like Kitty Hatton. Probably she would end up fat like her mother and sister, but for now she was all right.

"We just came from Turpins Falls," Ben said.

"Did you swim there?" Candy crouched over her bent legs and squinted at him.

"No, we jumped. The water was freezing."

"A man died there doing that." Candy wriggled and smoothed her wet hair with her hand. She leaned back a bit and let her legs slide long.

"Well, you have to pit yourself against it." He lifted his chest and made a sardonic grin, waiting to see if this would rattle her.

"Against what?" She pouted a little.

"Against death."

"You're crazy." She rolled her eyes.

"But when you win, then life feels great again."

Candy didn't reply.

"You want to swim across with me?" He wanted her to take her T-shirt off. She stared ahead at the water and straightened her back. A little frown on her face as she considered. She stood up and turned to him.

"Just so you know, I already know I'm alive, so we can keep the cheap thrills out of the water."

Ben laughed. He hadn't expected that. Maybe she wasn't uninteresting after all. Her legs looked better now that she was standing.

"I promise," he said.

"Is that your sister?" Candy was looking out across the water.

Ben looked. Tilly was in the water, over on the other side, sitting astride a Li-lo as if it were a horse. And Raff lay draped across the other end, his face twisted to look at her. He kicked at the water to move the Li-lo on, away from the reeds. But this was done almost haphazardly, so unconsciously that Ben could tell that neither of them was aware of the course the Li-lo took as it floated at the edge of the reeds, and that they were both caught in the kind of spell that happens when two people are attuned, one to the other. Ben didn't notice Candy take her T-shirt off. Something was happening between his sister and his mate.

"Are they going out?" said Candy. She stood before him in her polka-dot bikini.

Ben looked at her and back at Tilly and Raff. Were they going out? He pushed the thought out of his mind. It made him uncomfortable. He stood up. Why would Raff be interested in Tilly all of a sudden? Ben couldn't keep admiring Raff in the same way if he went out with Tilly. What about Raff's older girlfriend? That was more respectable, more enviable. Raff was probably just flirting with Tilly. Ben should warn her to take care. No, he should stay clear of the whole thing. He could watch it unfold and investigate it further later. Here was Candy Newton, without her T-shirt, relaxing, one hip thrust to the side, a tiny mole in the alluring hollow of her hip bone.

"Not that I know of." He smiled at Candy. "Let's go in, then."

23

Toby Layton was at the theater too. He was there with his mum, Mrs. Layton, and Ada had to be polite and sit next to him.

"Did you watch a movie at our house?" Toby said. Toby still knew nothing; he didn't carry a terrible secret like Ada did. Everything she could say would seem hard as a shield thrown up against the real truth. She wouldn't bother telling Toby about Gregory Peck and the happy-sads. Tilly said that some sadness gets buried so far away inside that it only gets unburied by something as accidental as happiness. What did she and Toby usually talk about? She couldn't remember.

"Our chickens got killed by the fox," she said. Ada kept going, swept up in her own satisfaction at having found the right thing to talk about. "And Mum had to ask your dad to come and bury them for us because our dad works too far away."

She shouldn't have mentioned Toby's father. Ada quickly jammed a fingernail in her mouth and gnawed at it. Toby's father would probably cry if he knew what Toby's mother had done with her dad. And he was a tall, kind man. He had buried the chickens and they had talked about Elmer. He had shown her and Toby the blue-tongued lizard. Her heart sank. There was nothing that didn't lead to it, no way of talking to Toby Layton without the secret bubbling up.

"Are you getting more chickens?" Toby's feet swung back and forth beneath the seat.

Ada nodded. "I guess so. But there won't be another chicken like Bolshie. She used to lay her eggs in our washing basket. She pecked on the window and we had to let her in and then she jumped in and laid an egg. Mum didn't like it because sometimes we didn't know it was there and so Mum broke an egg on the floor."

"Why did she lay her eggs there?" Toby asked.

"I don't know. She just did. Ben used to say, here comes Basket Case."

Toby didn't get the joke. He unwrapped his ice cream. It was chocolate-coated. Ada was always envious of Toby's lunch boxes at school, and now he got an ice cream too. Toby got chocolate biscuits so often that he was offhand about them. He didn't eat them at playtime, whereas Ada would have been counting the minutes looking forward to it. She eyed his ice cream with a furious longing. Ada's mum said Toby got certain things that Ada didn't because Toby had been a child they had worked hard to get. And Ada was lucky because she had a sister and a brother. There were times when Ada would have willingly swapped her brother and sister for chocolate biscuits. Older brothers and sisters went before you all the time, in everything, and there was never anything Ada could be first at. And Ben had told her the Easter bunny wasn't true: she had found more Easter eggs than he did in the hunt and he told her to get even. But she had worked out for herself about Father Christmas, because her mother used the same wrapping paper with gold candles as Father Christmas had. Ben said not to let on that she knew about that, either, because their parents wouldn't bother giving them Father Christmas presents. So Ada had to pretend on behalf of them all and that was a terrible responsibility. She'd only done it for one Christmas before she let them all down.

"Did you know the Easter bunny isn't true? It's your parents who hide the eggs," she whispered.

Toby didn't get the ice cream to his mouth. He stopped halfway, his mouth open like a trapdoor. For a moment he didn't say a word, and Ada watched his long face as thoughts dashed in and out of his mind. Toby closed his mouth and dropped his hand to his lap and let go of the ice cream.

"How do you know? Are you sure?" he asked. His voice was small and clip-clopping.

"Yes. Ben told me. I've known for ages and ages," Ada boasted.

Toby's face screwed up for a minute, as if he were trying to see the Easter bunny in the theater. Ada instantly regretted having said it. But she couldn't unsay it. She sucked in her breath. It hadn't been fair that Ada had to know everything, and Toby knew nothing, but now that Ada had told him, she felt worse. It wasn't the right thing to have done. Ada knew it and now she would be in trouble. Toby was squirming, and the movie was about to begin. Ada didn't know what to say. She leaned closer, panicking.

"But don't worry because Father Christmas really is true. And you don't need to tell anyone you know about the Easter bunny. Don't tell your mum and it won't stop happening. Does it make you sad? It made me a bit sad."

"No, I don't care." Toby tugged at his finger. He stared at Ada as if she were a frightening person.

Ada hung her head. It was all because of the chocolate-coated ice cream and the secret and how together they had built up a sort of pressure inside her, which exploded in that sudden, terrible way, and there was nothing she could do about it. She couldn't say sorry because Toby was pretending it didn't matter; yet Ada knew it did. In her mind she began to sing:

> *Miss Mary Mac, Mac, Mac,*
> *All dressed in black, black, black*
> *With silver buttons, buttons, buttons,*
> *All down her back, back, back.*

Toby still didn't eat his chocolate-coated ice cream.

> *She asked her mother for fifty more, more, more,*
> *To watch the elephant, elephant, elephant,*
> *Mop up the floor, floor, floor.*

When the movie finished, they didn't say anything else to each other. Ada was so worried she forgot how to be normal. The harder she tried to think normal thoughts, the more and more her thoughts would turn into Easter bunnies and Mrs. Layton in the nude. So she had to start singing again to scare them away.

By the time they left, the doom had crept in and Ada had the terrible pressing feeling again. And this time she had been the one to start it by breaking a bit of Toby's heart. The pressure she felt would swing like a wrecking ball, make PJ die, or roll a fireball over Tilly when she went to a party at night, and it would all be her fault.

24

Tilly would be in trouble for coming home late from the Res. She didn't care. She didn't care the whole way home. Her legs were stuck to the vinyl seat of Simon Marsh's car. She sang along to the radio, and the music made the day spin past in colors of sky, road, and sun. She stared out the window without looking at anything—a pleasant internal commotion danced her along with the song. Love was a boat she had sailed out to sea in, no matter what Alice said.

Alice was in the front seat—a red bikini tie poked through her curtain of gold hair. Tilly could buy bikinis now. Her dad had given her that twenty bucks, either for nothing or to try to make it up to her. She began to imagine the sort of bikinis she'd buy. Alice smacked Simon on the thigh, lit a cigarette, and turned around, puffing a halo of smoke.

"So?"

"So, nothing."

Tilly wasn't going to talk. Alice was wrong about Tilly's feelings. Tilly leaned back against the sun-warmed seat. She closed her eyes and basked in the window's patch of sun. Once Simon wasn't around she would tell Alice, and Alice would shine smiles of welcome. They could go shop for bikinis together.

When they dropped her off, Tilly ran inside, holding tightly to the happiness and getting ready to use it as a buffer. The kitchen was empty. It was clean too. There was an unfamiliar hush and stillness. Martha wasn't home. Tilly had never been so well prepared for the battle and there was nothing to contend with, not even a mess. There was just her, standing in the kitchen, let loose in the moment's perfection. Not even Ada was there to ruin it. She went toward the bedroom, preparing to wriggle her wet bathers out from under her dress, but stopped to listen to a noise coming from the front porch. Tilly crept closer and pushed open the flywire door. Ada lay crunched up on her side on the daybed sobbing. PJ was curled up beside her.

"Snug, what's the matter?" Tilly squatted next to Ada. "Where's Mum?"

Ada stifled her sobs. She threw her arms dramatically around PJ as if PJ could console her.

"Where were you?" she whined. "I came home and no one was here."

"Ben and I were at the Res. I didn't realize Mum wouldn't be here. Where did Dad go?"

Ada frowned and sat up. She wiped at her nose with her arm and squinted at the dazzling sky. Tilly stroked Ada's forehead, smoothing it out with her thumb. Poor little Ada—still such a baby.

"Dad dropped me home and he didn't come in. He had to go to a meeting," Ada said, sniffing. Tilly doubted this. No one does business on weekends. She didn't trust her father anymore, but she didn't want Ada to see it.

"Why didn't you go to Louis and May's?" she said.

"I couldn't." Ada perched on the edge of the daybed, her hands clinging to the sides, her brown legs swinging furiously. Tilly waited for the explanation. Shadows wobbled over the garden. A breeze tousled the heads of lavender. Ada's bare feet swept back and forth.

"Why couldn't you go there, Snug?" Tilly asked. She watched a sun-addled bee crawl across the edge of the veranda.

"I didn't go there," Ada said, glancing up at Tilly again. Her lip quivered, her face contorting into a strange solemnity.

The terrible abandonment that had struck at Ada's heart was affecting. Ada's swinging legs dragged. Tilly wanted to wrap the afternoon up in her arms and hold it still.

"Let's lie down," Tilly sighed. They could be like plants in the garden, letting the breeze blow away anything they didn't want. Tilly stretched out behind Ada. Ada watched her. After a moment she lay down too. They had to turn sideways to fit. Tilly closed her eyes. The sun couldn't reach them there.

After a while Ada confessed. "I did something terrible today. I've made something bad happen because of it. So that's why I couldn't go over there."

"Tell me what you did." Tilly was steady. She had never felt so sure of herself. She could make anything better. Love had made her tender. She loved the day, the stumbling bee, the feeling that life had crept out of a dark drawer and exploded in full color.

"I told Toby Layton the Easter bunny isn't true." The confession brought fresh tears. It wasn't like Ada to nurse this sort of anguish.

"But listen," Tilly said. "It's not so bad. Someone was going to tell Toby one day. We all find out sooner or later. Ben didn't care when he told you. Remember?"

"This is different. Something bad is going to happen now."

"That's silly. Nothing bad is going to happen."

Ada was so dramatic, so convinced by her own imaginings. It would have annoyed Tilly once, but not today. Poor Ada.

"Yes, it will. I know it. Am I going to get in trouble from Toby's dad?" Ada persisted.

Tilly laughed. "No, you won't get into trouble. Look, it's just what happens. Kids find out. No one will get cross. Nothing bad will happen. I promise." Ada was confusing one secret with another, or perhaps the weight of one was bearing down on the other. But it wasn't worth mentioning the other secret, the affair. It had become a monster in Ada's mind against which her childish imagination pitted visions of imminent retribution. If Tilly talked about it, that would make it more concrete. So far Ada hadn't mentioned Mrs. Layton; maybe she'd forgotten it and this was just the way Ada's mind worked anyway—with a theatrical sensitivity that sought out the darkness in things. It was best to draw Ada away from the whole business.

"Can I tell you something?"

"What?" Ada sat up and stared at Tilly. She was like a baby bird, waiting.

"I think I'm in love." This was a silly way to put it, but Tilly knew Ada would like it best if it came out in all its fullness, shining with fanfare. "With Raff Cavallo." Tilly blew a pretend trumpet.

Ada frowned and tilted her head thoughtfully, still not taken in.

"I saw him today at the Res. He—"

"But why didn't you take me?" Ada interrupted. Her voice was little and mournful. She started again to rock back and forth. Tilly took her hand and held it still.

"Because you were at the movies, remember? I will next time."

"Did you kiss Raff?" Ada said accusingly. She looked petulant.

"No, we just talked, on the Li-lo in the water. But I felt something. You know how when people fall in love in the movies they do swoony things? Well, that was how I felt, as if my head was about to float up into the sky."

Should she tell Ada how it happened exactly? How Raff had appeared there, before she'd realized he was at the Res. There he was, blocking the sun almost, laughing. She hadn't seen anything except the spill of laughter from his green eyes. And she hadn't had time for a thought to form before the sun came down in a flood of brightness and warmed every point of brittleness, so that moments passed like air. And the words skipped between them. His body shifted on the slope, his eyes roved over her. She could hardly remember how they ended up on the Li-lo.

"I'm going to show you a water bird, a white-faced heron," he had said. He didn't ask her; he told her. She liked his assumption that she would be interested to see a white-faced heron. When they got close to the reeds, the bird took flight and it was only them there. Everyone else was a distant dot on the shore. She thought about kissing him. What would it be like, if he came that close, if he touched her face? She glanced at his mouth. He was smiling at her, lazy and alert all at once, kicking the water away. The sun made diamonds on the water. The Li-lo bobbed like a lullaby. His hand was flung out right next to her leg. She liked his hand. She liked it lying so close to her leg.

"But aren't you scared of him? You said he was a criminal. Remember?" Ada was adamant.

Tilly laughed again. "Things change. You'll see. Someone you don't even notice at school will one day seem interesting to you, because you change too."

Ada shook her head. "I won't change." She began to swing her legs again, as if to shore this up. She was so determined it made Tilly wonder if it were true, if Ada would always be like she was, looking deeply into things and making up mysteries. She had expected Ada to be excited. Ada had always stuck up for Raff Cavallo and now she was playing another tune.

"*Helloooooo*. I'm home," their mother called out. The sound of her voice came like a poke in the head. Martha sounded as if she were someone else, visiting someone else's house.

Ada's face jerked anxiously. "Mum's home."

Tilly sat up.

"There you are!" said Martha. She lifted her arms dramatically. "I thought no one was home. Monkey, come and give me a cuddle. How was the movie?"

"Where have you been?" Ada gave herself up for the cuddle, though Tilly could tell she felt cross still. Poor Ada, she couldn't tell Martha she had been alone because she wouldn't want Martha to get angry with Tilly.

"Where's Ben?" Martha said, looking at Tilly, while clamping Ada to her.

"He's at the Res."

"Oh."

Martha seemed different. She wasn't bothering to find things out; she wasn't being Old Sherlock. She released Ada, slumped on the step, and kicked off her sandals. "I think we'll have eggs on toast tonight. I can't be bothered cooking. I've been out all afternoon."

"Where?" Ada persisted, still bearing her silent grudge. She looked at her mother's sandals on the step. "And why did you put my sneakers on the grass?"

"Where?" Martha echoed, giggling.

She'd been drinking—that was it. Tilly examined her mother's face, but as she caught her eye or Martha caught hers, there was a crash, a jolting recognition. Martha straightened up and looked with sudden severity at Tilly.

"Well, I'll tell you where I was. I was at Daisy Cavallo's." She glared with some satisfaction.

Tilly began to panic. She wouldn't care, she reminded herself; she had her other feelings, true and warm and joyous feelings that would float her above anything her mother shot out. She stood up, getting ready to go inside.

"Why did you go there, Mum?" she said.

Martha's head fell on an angle. Her eyes fluttered lazily. "Why?" she repeated, drifting elsewhere for a moment. Ada stared at her too, bewildered, and Martha frowned, pulling herself back and folding her arms across her chest.

"Well, what I would like to know is why you took money from your father?"

Tilly held her mouth shut. More than anything, she felt her failure to block her mother out. Even now, when she was so happy, her mother had got in and let all the bad feelings rush forward.

Martha's face was cold with inquiry.

179

Tilly went directly to her pillow, fished out the envelope, and returned, standing at a distance from her mother, her arm thrust out.

"I don't want it, anyway."

Martha reached out and took it.

"What's going on?" Ben stood there, grinning, hands in his shorts pockets. "Sorry, I'm late."

"Tilly's getting in trouble," Ada sighed.

The stern look on Martha's face melted instantly. She stood up and walked over to Ben, and, taking his face in her hands, pressed a rugged kiss on him. "Do you mind eggs on toast tonight? I'm tired out today."

Tilly slipped inside and headed for her bedroom. She wouldn't eat: she didn't need it. Instead, she would grope around for that faltering happiness; she would find it again. But it was harder than she thought, and for a while all she could think about was running away and never coming back.

Later Ada arrived with a boiled egg hidden up her sleeve. She climbed on the bed and passed it to Tilly.

"You didn't finish telling me," she said, settling in, "about Raff on the Li-lo."

And because Ada looked so reproachful and serious and ready, Tilly put aside her anger and her quest to rid herself of it. First she would tell Ada the whole story in exactly the sort of detail that Ada expected, and then she would work out how to leave.

25

Martha had woken up with a real migraine this time. It always happened if she drank, and she couldn't remember how many drinks they'd had. It was hot. Gin and tonic in the middle of the day.

They'd sat at the table in Daisy's kitchen. The blinds were drawn to keep out the sun. It was private and removed; the world retreated from view. Martha felt that Arnold Buch would have approved of Daisy Cavallo, and if anyone would understand Arnold, Daisy would. She was a bohemian. She didn't have a tidy house. She drank gin and tonic in the middle of the day. Her fingers were decorated with rings and red nail polish. Martha felt she could show Daisy her hidden self, show who she could have been if life had gone differently. She began to explain about Arnold Buch. And as she began to open up, understanding smiles drifted across Daisy's face, encouraging further disclosure.

Martha had seen Arnold Buch play piano once. In the large room at Mary Galmotte's party. At first he had simply leaned over and with one hand played a few notes, his ear turned slightly toward it. It was as if the sound had caressed him. His body followed, and he succumbed, seating himself on the stool. He held himself quite erect over the piano, rocking slightly, as he finished the last bit of his cigarette and squashed it down into his glass. He put both hands gently on the keys and curled over them like a dying flower stem, as if he and the piano were drawn to embrace or secretly converse. The notes rang out without any hesitancy. People turned and smiled faintly—some floated over and leaned on the piano. What he played was slow and sad and lingering. Some people wouldn't have appreciated it at all, not at a party. It fanned out through the room like a shaft of light, a glancing shadow of wistfulness, as the talking hushed and for a moment everyone seemed disorientated.

Mary Galmotte sashayed over. This wouldn't do. She pouted attractively and put her arm around Arnold, leaning into him and saying, "Darling, I never knew you could play. A man of hidden talents, I should have guessed. It's marvelous, but play something more upbeat, it's a party for God's sake, not a funeral. Then everyone could dance."

Daisy was amused. "Did Arnold oblige her with a boogie-woogie?" she asked.

Arnold was not the obliging type. He lifted his hands. The sad slow music stopped. He looked at Mary; his brows arched, either in mock amusement or plain disdain, and the sudden ensuing quiet accentuated his glimmer of cruelty. Mary Galmotte reddened but gathered herself. Arnold responded with a resounding bark of laughter. It was uncomfortable; it seemed that the whole room was waiting. The pause lasted a moment before Arnold leaned away from the piano with a mannered tilt of his head, as if he were in fact considering Mary Galmotte's request, which of course he wasn't. He stood up and grinned at Mary, his expression having recovered its distant wilting smile.

He said, "Well, Mary, you're right of course. Put a record on."

Martha had just met Arnold Buch, but she had already sensed in him something hidden and grand, something almost old-fashioned. It was a time when hats were being thrown off, gloves discarded, bread came already sliced, people were protesting, Martin Luther King Jr. had marched, women wanted equality, and people wanted to boogie. In a few years, a man would walk on the moon. But Arnold seemed impervious to all this. He had a timeless dignity, an almost regal demeanor which Mary had offended. What it showed both frightened and intrigued Martha. But she was ready for danger, wanting it. Here was an opportunity to crack open the heart of life and to get at whatever lay beneath. There she was, slowly getting drunk in Mary Galmotte's white house, in Imogen Ashton's green silk dress, with two men, neither of whom she had ever met before and each of whom stirred something in her. She felt like a crude version of Cinderella in her borrowed finery, and she gave herself to the night's atmosphere, thinking it was a game that would end. In fact, it was the looming inevitability of the game's end that hurled her into it. Mary Galmotte would never have done what Martha did that night, but Mary didn't have to. Mary belonged there, in her elegant white house, throwing parties, waiting to trap a respectable, wealthy husband.

And there was Mike, who had impressed her with his unaffected gallantry, with the flash of his boyish smile as he appeared at the bottom of the staircase. He was an innocent. She trusted him immediately, and once he had relaxed into himself, he was alluring in his way. He leaned back, arm across the window ledge, and opened himself to the whole of the room's possibility. Whereas Arnold Buch sat straight up with one leg crossed over the other and jiggering. He looked at Martha with such brazen intensity that her heart scuttled for cover. His complexity excited her as much as Mike's straightforward masculinity drew her to him. She moved between them like a cat, performing a version of herself she hadn't yet encountered. The emerald dress transformed her, entitled her. And those two men saw her perched on that window seat, by the piano, radiant with stolen confidence and champagne giddiness.

If Arnold Buch hadn't played the piano and Mary Galmotte hadn't offended him, they would have stayed the whole night there, but Arnold's mood was turned. The party soured under his scrutiny, became a mere parade, a spectacle. They were separate from it and better than it. Martha felt she had to impress Arnold; she had to prove she was better than the others. He said he was going to drive to the ocean—who wanted to come? Martha rose instantly. She glanced at Mike. She knew he would come too, but she wanted to make sure.

Daisy seemed delighted by the story. She interrupted. Which one, she wanted to know, had Martha fancied?

Martha hadn't known, but she thought she couldn't have liked one without the other. She wouldn't have trusted Arnold without Mike and wouldn't have found Mike interesting enough on his own. Arnold was fascinating in a way that Mike wasn't. He was unpredictable, his intelligence was disarming, but she glimpsed a coldness, and she bounced right back toward Mike, who was there, warm and waiting.

Daisy wanted more. "Was Arnold Buch handsome?"

He probably was to some, but not to Martha. He was tall but all head, as if his body were just there to carry it around. Except when they had played pool. He was surprisingly good at that. It was the only time he looked to her like a man and not an intellectual. Mike had exactly what Arnold lacked; he was alive in his body.

It was hard to know who was leading the whole thing. Arnold at first because of the car, but afterward it seemed to be all of them leading and following at once. Perhaps Arnold always was, but he let them think they were too. He was clever enough to do that. He drove like a madman, nearly hit a cat. A good omen, he claimed. He sang a lot, telling them to sing along. Songs like "Don't Let the Sun Catch You Crying." He liked those melancholy songs. Mike didn't sing, he still didn't sing. They drove for nearly two hours. They were all drunk. The ocean appeared, and the moon hung like a huge pearl above it, and they went straight to the beach, took off their shoes. Mike ran and jumped at the shoreline; Arnold plunged forward, still talking. Moonlight rippled over the sea. They took off their clothes and went swimming. Martha was drunk enough to feel porous and blank, guided by senses, lying between sea and air. Either they were playing at being free of any future or past, or for that moment they really were. They stayed up till dawn, watched the orb of sun peep over the horizon while they shivered in a huddle beneath the suit coats. Martha buried her wet feet in the sand.

Afterward they went to the Continental Hotel. Arnold stopped the car, leaned over the back seat, grinning.

"Two of us should book the room. Martha, who will you take with you? Do you want to be Martha Buch or Martha Bloom?"

He had laughed at this, either to hide or accentuate the discomfort this question raised. He didn't give Martha time to reply; he said that it was far more beautiful to bloom than to buck. He ushered her and Mike in together, as if they were his underlings or accomplices, pieces in his game.

"Mr. and Mrs. Bloom," he said and bowed.

The hotel was old and grand, a sandstone building with verandas all around and a view of the bay. They smuggled Arnold up the back stairs. Mike had the key and pushed open the door, already with a proprietary air. The room had languished through winters and decades; its furniture was elderly and polite. There was a pale-yellow bedspread, an armchair, and a dressing table with a round mirror. They all edged in. The intimacy of the room made Martha uncomfortable, and she went to the window and yanked it open. The early morning flooded in. The air smelled of the sea, and the baker's truck shuffled past below. Arnold hauled the armchair across the room. He faced it to the window and sank into it, hoisting his legs up on a padded stool and closing his eyes.

"I'm taking a nap," he said.

Mike had already lain himself flat on the bed, perhaps too exhausted to care, or perhaps because he was Mr. Bloom. Martha didn't know. She peeled back the bedspread and curled, careful as a cat, on her side. Mike's body shifted closer to hers. Like that they slept until the late afternoon, when Arnold roused them with his singing, his frenzied eyes, holding aloft a bottle of champagne. The night began again.

"How did it end?" Daisy asked.

End? Martha threw her hands over her eyes. The end always came with you. "I thought you would have guessed. That hotel. It was where I conceived Tilly."

Daisy leaned closer.

"With Mr. Bloom?"

"Yes," Martha lied. At the last moment she lied. "With Mr. Bloom."

26

Who was Tilly Bloom? Tilly didn't know. Alice had said, "Just be yourself." That was the whole problem; Tilly didn't know how to be herself. It was something so natural, so normal for Alice, but not for her.

She was on her way to her first piano lesson and it was such an awful day, so hot and muggy the air would sweat if it could. The sky had been drained of its blue and was scorched a dirty pale color, a color that couldn't announce itself.

Tilly wished she hadn't admitted to Alice that she liked Raff. But Raff Cavallo was going to change everything. She would sit with him on a Li-lo and sail downstream. Her life had moved longingly toward that moment at the Res. While he had lain there and talked so easily to her, turning his face toward her, her body had exhaled a long-held breath and the tips of her sprang to life. And if she did have a self it had burst out of hiding and filled her so well that she felt expanded with it. Life was different. Larger, deeper, nearer. And all this had made her so much better, so much closer to Tilly Bloom than ever before. Now it was worse than humiliating to think the moment with Raff and all its attendant possibilities might have already passed into history. Her heart stumbled around inside her like an animal trying to get out. Tilly had expected love to unwind easily, naturally, like the opening of a letter, but instead she had folded herself up and begun to fret.

Alice had met her in the park on the way to her lesson. They shared a cigarette. Alice's face had that terrible reassuring expression, but Alice couldn't possibly understand.

"So, what's happening? Have you talked to him?"

"No."

"Doesn't mean anything. He probably doesn't even know you like him." Alice dragged her close and slipped her arm over her. "Of course you like him more the more unavailable he is. That's what you do," she said.

Tilly's heart was unsteady, flammable.

"Well, that's how he is, though. He never makes an effort," said Alice.

"I'm so embarrassed to be going to his house for piano." This sounded dismal.

"Be yourself." Sometimes it felt like Alice was wiping her clean with a Wettex, dusting her off, plumping up the cushion of her spirit with a sharp pat.

Tilly had looked away, holding her feelings tightly inside again.

Now as she trudged along, alone in the heat, she understood why Alice's advice had been irritating. Alice made it seem that being yourself was the simplest thing in the world. As if everyone were busy being themselves: announcing their love, their soreness, their little vertiginous hopes—stomping forward, saying this is mine, this is me. Did they all know how to fail, how to fall over, how to be dirtied, half-built, black-eyed, heart limping, pounding, and afraid, too?

When she tried to picture the self that lived inside her it was like looking for a ghost. Tilly had steered herself through life so far without it anyway, by watching which way to go, by stepping carefully, by checking herself against others. She studied people's ways, how she was in their eyes. She shaped herself to fit into the places between them, sliding in unobtrusively, like a girl without a ticket sneaking a seat on the bus. But she wouldn't know how to behave when she saw Raff. She didn't trust herself to be true. This was what hammered at her as she walked.

She almost laughed at herself: to think she could lose something she had only imagined having. And yet that was what had wrenched her open—the sense that she had lost something and the feeling of it bleeding out.

She didn't have to go to her lesson. She could write a note to Daisy and slide it under the door saying she had unexpectedly had to hurry home to look after Ada. She could go lie down under the tree that Ada called William Blake and wait till it was time to go home.

27

Martha hadn't told anyone the truth. It had become so conveniently blurred that she could hardly see it anymore. What had happened between her and Arnold closed the space in which possibility had lived and brought on a terrible disquiet.

She had always blamed the delirium of the night. She felt they had made an unspoken pact. It was a game and she was the one who lost. For a long time afterward, she had tried to see it like that. Then she had tried not to see it at all.

She had been asleep when Arnold heaved himself on top of her and did his jagged dance. She had caught sight of the yellow curtain fluttering and her own confusion all at the same time. The air came in silently. She could still hear Arnold breathing heavily at her neck, after he had finished.

For a while he lay on top of her—a dead weight. His body began to shake. He rolled off her and crumpled. When he began sobbing, she was appalled. She was the one who had been abused. Not him. He wasn't the man she had thought he was. The sophisticate. The dark gentleman. He had invaded her and he was playing the feeble and broken one. She said nothing. She turned her back on him and listened to his sobs, each one a fist beating against her ear.

She had never asked Mike where he had been for fear that he would ask her what had happened. And she could never tell him. Their lives had grown from this silence like flesh over a wound.

Mike woke them early in the morning. He had the car and he wanted to leave. Arnold was so hungover that Mike had to almost carry him to the car. They put him in the back seat. He lay on his back, his head to the side and his hand dangling from the seat, limp as an uprooted flower.

Mike ignored Arnold and hardly spoke to Martha. He sped her away from it, as if he knew what was needed. He drove the car with a gallant straightforwardness that she was grateful for. When, weeks later, she discovered she was pregnant, she chose him to save her again.

She blamed Arnold for cutting off her youth. Arnold and everything about him became repellent. He had insulted her, first with his body and then with his sobs. In comparison, Mike was all substance. In his arms she was prized; beneath Arnold Buch she had been violated. From this she had lurched, wiped her eyes, and in the struggling light of summer, flung herself toward Mike.

She had loved Mike. But it became harder as time went on to love the man she came to know and not just the man who had adored her. The man whose opinions and aspirations were predictable and small, the man who pestered her in bed, the man whose competence and conformism had once been appealing, even soothing, but now were so stultifying. He had offered her a worthwhile and feasible happiness. By the time she realized it was an enclosure, she couldn't get out again.

But she did still love him. She loved him because he was there. His reliable arms wrapped her life up in his, as if they were a present to each other that neither had given. But that love was tired and old. That was the way it went. Love frayed like old clothes that you kept because your life had been lived in them. She had made the right decision without ever realizing it. She should love Mike back. She should show him that she could.

Despite all her efforts to block him out, Arnold Buch still crept into her mind. Especially when Tilly played the piano. He had ensured his own mystique by leaving, but he had left this behind, the musical ability. He was an uneasy memory that had emerged dusty and formal to perch on a chair in her living room after all these years. He was so harmless, impotent. And if he suspected anything about Tilly, he didn't say. Her fear of him asking her meant that as soon as he got there, she had wanted him to leave. It was too much, having them all in the same room and Mike telling him how Tilly played piano and the awful tangibility of her secret hovering between them, a ghost that only she could see, but which they might glimpse. It was enough that they had had to entertain Arnold. She had put on her dress because she had wanted him to see how well they were doing, she had wanted him to envy Mike, she had wanted to win this time around. In the end, what did she care about Arnold and his opinions?

She didn't want to think about it. Her head throbbed.

It was already midday, and everyone had left her in peace. Mike was playing tennis. Tilly had her piano lesson, Ada was next door, and Ben was probably cruising the streets. Martha padded down the hall, still in her nightie. She would go back to bed once she had gotten a glass of water. She stood at the kitchen window staring out at the garden. The poor trees. Maybe she could sit in the shade of the elm tree. It was no cooler inside than out. Her limbs ached. All she wanted to do was lie in some dark, cool place.

A fox slid past the trees. Or was it her foggy head not seeing properly? Surely a fox would not be there in the middle of the day? It must have been someone's dog, a red heeler. But it came out from the shadows of the hedge and sniffed at the base of the olive tree, in broad daylight, as a dog would, but with its blackened socks, brushy black-tipped tail, and unmistakable fox face.

Martha was astonished. Here was the fox that had killed her chickens. Seeing it was like finally seeing the unseen. The hidden showing itself, the darkness standing there in the light. It was the fox of all her childhood stories. The fox that tried to eat Henny Penny, the fox that cunningly lured the duck from the pond, the bird from its perch, the lamb from its mother. The one that had bitten off Peachie's head and broken Bolshie's neck. She was filled, almost childishly, with a primal fear. It was as if her own dark secret showed itself in the blank, white sunlight, sniffing, as if it were a dog. Martha's skin prickled.

She opened the door. The air was unbearably hot. She would be sunburnt in an instant. She should forget it, but she was walking quietly toward the fox, and the fox had stopped sniffing and was looking at her. It was larger than she had expected—probably a male. Martha stopped and stood still. She expected it would slink away, but it came closer. She waited to see how close it would dare to come. It walked toward her, its head at an angle of inquiry. Martha leaned back, momentarily frightened by how close it was and how it looked up at her. Foxes were scared of people. She shouted "shoo" and kicked out at it.

The fox sprang at her foot and sank its teeth into the bare skin.

Martha screamed. The scream came again as if from someone else. This didn't happen. Foxes didn't attack people. Martha shook herself from her own disbelief. She dropped, and her hands pulled at its jaws. The pain was terrible. She shouted at the fox, as if it were a dog. As if it would obey. *Stop it.* Blood ran from its teeth, her blood. Its grip was like a steel trap. The fox was quiet, experienced, a calm predator. It didn't growl or writhe, it just bore down, ignoring her commands. Her fingers weren't strong enough. Her palms sweated. It was her strength against the fox's.

No one would come. Martha realized this with horror. Did animals fight till the death? This was killing. She was being attacked, as the chickens had been. The fox that killed Peachie was trying to kill her. She kept screaming at it, as if the fox would respond. It had made a terrible mistake, an error of judgment. She was a person. She wasn't prey.

Her hands worked desperately to open the jaws. Without warning, the fox let go and with a flicking snap latched on to her hand. She heard her screams as if they belonged to the air; they were hysterical, mixed with breath, high-pitched. She ran toward the large trunk of the pine tree, dragging the fox, and slammed it against the tree, her cries now like grunts. Still it held. She sank to the ground; the fox was on its side, its yellow eye staring intensely at her. Her knee pressed heavily on its throat. The fur was warm. She felt the animal beneath her and leaned all her weight onto it. Now it was she who was crushing. Her breath came fast. Between them, Martha and the fox, something locked, as if neither could give way without giving everything. She pressed harder.

The fox lay motionless on the ground. Could it be dead? She felt a hot rush of relief, and her head dropped. Her foot throbbed. All she wanted was to get away from it. She lifted her knee slightly. The fox didn't move. Its mouth fell open, and she took her bloodied hand away. The fox lay still. Martha stood up and her knees buckled. She closed her eyes for a moment.

The fox was just a small animal that had made a terrible mistake.

Martha stumbled to the house and slammed the door. Her breathing was still fast. She put her hand to her chest, tried to slow her breaths. She was covered in sweat and blood. Her nightie clung to her. She had to look at the foot. The blood was thick and sticky around the jagged wound. There were gashes on her hand where the teeth had dragged. She went to the bathroom, stuck her foot under the bath tap, and washed her hand at the same time. The blood ran; translucent red ribbons of it poured over her foot. She found a bandage and wrapped her hand in it and plugged the holes in her foot with cotton wool and wrapped a sock around the foot. She limped to the phone and rang the hospital. A woman answered.

"Do you mind waiting, please?"

"No, I can't wait, no." Martha's voice choked.

"All right. How can I help you?"

"A fox attacked me." A sob escaped her. "And I killed it."

28

When Ada got home, Martha was lying on her back on the couch. She looked like someone who was dying. Ada tiptoed forward. Martha raised her head and gave a feeble smile. Ada leaned on the edge of the couch.

"Have you got a migraine?" Ada asked.

Martha sat up and shook her head, raising her bandaged hand as an exhibit. "The fox attacked me. I have to go to the hospital. Anne Dresden is coming to pick me up."

"The fox that ate the chickens?" Ada stared in disbelief. "Did it really bite you?" Ada had never heard of a fox biting people.

"Yes, and my foot. Look. And I killed it. I had to kneel on its throat to make it let go. I feel terrible."

"Oh, poor Mama!" Ada was exuberant. This was something. It was alarming in the best way. The doom. The fox. The lurking feeling. And now an attack.

"How did it happen?" she whispered, as if this were the greatest secret of all. Martha told her. Ada's hands flew to her mouth in horror. To think of the fox clamped on the end of her mother's hand. Ada patted her mother's good arm. She wouldn't tell her what this meant. Her mother was too ailing already. Instead she had to take charge.

"Mama, I'm going to see the dead fox." Her mother recoiled.

"I don't want to see it. Can you get Ben or your father to bury it as soon as someone gets home? Anne should be here any minute."

Ada flew outside and ran to the pine tree. The dead fox lay on its side. A fly already buzzed around it. Her mother was right. It was dead. The fox wasn't inside its body, like socks sometimes don't have feet in them. And now that it was dead, Ada was surprised that she didn't hate the fox anymore. Because it was a poor thing— its eye white and rolled back, never to peep again, its body like a jumper someone had thrown off and left by the tree to become damp and forgotten. "Poor fox," Ada whispered. It shouldn't have tried to eat Martha. "Couldn't you tell, little fox, that you were too small to eat a person? Couldn't you tell?" She had to say it twice, like she did when she talked to PJ, because animals can't answer even if they are alive. What had happened to its cunning? It was a little animal. Did she want to touch it? Just to see what death felt like. Poor fox—as dead as the chickens.

Ada reached toward it. She changed her mind and pulled her hand away quickly and hid it under her arm. She'd probably catch a disease—gangrene or leprosy, gruesome old diseases that rotted your limbs off. And to be fair, if Ada were dead, she wouldn't want the fox to touch her. It was taking advantage.

But she had to do something. Death was in the garden again. It would keep returning if Ada weren't careful. She went over the events in her mind. The fox had killed the chickens and her mother had killed the fox. Her mother would be next in turn. There was a pattern to things. Ada saw it everywhere. Spider webs, seasons, ocean waves, seedpods. Her mother would be the next to be killed. Ada stared hard at the dead fox. It had to be wiped away and removed from the garden. Perhaps Ada could make it that the fox hadn't died after all but had just run away.

Ada knew exactly where the fox could be vanished forever—in the old windmill's hole. Down at the bottom. No one, not even the sun, would know. And her mother would be safe.

But how would she get it there? She didn't want to carry a dead fox. She would have to drag it on the picnic blanket, which she went and found rolled up in the chest with the badminton and the tent and the totem tennis bats.

She squatted and took hold of the fox's paws. What if it were pretending to be dead? She watched its face. Would it open its eye to see who was holding its paw? Its face showed nothing. She dragged the fox onto the blanket. She was relieved there was no blood. No guts or sticking-out bones. Nowhere for things like diseases or curses to come out. But still, poor fox. Poor chickens. Poor Elmer with no eyes. Poor PJ because he was old too. Ada's heart grew bigger in her chest to fit them all in. She frowned for a moment and waited, in case she would cry. But she didn't. She wrapped the dead fox in a bundle and lifted it up. She had never carried a dead animal before. Did you hold a dead one in the same way you would hold a live one?

She hadn't reached the gate before Tilly arrived.

Tilly frowned. "Ada, what have you got?"

"A dead fox. I thought you had a piano lesson." Ada stood still. Should she tell Tilly? If only Tilly hadn't grown up so much lately, she would understand and they could do it together, but Ada couldn't be sure whose side Tilly would be on.

"Where did it come from? How did it die?" Tilly put her hand up to shield her eyes from the sun. She was wearing jean shorts. She looked like she was going to the beach. She wasn't dressed for a death mission.

"Mum killed it, because it was biting her. She crushed its throat."

Tilly rubbed her face. She looked astonished. "Mum killed it? I can't imagine Mum killing a fox."

Ada didn't respond, and she hoped Tilly wouldn't ask any questions so that she wouldn't have to decide whether to let Tilly in on the problem with death. This could be the last chance for Tilly to join in with the meaningfulness of life. Tilly was cutting herself off from death and life and foxes. She wouldn't understand how the fox was a part of everything. It would be better if Ada told her something that would keep death's doom out of it.

"Can you help me take it to the windmill? Mum doesn't want to see it. She's going to the hospital and she has a migraine and bandages on her hand."

Ada was pleased with this account of events. It had skipped over the meaning of everything and just made it facts. Tilly was still trying to understand how it could have happened, and because she was stunned, she just naturally took the fox from Ada.

Ada was pleased—not only did she have a mission but she had her old accomplice, and this was exactly how she liked life to be, with secret purpose and great meaningfulness—and with Tilly. All these things added up to great happiness.

But it didn't stay like that. Once they got past the gates and turned to head up toward the bush, there came a shout. It was from Ben. He was with Raff Cavallo, and though Ben sometimes did come home with Raff, it was different this time because Ada knew

Tilly had danced with Raff. She glanced quickly at Tilly to see if she still looked at Raff as if he were a criminal or if she looked at him as if he were a dancer who knew tenderness and listening.

"What have you got?" Ben shouted.

Tilly stopped. She looked at them. Her face was gentle and shy. She was hiding something—there was an artfulness behind her expression that only Ada knew. And she wasn't looking at Raff as if he were a criminal.

Ada was cross. She was at least going to be the first to tell. No one knew it like she did.

"A dead fox," she said with pointed drama. She wanted to keep going. She was afraid that Tilly would leave the mission and that Raff would look at Tilly in a different way too and that these differences were exactly what was straining everything. They excluded her in a dreadful way and the mere fact of them was pulling Tilly away, just when Ada had brought her back in.

Raff stepped forward. "Shall I carry it for you?" He smiled at Tilly. He asked Tilly, not Ada. He looked directly at her and held out his hands, and Tilly gave him the dead fox in the blanket even though it belonged to Ada and even though Tilly could have carried it herself. Something passed between Tilly and Raff, something more than the fox, and it looked as if they both knew it. Tilly went red.

Ben, at least, was as appalled as Ada. "Suit yourself, mate. I'm going inside. Too hot out here."

Ada called out to Ben, "Well, don't tell Mum. I'm telling her the fox didn't die and it ran away. Because she feels terrible about killing it."

Ben nodded. He didn't care about dead foxes.

The fox had been passed from Ada to Tilly and from Tilly to Raff, and Raff carried it in his arms as if it were a baby, which made him look like a grown-up man. Tilly walked beside him. She was alert and brimming and skipping along on her long legs like a deer, beautiful and frightened of everything. Ada had lost her. Nothing could be crueler. Ada wanted to run up and hit Tilly and make her stop it but instead she put her head down and forgot even to look at the trees. She was lonely and sad and whatever the other two said to each other just sounded like faraway music that wasn't playing for her.

The old windmill didn't look the same as it had when Ada first discovered it. It didn't look like anything except a windmill. Ada knew it was because Tilly and Raff were there too and the old windmill was hiding its true self from them, just like the trees were. The three of them stood there and Raff held the fox, and no one said anything for a moment.

"Do you know there is a wallaby around here and her name is Emily Dickinson?" Ada said.

Tilly looked at her as if she were just a kid.

Ada continued, undeterred. "You know, I found the old windmill." This was directed at Raff.

"Ada makes friends with the trees here. She has names for them. This is her patch of bush," Tilly explained. Ada didn't need it to be explained. Explaining it was ruining it.

Raff smiled. "When I was your age, I had this place, a vacant block that's been built on. It was all overgrown and there was this tree that had fallen and it was covered in ivy. I called it the Ivy Palace. Because it was like a throne. I used to go there and feel like I was a king."

You are a king, thought Ada with a deep breath. Did Tilly even notice he had said that? Tilly stood still, staring at the hole. The sun flared and made her look as if magic had struck her.

Raff watched her for a moment. "What shall I do with the fox then?" he said, squatting at the edge of the hole.

Tilly turned to Ada. "Should we just drop it down?"

"First we should think nice things for it."

"It didn't think nice things about the chickens when it killed them," Tilly said.

"I bet it did. I bet it licked its chops," Raff said.

Tilly smiled at him. Again, something passed between them, a secret understanding, and it made Tilly look sly and beautiful in a way Ada didn't like.

"You know why this hole is so awful?" Tilly said, turning back to the hole. "Because you can't see where it goes. So it makes you wonder."

"It's Wonderland!" Raff said.

Tilly smiled as if only she could understand what he meant. "I doubt there's any rabbits down there."

Ada knew they were talking about Alice in Wonderland and she wanted to prove it. Tilly was still wrong about the hole.

"It's not that type of hole. I went in it."

"We know. We're just saying how a hole is like—it's like something unknown, and what we don't know we imagine instead."

We? Tilly had said *we* as if she were speaking for him as well, as if they were having one thought together and Ada was having her thought alone and differently. How did Tilly know if Raff were thinking what she was thinking or if he were thinking what Ada was thinking—that the hole was a hole of doom? She looked at Raff. He was squatting at the edge of the hole. The bundle of dead fox was at his feet. He looked straight back at her and grinned. His eyes were still the eyes of a villain. Shining with plans. Ada couldn't tell what the plans were, though.

"Let's drop the fox into the hole," she said. This had been her plan, after all.

He nodded and picked it up. "Then Tilly will know what's down the hole and she won't have to imagine things anymore."

Tilly said, "But I'm not looking." And she turned her back.

Ada was glad. That left her and Raff to be the important ones together.

She gave Raff a grave nod to go ahead and he took the poor limp fox out of the blanket and lowered it in the hole. Tilly didn't turn to see it. She even put her hands over eyes, just like Martha would have. Ada and Raff leaned over and watched it fall into the darkness, but they still didn't hear it land.

29

Susie Layton had rung Mike at home. She said Joe was out for the whole day. He had a job in Elphinstone.

"Can you take an hour off? Come here?"

There was the deep, breathy voice, the throaty giggle and the well-worn line. It was all so calculatedly cheap, but that was what got him. She turned him into a player. They'd never done anything at her house. This was a riskier transgression. He looked at his watch, pretending to himself that he was considering.

"I'll come now," he said. After all, it looked like Martha had a migraine coming on. It was better he leave the house.

As he drove he wondered whether he would tell Susie that Ada had seen them and that Tilly knew. If he did, he would do it afterward. It would ruin the mood if he did it before. But afterward . . . afterward was already becoming complicated. Susie had started to linger, snuggling up to him and talking about things. He hadn't wanted to hear why she married Joe (because she was desperate to have a child), how Joe had problems sexually, how he loved her, though, how he would do anything to please her, how he still read stories to Toby at night, and how her own father had died suddenly and she still hadn't recovered. It wasn't that her stories bothered him, it was just that he wasn't interested in knowing her in that way. He didn't want to become close. He never asked her anything, yet she spilled herself all over him, showing him a woman, just like Martha was a woman, a woman whose body was exposed and lying beside him on a hotel bed in the late afternoon. The instant she nestled her head onto his chest and spoke of love, she weighed a ton. He wanted to fling her off before she buried him. He didn't want her love; he wanted her hunger for him.

No, it was better he tell her nothing about Ada and Tilly knowing. Better not to encourage this sharing of confidences. As it was, she would be exactly as he liked her: she would sweep him up, pounce on him as soon as he walked in, lead him where he wanted to go. He imagined what she'd be wearing. She would have prepared herself. His mind happily succumbed to a stampede of possible scenarios.

He drove fast. Something of the hunger of his youth, the sense of anticipation, seized him. But it wasn't the same; it was dirtier. When he was young, everything was explosive and ardent and dreamlike. That's how it had felt when he met Martha.

But Arnold Buch had ruined that night. And Mike had fled from it for good reason. Arnold had broken every rule. Those rules had the rigor of a sport; they were played on a field with boundaries marked in fat white lines. Mike should have seen it coming. But it was so fluid between them with their complementary tactics, that Mike hadn't noticed the shifting terms. Had Arnold? Had it been part of a master plan from the beginning or was it just the culmination of the night's lawlessness? And afterward, Mike cut him off. He'd had to. He flinched at the memory of it.

Martha had been asleep on the bed. He and Arnold were drinking. They sat at the window. Mike lounged back in the old armchair, half dazed and sodden, while Arnold perched feverishly on a bedside table, issuing wild observations which became more incoherent and passionate the drunker he became. He lapsed occasionally into moments of absorbed quiet from which welled the sound of the ocean as it shifted its great bulk on the world's surface. Finally, Arnold began reciting poetry. Mike closed his eyes, bored.

Arnold had demanded he listen. He had claimed that if Mike did not listen to poetry then he did not have a soul.

Mike didn't understand poetry, not even when he was drunk, and he had no intention of listening. All he understood was that Arnold was making some sort of criticism of his nature. If he did have a soul, and Mike didn't even believe in such things, it was a utilitarian one, and he liked it that way. The words still sailed over him, like the sound of the sea and the salt wind that came off it.

When Mike's eyes opened, Arnold was bent over him. His face, through the darkness, showed an unfamiliar expression of pain or, thinking about it now, maybe it was ardor. Mike began to sit up properly, but Arnold seized his face and, with unrestrained fervor, kissed him on the mouth.

Mike's mind twisted at the memory of it. It can't have been his fault. Had he loosened his grip on himself? Arnold's speech had swum over him, like a story he wasn't paying attention to. In fact, he had been in his own sort of pleasant swoon for Martha. But Arnold's mouth was crushed against his before his mind could even register what was happening. He had been ambushed. And he was pissed. It took him a moment to pull himself back together and when he did, he pushed Arnold off him, of course. He should have done it sooner. Not submitted, like a girl.

Arnold stumbled and fell. Mike got up—not to help Arnold, but to get away. He'd shouted at him, called him a homo. Martha stirred on the bed but didn't wake. They'd both stared at her. She was a woman—not a part of this, but the point on which everything pivoted.

Arnold had begun again on his damn poem, as if life would go on as it was before, and night would raise its curtain on a new day, clean as the baker's truck.

Mike saw it all. Arnold Buch was soft and mad and queer. Their whole friendship turned on its side, twisted and gaped open, the past lifted like flesh from a bone. Mike turned away from it. The night sky leered, stars mocked. Everything he had known to be true jeered at him with the maniacal persistence of Arnold Buch's poem. He didn't know what else to do but to get out as fast as he could.

And from there his life sped away, on the run from such sinister uncertainty. When he and Martha managed their own courtship and headed straight down the Calder Highway, right back to the plain country, back to the heartland of the gold mines, it was because he was still running. Martha's pregnancy brought the sobering necessities of marriage and a job. He had rung an old mate whose father managed the Wattle Gully gold mine. And they were back there, in the first wave of new residents to the old towns. Most of the others were "earthenware" to him: ceramicists or beekeepers, long-haired people in overalls who built mud-brick houses and grew their own vegetables. But Martha was happy; she had a new baby and her own house. She made friends with the hippies, even if Mike never would. Mike was as suspicious of hippies as he was of homosexuals. Ever since Arnold's kiss, everything he did—his marriage, his work, his self-assurance—built his case: he was not a homosexual. He had proved it over and over. When Mike heard that Arnold Buch was going overseas, he had been relieved. It would end the story and the threat within it.

And perhaps it had worked. Arnold's visit hadn't aroused in him anything except a distant sort of fondness. Mike was not as sharp or quick or startled; life had worn him down. He had even wondered if he and Arnold could be friends again. After all, here he was, the adulterer, on his way to see his lover. It was hard to be good.

Susie opened the door wearing nothing other than a floral apron. He was more amused than aroused. His memory contained a select picture of Susie. It took him a moment to adjust to the embodied version. Did some hurt darken her eyes? She had seen his hesitation. But she rallied; she stepped closer and slapped him on the shoulder, lifting her chin, jaunty as a schoolgirl. She eyed him, challenging him. How dare he hesitate, how dare he temper this moment with doubt? Mike laughed inwardly at her defiance and, detecting this shift, she drew him toward her, holding his head with both hands, tunneling her gaze into his.

Over her shoulder Mike could see Toby's drawings of a house and family stuck on the fridge. The dog lay in its basket.

He suggested she take him to the bedroom. But there, he was even more uncomfortable. There was Joe's side of the bed: a sachet of pills, a watch, a half-drunk glass of water. On her side, there was a pile of books, just like Martha had. He closed his eyes.

He didn't see Joe Layton walk in. He heard Susie's gasp, like a fish dying in the air. She began to yank the apron off as if she would be more decent in just nothing. Mike lifted his head. "Shit," he said.

Joe was staring directly at him and at Susie as if making sure they were both real. Susie said, "Joe!" He started saying, "Honey, I'm sorry, honey?" but she was fumbling with the apron tie and struggling to get her legs out from underneath her so she could go to him. He didn't answer her. He wobbled as if he had just taken a hit and his eyes screwed closed and he turned away, his hand raised at her in a stop gesture.

By the time Mike sat up, Joe Layton had left. The front door slammed. It opened again. Mike reached for his pants. For a moment he thought he was going to have to fight. But the door slammed again. Mike waited, listening. Susie was crying. Minutes passed before he was certain that Joe Layton had gone.

30

The afternoon light struck the trees, flung shadows down. Tilly walked silently next to Raff. The ground was hot and dusty; wind-roused leaves scampered over it like little animals. Ada's brown arms swung and her singing drifted back toward them as she skipped ahead. She was eager to tell their mother the fox wasn't dead after all. She loved to be the one to tell, even if it was a lie. Ada's problems seemed so enviably simple. Tilly couldn't remember life ever feeling like that, solvable, answerable, reasonable. But it must have been. She must have been as happy and lucky as Ada was. Maybe Ada would change too when she got older. Maybe that's what getting older was—realizing the unwieldy immensity of your own interior. Trying to make your inside match your outside, which was like trying to make a hand-drawn sewing pattern match up even though the inside seams are too large. She was always running fast over the mistakes, stuffing her big feelings in like toys in a Christmas stocking no one ever opened. It made her feel untrue—her inner self was far away from the person who was representing her out there.

The moment Ada was out of sight, Tilly missed her. Because Ada had made it easier: Ada made it three. Whatever was between her and Raff was diffused by Ada and also inconspicuously allowed. The air bristled with bird sounds and a sense of portent. She and Raff were alone, but the distance between them was stretched thin.

"Well, I'll be glad to get out of this town one day," Tilly said. She hadn't prepared herself to say that at all, to create an impression of someone with direction, a false impression. Yet it didn't feel like a lie; it felt like a reach for the self she wanted to be, the self that had tottered forward, without even a push.

"Yeah? Where will you go?"

"Ice skating first of all. At St. Moritz."

He frowned.

"I thought you meant you wanted to live somewhere else?"

"Yes, I do. Ireland."

"Why Ireland?"

"Because of their voices . . ."

"You're funny."

"Well, I try to be very normal."

"It wouldn't suit you."

"I could pull it off—you'd be surprised. I have good manners, for one thing."

She thought if she could put her hands on his face she would hold it as if it were the most precious thing she had ever held. He picked up a stone and turned it over in his hand.

"Do you sing?" he said.

"Only to myself."

"I do my best singing to myself."

Why had he asked that? Did it count for him? Was he checking off requirements? Could he only love a girl who could sing? And what if he asked her to sing and she couldn't after all and he would think she had told a fib just to impress him when she had just meant she sang in the way everyone sang, not in the way real singers sing, the ones with lovely voices. Should she tell him, to clear it up so he wouldn't be disappointed should she ever have to sing in front of him? Probably he could sing well, because he played the trumpet. That other girl probably sang, the one with the Shirley Temple hair. She looked like she was a singer. She was even sort of golden, like a canary. She probably purred too. She'd have a sultry voice, and growl Nina Simone love songs with her flaxen curls and high heels. She probably had experience too. She wouldn't be frightened of sex and all the other stuff that came before it. She was like a movie star, directing her inviting smile straight at him.

Raff was rubbing at his forehead, as if it hurt. "I got this song stuck in my head. It's terrible. Because of the fox."

"What song?"

He began to hum. She knew the song.

"'Fox on the Run,'" she told him straightaway. He was nodding and singing in a laughing way. She had gotten it right. There they were, walking down the street past the house that overflowed with children and goats and odd bits of furniture, past Beryl Minister's house with the lawn always closely shaved and past Doug's copse of thin elms all swept clean because of fire risk, and beneath the flat, blue sky and glinting tin roofs and past everything that was always there. But the world had shifted into a bright, unfamiliar perfection; it all seemed different, bolder, bluer, clearer—even astounding.

Tilly chimed in on the chorus. And everything conspired to belong to it: the neighbors' houses, the hot gray road, the heat and birds and air, her and him, their dance of voices, the brilliant dust. When the song ended she realized nothing had really changed except that her own bedraggled soul was sauntering like a dandy past the shabby familiarity of her street.

Home, when they arrived, clamped its old ways over it all. They paused at the door. She thought it was all over, but he kissed her—he grinned for a second and pulled her toward him and kissed her on the mouth. It lasted long enough that she knew it was a real kiss and she had time to blink and blink again, glimpsing his jaw, his ear, and his neck. He looked at her in a tender way and stuck his hands in his pockets. She stepped back to see his whole face and to see if she could tell what he felt, but he was already saying something, quietly and with a frown.

"You know I'm moving to Melbourne next week?"

"No." She deflated instantly.

"It's a shame in a way, but I planned it ages ago."

"Are you saying that was a goodbye kiss?"

He laughed.

"Maybe."

"Maybe I'll move to Melbourne too. Once I get my results."

"Maybe you will. Look me up if you do."

"What will you do there?"

"I don't know. Explore. Play music."

She gave up. She thought she might just sit on the step and wrap her arms around her knees and feel sad. She stayed silent. He must have sensed it.

"You can visit. I've got a room with my cousin. You and Ben are pretty different," he said as he turned to go.

"He's much more handsome," she said.

He no doubt meant that Ben was more fun than she was, but the difference between her and Ben came out of his maleness, which made him special to Martha and to the world. None of it was true though; she could be just as sporting as Ben. She could also explore.

He leaned back toward her, but he didn't take her hand again. He smiled. Did he mean to kiss her again? Once was enough. It was alarming. She turned quickly to go inside. She didn't know how she felt. But here was her chance. Everything depended on it. As if it were a test, as if Raff Cavallo's unconsidered kiss had left him weightlessly but landed within her with all the bundled-up gravity of an imminent explosion. And now he was leaving.

31

Ada arrived home from the windmill and raced in to tell Martha the altered version of the story. Her mother hadn't killed the fox after all. Ada sang it to herself as she skipped down the hall. But no one was there. She flopped on Martha's bed, flat and wide as a star. She had rehearsed how she would say it: *Mama, I looked everywhere but there is no dead fox in the garden, so he must have got up and run away after all. He was only playing dead.* Ada had been looking forward to declaring it because there was the force of God's thunder in it. Ada would deliver fate a blow, swerve destiny back on course. She could save her mother from the universe's plans because she had undone life and done it up a better way. Her mother had not really killed anything. Maybe Ada had outsmarted God. Just in case he should hear this impertinent thought, she began to sing a song quickly to drown out her uncoverable thoughts.

> *Hey, ho, nobody home,*
> *Meat, nor drink, nor money have I none*
> *Yet I will be merry.*
> *Hey, ho, nobody home.*

But Ada couldn't save the day if she couldn't tell Martha. Ada was cross with her mother for not being there, for jeopardizing the important moment. She lay still on the bed. Maybe she could pretend she was dead. How still could she be? Almost immediately her nose itched. God was testing her.

"Ada?"

It was Tilly. "What are you doing, Ada?"

Ada heaved a sigh. "I was pretending to be dead. A dead star. But you ruined it."

Tilly lay on the bed too.

"Where's Mum?"

"Gone to the hospital, I suppose. Anne Dresden was coming to take her."

"Poor Mum." Tilly sounded worried.

"Don't worry. She won't die," Ada said with the kindly knowing tones of a doctor. But Tilly hardly noticed. She was already wearing a dreamy smile. It was as if she hadn't heard a thing. Ada remembered she was still cross with Tilly, but she didn't know exactly why—it had something to do with this love spell she was under. She didn't want to ask in case it made her feel lonely again. And, anyway, what about dinner? Ada was hungry. Who would make dinner if Martha wasn't home?

"Are you pretending to be dead again?" Tilly asked.

"No," said Ada carefully. "I'm worrying about dinner."

"We'll just probably have baked beans," Tilly said. She sat up. "Actually, I'm going to cook something for dinner, but first I have to call Alice."

Ada frowned. She didn't believe Tilly could make dinner. Dinner was Martha's job. Tilly was hopeless. Martha always said she was.

Tilly went to ring Alice. Ada picked up the receiver on the phone by their parents' bed, quickly, before Tilly picked up the other end so that she wouldn't hear the click. She lay on her back and crossed her feet. She liked listening to phone calls. It was like going to the movies.

Tilly said, "Guess what," and Alice said, "What?"

"We pashed," Tilly said. Ada frowned. She wasn't sure what this was, and it annoyed her that she didn't know. Without knowing she couldn't be properly disappointed.

"Wow. You and Raff?" Alice said.

"Yes. He came over."

"Did you like it? Is he a good kisser?"

Now Ada knew.

"I guess so. What would I know?"

"Well, you should be able to tell. Bad kissers are all mouth and tongue. Good kissing comes in slowly, like nudging . . ."

Ada didn't like this talk of kissing. She closed her eyes and imagined cheesecake.

"When did you become the kissing expert?"

"Did he try anything else?"

"No. He just told me he was moving to Melbourne next week. Maybe I didn't kiss him back properly." Tilly sounded pained.

"Maybe he was shy," Alice said.

"He's not shy. He probably thinks I'm frigid."

"Oh, who cares what he thinks."

"I do."

"Are you scared?"

"No. I don't know what I am."

"Do you trust him?"

"Trust? I don't even know. I don't know about trust." Tilly laughed, but it wasn't funny.

This was sex, thought Ada. This was where it was going. Sex wasn't one bit funny and neither was trust. Ada knew what trust was. Why didn't Tilly? You could not trust a fox. You could not trust the headmaster, or the windmill. You could not trust the weather. You might not be able to trust Raff Cavallo, just like you might not trust Ben, or their dad—even he couldn't be trusted. But you could trust William Blake. You could trust PJ. Ada wanted PJ. She hung up the phone and went to find him.

Ben was in the kitchen. He was drinking a can of beer and reading the newspaper—the sports section. Ada forgot about PJ because she realized that Ben was just sitting there and that he didn't know what she had just found out. In fact, he didn't know anything. She leaned into the bench and began to hum. He didn't know what they'd done with the fox. He didn't know Tilly was going to have sex with Raff. She liked the feeling of having a secret Ben didn't know. If there was anyone to keep a secret from, it was Ben, because he was the one who always knew everything.

"Mum went to hospital with Mrs. Dresden because she got bitten by the fox."

Ben looked up and took a swig of beer.

"Seriously? How the hell? That dead fox?"

"You swore."

Ben wiped his mouth.

"Okay, well, what happened? Were you there?"

"Nope. Tilly and I put it down the windmill hole, so we can tell Mum it just ran away."

Ben shook his head.

Ada realized she had given too much away. She sat on her hands.

"Ada, why do you want to tell her that?"

"I know something else, too." Ada took her hands out from underneath her and leaned forward. She wasn't going to explain about the death coming in the garden. Ben wouldn't understand. She was going to taunt him instead with her other secret.

"I bet you do."

"It's about Tilly."

"Uh huh."

"And Raff Cavallo."

Ben jiggled his beer can to see what was left. He leaned forward, grinning.

"Are you going to tell me? Tilly was showing off, wasn't she?"

Ada wasn't going to tell. No way on earth. She shook her head and pressed her lips together. Shut. But she couldn't help saying just a little bit.

"It's to do with sex."

Tilly walked into the room. They both turned and stared at her.

"What?" said Tilly.

"Nothing," said Ben.

Ada shouldn't have told Ben anything at all. She wished she could take it all back. Now that she saw Tilly standing there, looking so scared and so happy with her eyes so wide open anything could sail into them. What if Ben said something, something that would crush her, because that's how she looked, as breakable as glass. Tilly wouldn't trust Ada again. And Ada wanted to be trusted.

Where was PJ? She jumped up and flung the flywire door open, calling to him. Inside the phone was ringing. Everything seemed so urgent all of a sudden—as if Tilly was about to do something terrible and Ben was about to say something crushing, and the fox was dead in the forever hole.

PJ hobbled up to her. She bent and put her face close to his.

"PJ," she gulped. She pressed herself close. She was going to have to tell him her big secret. Because it had all accumulated within her and she had to get it out of her. But she didn't know what to tell him. She didn't want to tell anything anymore. She just wanted to be Ada and PJ. And nothing else.

Tilly came out and stood looking at the sky. It wasn't yet dark, but the day was in shreds, the blue drained away, the shimmer of the evening welling up. Why would she stand there and stare at the sky?

"What are you doing?" Ada dreaded the answer, but she had to ask.

Tilly turned. She blinked. Her hands just seemed to drop as if she had let them go.

"Well, it's so strange. Mum just rang and she isn't coming home tonight. She's staying with Anne Dresden. Of all nights."

"What do you mean?"

"Nothing. It's just such a strange hot night."

Tilly felt it too. This was so wonderfully reassuring that Ada wriggled out of her turmoil and sank her head onto PJ and listened to his body heaving. This always made her sleepy. The cicada chorus had started up. The strange hot night was under way.

32

Nothing happened in the night. Ada forgot to stay awake and see if Tilly snuck out to have sex with Raff.

The next day she walked home from the pool. It was too hot to skip. It was even too hot to walk, but she had to, so she clung to the fences where there was sometimes shade from trees. It was like walking in an oven, the sun baking her like a biscuit and the sky just tired out and sucked of all color. Everyone had said the cool change was on its way. As far as Ada could tell, the heat was fighting it. But her thoughts were drowned out by the wail of a siren, and a fire engine sped past her. Ada took off her hat and looked up. A funnel of dark smoke dirtied the sky. Another fire engine sped past.

It occurred to Ada that her house may have burned down. But she shook her head. Her dad said fires come from the north. And fires don't jump the train tracks either. So it couldn't be her house that was on fire.

She stared at the great cloud of dark smoke. Ada wasn't sure. She used to believe her dad knew everything, but she didn't believe that anymore. The air was solid as a wall and it smelled of burning leaves and charcoal. Specks of soot swirled in the sky. Ada remembered the stalking death and the fox and the chickens. She remembered the terrible thing in the living room. And the terrible thing she had done to Toby Layton.

She stopped. Her swimming bag slid off her shoulder. Ada was frightened, not for herself, not for Toby. Ada was frightened about the fire and where it was going and who it was aiming for. Someone in her house? PJ?

Ada marched up the street. She would need to protect that person, or PJ, with a blanket. The foreboding jiggered inside her. The fire was the terrible thing. It was there. Finally. She had known it all along. She had to get PJ out of the house. Or someone.

People were coming out of their houses. They could smell the smoke and hear the fire engines. What if it was Tilly who was up there? It wouldn't be Ben because Ben would have known how to get away. If the fire were to get anyone it would be Tilly.

Ada had to get a blanket. They were in the laundry, in the cupboard, on the top shelf. She would need a stool. The smoke wound around her. Her eyes began to sting. Tilly had told her of the blackened skin. She shouldn't have. But Tilly had changed; Tilly was sly now, and pretty, but she was still Tilly. And she hadn't meant to change. She didn't mean to love Raff. She just did it because life had put its weight behind her.

But what her dad and Mrs. Layton had done in the living room was on purpose. The fire was not because of Tilly, but because of them in the living room. God had seen it and thorns of rage had sprouted on his back and he'd breathed a hellfire down on them, on their house. The sky was gray, the road stank, the grass was scorched yellow and brittle as paper. People stood in their dry gardens, sheltering their eyes.

It had happened: the fire had exploded; the flames were licking up the trees and burning them into nothing. Ada began to run. The cinders were already twirling in the air like falling confetti. She had to get the blanket. In her mind's eye, she could see a ball of flames hurling through the sky.

"Ada!"

Ada spun around. Ben was on his bike, coming up the hill. He was shouting. His face was red.

"Ada, don't go up there."

But Ben wasn't the boss. Ada shouted back. "I'm going to get PJ. And Tilly."

Ben caught up with her. He stopped and wiped his forehead and said it was too fucking hot. He told her not to be bloody stupid. There was a fire. She had to wait. He would get PJ. But he didn't say anything about Tilly.

"Where's Tilly, though?"

"I don't know, probably on her way home."

Ada shook her head. She was going for the blanket. Cars were coming down the street. Mr. Staum tooted at them and leaned out his window and told them to go back.

"Give me a ride," Ada ordered. She climbed on. Ben scratched his head and swore again. He said the deal was if he turned back, she was coming with him. Ada didn't care for deals.

But a fireman came striding down the street, waving his arms wide like windscreen wipers. "Hey," he shouted at them. "Go back."

Ada squeezed Ben like a horse she was giddying up, but Ben stopped. Ada pressed him forward. "He's not the boss of us," she whispered. But Ben didn't move. Ben didn't really understand. He didn't realize the fire's intention. He didn't know about the living room. He hadn't felt the dry sucking of death in the air. He didn't even know they needed the blanket.

Once the fireman was close enough, Ada yelled, "We have to go home. It's our house just up there and our dog PJ could be there, and he only has three good legs. And we don't know where our sister is."

The fireman wore a hard hat and a shiny yellow coat. He had brown skin and gray hair on his face, just like Mr. Layton. He put his hands on his hips. He wouldn't let her through. He wasn't as nice as Mr. Layton. He was closing the street. He told them to go and wait at the oval. He said all the houses had been cleared already. No one was there. He said the fire was in the bush block. It was the one between their house and Toby Layton's house.

Ada paled. Her patch of bush. William Blake would die. And Emily Dickinson. She shook her head. The fireball was af- ter them. She climbed off the bike and began to run again. Ben called her back. The fireman grabbed her by the arm.

Ada shouted at him. "What about our sister, Tilly? She's al- ways in trouble. And our dog, PJ. He only has three legs!" Ada couldn't tell him about William Blake. The fireman wouldn't un- derstand.

He let her arm go and looked at her with a frown. His voice softened. "Your sister can't be in the house. Everyone has left. I'll make sure your dog is taken away too. But I'm not going to let you through."

Ada didn't know if she could believe him. She was too afraid, and her mind was twitching. She couldn't hear herself. Ada felt it in her bones. She couldn't explain about the terrible thing, the old windmill's doom, because no one would understand her. No one could see it except her. Ada pointed up the hill. "Our house is the one on the corner just up there. The one with the pointy tree by the gate. PJ will be on the veranda. Call his name loudly because he doesn't hear well."

The fireman nodded. "Where's your mother? I bet she's on the oval with PJ wondering where you are. You should get going."

Ben began to turn the bike around. Ada twisted back and watched the red glow spread like a stain over the sky. Now the fireball would come. And she couldn't get the blanket. She pressed her hands to her eyes, but the tears came anyway, so she closed them, and in her mind she began to plead with the fire-breathing god.

33

Mike was already on edge because of Joe walking in, and not long after that Martha had rung him, hysterical. She had sobbed into the phone. He'd braced himself, thinking Joe had gone and told her. But no, she was at the hospital. A fox had bitten her. He didn't even know foxes bit people. The hospital woman had told Martha that hand wounds were the worst, and it would require treatment as soon as possible. Foxes carried tetanus.

Martha's voice became high pitched. "All sorts of infections, Mike," she wailed. "I could have rabies, and I had to kill it, I knelt on its throat." Mike had tried to reassure her. He was so relieved his betrayal hadn't been reported that he felt almost grateful for her neediness. And she had sighed as if she had really believed him. As if she would let him be a man after all. She said she would stay at Anne's for a while because she was too distressed and exhausted to face everyone at home. Mike had been relieved. He had encouraged it. Yes, stay there, that would be fine. He would deal with the kids. He didn't want to face her.

First Joe and then a fox and now a fire. Hell was raining down on him. And had he cleaned out the gutters? Had he renewed their insurance? His reprieve had been short. He was a man with problems again. He was harried, neglectful, unprepared for the season of fires. Usually they came from the north. So he hadn't bothered. And he had jeopardized the safety of his family.

By the time he arrived at the oval, there was a small crowd of people under the oak tree. He was relieved to find Ada and Ben and Susie and a handful of other neighbors. Toby lay with his head on Susie's lap, reading. Susie acknowledged Mike with a nod. She and Toby sat slightly apart from Ada and Ben. Ada didn't rush out to greet him, as she usually would have.

Ben seemed unaffected. He glanced at Ada as Mike approached and explained, "She's worried about Till and PJ. Do you know where Mum is?"

"I assume she's still with Anne, if she isn't here. She's in a state about rabies."

Ada startled out of her thoughts. "Do people die from rabies?" she said.

Mike shrugged. "She hasn't got rabies. Where's Tilly?"

"No one knows," said Ben. "Ada is worried she was in the bush that's burning. It's the block over the railway, apparently someone lit it. That's the word around here, anyway."

"Why would Tilly be there?" Mike asked.

"She wouldn't, it's just Ada's got a thing going. She's, you know, seen something. It's her bush that's burning; it's where William Blake is."

"A fireball, that's what I've seen," said Ada severely. "And PJ is there on his own."

Sweat had spread on Mike's shirt and now it stuck to his skin. The clouds were darkening, or perhaps it was just that smoke had filled the sky. And the fact remained: he had cheated on his wife. He couldn't dispel Ada's visions of fireballs. Nor could he make things better for Susie, who was wearing a boldly patterned sundress disturbingly reminiscent of the floral apron she had tried to undo. For once, despite the dress, she looked strangely timid, as if stunned into a disconcerted reserve.

And where was Tilly?

Mike rolled up his sleeves. He would go and look for her. Should he talk to Susie first? Would it be rude not to talk to her? He should ask her if she was all right. Of course she wasn't, though. And Toby was here. Whatever he said or didn't say in relation to Susie would feel wrong, to say nothing, to say something. And why weren't Ada and Toby playing? He should find Tilly first. Then Ada would calm. She would stop this embarrassing praying, and he could avoid Susie. Just seeing her made him feel bad. He didn't want to see her anymore. His feelings for her were dead. Joe had killed them. The disgust that had deflated his face had reflected their ugliness, Susie trussed up like a chicken in the floral apron she'd tried to tear off. He cursed his mind's eye for returning the scene to him.

He crouched by Ada. "How about you and I go look for Tilly. We'll get an ice cream on the way."

Ada didn't even move; she opened her eyes and fastened an unerring look of reproach on him. Did she know about Joe? Ada never refused an ice cream. Mike stood up and shook off her stare.

After a moment she said, "William Blake is probably burnt to the ground. I'm waiting here for the fireman and PJ. You go with Ben and get Tilly."

"Well, I need a beer," said Ben, standing up and dusting off his jeans.

For God's sake, Mike needed one too. He would have to leave Ada here with Susie. He could tell she wouldn't be persuaded. If an ice cream couldn't ease her out, nothing would. And he had to find Tilly. He glanced at Ben. Ben wasn't legally old enough to drink. But today was not a normal day. He fished into his pocket, pulled out his wallet, and handed Ben a two-dollar note.

"Ride to the bottle shop and grab a stubby. I'm going to go look for Tilly."

Ben raised an eyebrow. He tried not to make a big show of it. He slipped the money in his pocket, swung his leg over the bike, and slid away in an instant. Mike watched him anxiously. Why didn't he trust Ben? He began to wonder if he shouldn't have done it. Ben's self-assurance was unsettling. It was as if he knew the ropes so well he didn't need to use them anymore. He was too well wired for his own good—all savvy and charm and not enough truth. He was almost the opposite of Ada, in whom truth burned so bright it made her fierce.

A shout came from behind him. Mike turned. There was the fireman, leading PJ on a piece of rope, exactly as Ada had said he would. Ada jumped up.

"PJ," she shouted, running toward him. The fireman was a hero. He was not a man who cheated on his wife. He was a man who had cleaned his gutters, joined the local Country Fire Authority, and rescued an old lame dog. His life was tidy, praiseworthy. Mike resented him. Everyone on the oval wandered over to hear his tale. Ada stood by the fireman hero, patting PJ. She gazed up at the fireman, smiling.

The clouds had gathered above them. The sky was turbulent, aching. Any minute it would crack with thunder. But the fireman smiled at them all. He beamed like the sun itself. He said the fire had been contained and it was safe to return to their houses. No house had been burned. The police would be going into the bush block as arson was suspected. People murmured disapprovingly and began to collect their things.

The fire had been contained. The word *contained* struck Mike as a human inclination; it seemed to diminish men in the face of something greater. Fire, lust, life . . .

He found himself standing close to Susie after all. "You okay?" he said.

She stared at him as if she had just seen him for the first time; her face was as unsettled as the sky, her mouth trembling and her gaze rushing frantically all over him and past him too. Could she see it was over?

She shook her head finally and clasped Toby to her. "I haven't seen him," she whispered, and as she turned to leave, the first fat drops of rain began to fall.

34

Once the rain came it didn't stop. The sky opened up and let out everything it had withheld for so long. It hammered the tin roofs and sloshed over the gutters. People were overjoyed. A true downpour—finally. Kids galloped to the creeks to see if they would fill. Ben stood in town, stubby in hand, and watched the dripping awnings, the steaming road. He smelled rain, hot wet tar and damp clothes. The air cooled instantly. He rode his bike home slowly through the rain alongside the drains that were coursing like small streams. Water dripped down his neck.

He was thoroughly soaked by the time he walked in the kitchen door. Rain pelted the roof loudly. A bucket on the floor caught the drips inside. PJ huddled unhappily at Ada's feet. Both Ada and his dad stood staring out the kitchen window. They turned to Ben as he stood there, dripping.

"It's even cool," he said. He was the messenger delivering the sodden, soaking fact of rain. He grinned. The world was clean-scrubbed. And he began to shiver.

"Have you seen Tilly? I can't find her," Mike said.

"She's probably with Alice," Ben said.

"No, she isn't. You should go get out of your wet things," his dad said. "Your mum will be home any minute."

Ben smiled lazily. He turned and headed for the bathroom. And then he thought of the fox. "Is Mum okay?" he called over his shoulder.

Ada ran up close to him and touched his wet shirt. "Don't tell Mum about what we did?"

Ben nodded. He was no blabbermouth.

Ada raced back to the window where she glued her face, watching for Tilly.

"Yes, she's fine, just a bit shaken," said Mike.

Ben peeled off his clothes, discarding them in a pile on the bathroom floor. He stood in a hot shower for longer than he was meant to. But the drought had broken, and he wanted to remember how it was when water wasn't scarce, when they were kids and they played endlessly under the sprinkler and had their baths as deep as they liked. The rain still thudded down. The tank would fill. The dams would rise. Maybe even Cairn Curran would fill. He could stay under the hot water.

Mike thumped on the door and told him to get out. Ben, wearing a towel and holding his wet clothes, was headed out the door to his room when he saw a car pull into the driveway. It wasn't Martha's car.

He called to Ada, "Someone's here."

Ada flew back to the window. They both watched. For a while it seemed no one would get out of the car. Finally the passenger door opened. It was Tilly. She sheltered her head with her arms, speaking quickly and smilingly at the driver, and she ran toward the house.

Ada ran at her as soon as she entered.

"Where have you been? There's been a fire. William Blake is dead. We weren't allowed to come home."

Tilly wiped the rain off her bare arms and stared at Ada uncomprehendingly. "Wait, so where's Mum? Did your tree really burn?"

"Who drove you home?" said Ben.

Tilly ignored him and stared questioningly at Mike.

"Your mum's on her way home from Anne Dresden's," he said.

"Where were you, Tilly?" Ada wore the gravest expression.

Tilly tilted her head and examined the room as if to make sure it was all there.

Ben knew where she had been. He could tell. She was cagey, wide-eyed, distracted. Why should that ruin his mood? He fought against it.

"I went to my piano lesson. That's all. Raff drove me home. Because of the rain." Tilly eyed Ben with a forbidding glare. He wasn't to comment, obviously. But Ada did.

"Is he your boyfriend?"

"No." Tilly blushed and plonked herself on a stool. "What started the fire?"

No one answered. No one knew yet. The sound of the rain seemed louder for a moment and they all looked outside. The sky was streaked with the metallic rain. Ada's sneakers out on the grass were soaked through.

The telephone was ringing. Ben could hardly hear it. "It's like Armageddon," he said. The rain belonged to him. It was he who had seen the town submit to the downpour. Neither of his sisters answered him or even registered his observation. They stood together at the window in a way that excluded him. There was a quiet between them. He could tell something else was there too, something unconscious and constant. Their instincts moved in relation to each other like a dance. Something had drawn them to the window and pressed them into a gentle, silent awe. It irritated him because it joined them against him, against the moment he had meant to own.

Mike was speaking on the phone. The rain was so heavy Ben couldn't hear what he was saying. He would wait for it to ease and then he would run out to his room as he had planned.

But Ada ran outside instead. No one stopped her. She stood on the grass with her arms up, her palms cupping the rain, her face bracing to receive the splattering of water.

35

Anne Dresden drove Martha home. Martha was grateful. At least there was Anne. Anne's broad arms, her flat-shoed, unerring practicality, her ox-hearted steadiness. She had been exactly what Martha had needed. Susie would have made jokes, been flippant, even. Anne had stayed with her and taken charge. At the hospital they'd given her antibiotics, injections, wrapped her in bandages and recommended rest. Hand wounds were the worst. Anne had nodded sensibly, patting Martha. Martha burst forth with her visions of mad salivating dogs. She was nauseated.

Anne took her home to her place, initially just for a cup of tea.

"You've moved?" Martha had said as they pulled up to a small house on Duke Street.

"Yes, I told you. You don't remember?"

Martha remembered. Anne wasn't a close friend; she was one of those good women Martha couldn't relate to, though she liked her and even admired her goodness. But Anne made her conscious of her own selfishness. So Martha hadn't asked about her move, but had felt afterward that she should have. She should have given Anne the chance to tell her, because maybe Anne needed to.

"Oh, yes, I remember. Why did you move?"

"Greg was having an affair. I've got the kids." She shrugged. "Don't worry, I'm doing fine. A relief to not have to clean up after him as well as the kids."

Martha was so ashamed. Her own injury seemed hysterical in comparison, and Anne was tending to her, giving her a cup of tea. She began weeping again. "Oh, Anne, I'm so sorry."

"Don't cry on my account. Come on, have some cake."

Anne had squeezed her for an instant with her broad brown hand, and Martha had felt better.

Anne was driving her home through the downpour and Martha was preparing herself for her entrance. Anne Dresden wouldn't do such a thing: contrive her arrival for maximum effect. But something had happened to Martha; finally, something had happened.

To be attacked by an animal was not just unusual. It set off a deep, thrilling, primordial fear. Martha had been dragged to the edge of life. She had bled. She had a tale to tell. And while she had survived the attack, the possibility of infection still hung over her, so she was owed not only enthrallment in her story, but also ongoing solicitude for her threatened health. They should all see how shaken she was, how fragile and shocked. They should understand, as Anne did, how frightened she had been, how upsetting and brutal it was to fight to the death. This would all be conveyed by her appearance, her bandaged hand and foot, her limp, her war-weary expression. Because, once the initial questioning was over, she would lose their attention. Martha had already anticipated this and was hurt in advance. She would have to hide this brittle aspect of her feelings if she were to be received with tenderness. She wanted to be cared for. No one could deny that, after such a terrible attack, for once she was deserving.

Only Ada would understand the fabled portent of the attack. Martha's hand rose to her heart; she had become aware of both this embarrassing need to be attended to, and of a deep, nameless grief that was at the root of this need and which now overwhelmed her. She was alone—surrounded by people, but alone. All this emotion—the tears, all for nothing or for everything, it didn't matter which. It was the fox who had died, not Martha. It was Anne Dresden who had lost her husband. Martha wrung emotion out of air, weather, even foxes. That was why she was sad.

But this was how it always was. She wasn't poor or ill or divorced or childless or otherwise slighted. She was privileged. Her husband didn't cheat on her or beat her. She had nothing to complain about. And yet she was unhappy. But to be unhappy when she had so much was all wrong and shameful. It showed deep personal failure. If Anne could smile and roll up her sleeves, why could Martha not do the same? But Martha wasn't like Anne. She never would be. She had a miserable case of quiet, unspectacular, unwarranted unhappiness. And the realization just made her worse.

She leaned out the window so Anne wouldn't notice, gulped in a deep breath of the rain-washed air and turned on the radio. She had to stymie the swelling of this. She had to stop thinking. She had to prepare mentally for the theater of her return, where for once she would get her due.

36

When Martha came in dragging Ada by the hand, Tilly felt everything contract.

"I can't get a word out of Ada," Martha said. "What was she doing in the rain?" She stood there, pulling off Ada's wet clothes, even with her hand all bandaged up. "Tilly, help me please, my hand . . . Can you run the bath?" Martha held her bandaged hand up like an exhibit. Her tone of irritated self-sacrifice was so familiar that they all responded not to the wounded hand but to the ordinary pattern of life she brought with her.

Mike stood up. He looked as if the rain had washed him out. "Susie Layton rang. Joe is missing."

Martha bent to get Ada's sandals off. She frowned. "Knowing Joe, he probably went out to help someone who got stuck because of this rain."

Tilly felt an unfamiliar churning of pity for her mother. For the first time Martha was the one who was innocent. Martha was the one who had been wronged. And she didn't even know it. Martha, who had to know everything, didn't know the thing that mattered most. Mike said Martha was probably right, but he had answered so dutifully, he appeared to Tilly like a stunned child reciting a lesson he hadn't prepared for. Tilly suspected he knew more about Joe being missing than he was revealing. Even if Martha saw this, she wouldn't understand why.

Ada turned to Martha and said loudly that the fox hadn't been killed and could she see Martha's bites. They had all forgotten about the fox attack. Poor Martha. Tilly had seen her mother's bandaged hand but hadn't wanted to think about it. She should be more caring. She should offer to make her a cup of tea.

But Ada had already reached out to take Martha's bandaged hand and was examining it. Ada gauged the importance of an injury by the amount of blood that issued from the wound. When she found none, she returned her attention to the fox.

"We couldn't find the dead fox anywhere," Ada lied with too much portentousness. "Does it hurt, Mama?" At least this was sincere.

Martha looked bewildered. "You think the fox is alive? I was sure it died. I knelt on its throat." She turned to Mike in a panic. But Mike said nothing.

"Mum, do you want me to make you a cup of tea?" Tilly pulled herself together. She could do the right thing after all.

Martha's eyes filled with tears. The sight of her mother crying always upset Tilly, and she looked away. Mike finally put his arms around her. Tilly couldn't tell whether this was consolation for the fox attack or for some other private sadness between them. She couldn't tell what exactly had moved Martha to tears. But whatever it was, Martha accepted Mike's embrace as if it were the haven she had been seeking all along. She leaned her head into his chest and closed her eyes. Her bandaged hand hung limply by her side and Mike bent his head over her shoulder and stroked her back. They looked like two people who loved each other.

But Tilly rarely saw them hold each other and it unsettled her. Ada stood, transfixed. If life had swerved even their parents so far off course that in the middle of the kitchen they sought out the shelter of each other's bodies, then no wonder Tilly was afraid to ask either of them what had happened to Mr. Layton.

37

Mike didn't go to work the next day. He wasn't like his father after all. He couldn't just keep going, though how the hell would he not keep going? It wasn't that he had lost direction; it was that direction had lost him. The life that, up till now, had accommodated his lust and ambition, and also his boredom, wasn't there anymore. Some other life was, and he didn't like it. He lay in bed while the rain eased and sorrow knocked. His guilt was stone hard, and he couldn't chase it away. The rain had gone on all night, and while the clamor of it rose and fell, he thought again and again of his children: how Tilly had accused him, but Ada had known and said nothing. And, worst of all, Joe Layton wouldn't leave his mind. Mike kept replaying the moment of his arrival at the door, the shock, his departure, and then what? Mike tried to arrange the events. Had he gone out and come back? Had he come back for the salve of alcohol? Had he walked like a blind man with a bottle of whiskey to a private place to drown his humiliation?

Mike needed to tell someone he was sorry. Martha's mouth was slack with sleep; she twitched and turned her back to him.

He should have taken her trauma more seriously. But he was so trapped in his anxiety, he couldn't get out of it.

He got up early and started to dress. He would go for a run.

Martha was surprised when he said he wasn't going to work. He told her he had hardly slept. She frowned, momentarily perplexed. Mike always slept. She got out of bed too and came over and stroked the back of his neck as if he had finally proved that he too could feel deeply. But this tenderness from Martha just curdled inside him. He barged out.

He found himself beneath the old pine tree where the chickens were buried. The remnants of Ada's wreath of flowers were brown and sodden with the rain. There was no reason to be standing there. He had just fled from Martha's caress and the resentment he had felt. Why now? Why did she never touch him lovingly, not until he didn't deserve it? It was too late. He stared bitterly at the distant skyline as if the distance had something to offer. There was mist and the smell of wet ground, which was forgiving in a way. But it wasn't right to just stand there, staring out. Something had to be done.

Maybe he should go to work after all. Work would contain all of this, bring it into perspective. He had made a mistake, and because of it, Joe had fled. That was it. This was what he had to contend with. His body loosened itself around this fact.

"What are you doing?"

It was Tilly. Was no one sleeping?

"Nothing," he said. He was too tired to make something up. Tilly didn't even realize what sort of secret she held and how it would smash everything to pieces if she let it out. Martha would despise him. The marriage would end.

"Aren't you going to work?"

"Not today."

"Why not?"

Mike rubbed at his eyes. "Why are you up so early?" he said.

"Ada woke me. She's gone to see the burnt bush block."

"I bet it looks awful."

Tilly shrugged. It annoyed him. Always this nonchalance. She had closed herself to him. He had kept trying. He had given her that money for a new dress. Usually she would have beamed. But she had just been polite. Her smile was cold. As a kid she had adored him, climbed all over him, sang him made-up songs. He had tried to put the change down to adolescence, but it wasn't that. It was a blanketed hostility toward him because of what Ada had seen. This is what happens when you break the law: the judges come after you.

He missed Tilly. In time she would forget. After all, he loved her, and love prevailed, surely. Once she gained some maturity she might even understand.

Ada came running across the yard toward them, PJ hobbling behind her. Her hands were covered in soot. She was holding a handful of gumnuts, which she dropped when she saw Mike. She frowned at him.

"Why are you here?"

"Why? I live here, for God's sake. Why is everyone asking me?" Surprised he had shouted, he turned away. It was all getting to him. And here they were, accusing him just for being in his own home. He was the one who had showed up every day in that stuffy office and slugged away arranging other people's affairs so he could pay for that house he was not meant to even be in. No wonder he was mad. He had to make it up to Ada, though. He turned around to say sorry, but she glared at him, dropped to her knees, and wrapped her arms around PJ. Tilly turned and walked away.

He couldn't just keep standing here beneath the pine. He needed to do something. He could try to talk to Ada. Or Tilly. His own daughters—the keepers of his terrible secret. He looked at Ada, but she turned and ran after Tilly.

Mike rubbed his face again. He called out to PJ. He would take him for a walk. He never did this. PJ ambled over and stared up at him expectantly. He was almost deaf. He couldn't even hear the word *walk* anymore. Yet there was something about him that just continued so solidly. Lucky PJ. He didn't see Mike any differently. This was immensely reassuring. Mike turned and slapped at his thigh, whistling for PJ to come. He would walk toward the Laytons' house. If there was no one there, he would go in. He had to do something.

38

Everyone was thinking about the fire and Mr. Layton. Alice was worried. Tilly was worried too. Mr. Layton wouldn't desert them. He would come back.

Was it lying if Tilly said nothing about her father and Mrs. Layton? What if it was all mixed up together? The fire had rushed through, eating up everything, even Mr. Layton in some way, but all the torrid urgency of her secret was still there. Maybe it was worse.

She left the house, creeping out into a world that felt all enlarged and imbued with the scorched remains and the disappearance of Mr. Layton. She went to Daisy Cavallo's.

"I have a plan," Daisy whispered, at the door. She held up one finger. "We're going to lie back and just listen for a while. Come in. I'll put a record on. No, you put it on. You choose? Anything but the nocturnes. I'm too melancholic already. Is there any news on Joe Layton?" Daisy flopped on the couch, like a fainted Victorian.

Tilly paused. She wished Daisy had not mentioned Mr. Layton. And she didn't know which record to choose. Daisy's records weren't what you would expect for a piano teacher: Jimi Hendrix, Bach, Thelonious Monk, Nina Simone, but also Neneh Cherry, Hank Williams. They were just names to Tilly.

"It's terrible that we don't make a practice of listening. Just to fill ourselves with a beautiful song? Everything is too intentional. Did I tell you, next week I'm going to a women's peace camp at Pine Gap. I'm taking my accordion."

Tilly felt immediately ashamed of her own escape plan.

"Can I come?"

"Well, you could, but it's a long way. I'm flying there. Make me a sign, though, and I'll carry it for you." Daisy gestured toward the records. "Surprise me!" she sang. Tilly chose Dollar Brand, slipped the record out of its inner envelope. She didn't know who Dollar Brand was. When the music started, Daisy smiled, closed her eyes.

"See, I knew you would make a perfect choice. Close your eyes. It helps. Let's listen together."

Together. Daisy was her secret companion, Dollar Brand their accomplice. Dollar Brand played the piano. Tilly lay over the armchair, let her arm dangle. She tried to rid her head of plans.

Daisy opened her lazy eyes. "Are you listening, chicken? Doesn't he make it sing?"

"Yes, I'm listening."

"And what now?"

"Well, I'm going ice skating."

Daisy sat up. She stretched her lovely neck. "Oh, now that it's cooled down . . ."

Dollar Brand kept playing. The music was lilting, like something running up and down a hill.

"If I was your age," Daisy said. And she stopped speaking and kept listening. Tilly waited for her to continue. It was odd just waiting there with the piano and everything languorous and damp, as if ready to take flight. She felt like a seed wedged in the earth, just beginning to push up.

Daisy let out a long sigh. "Whatever you do, you must do it all before your legs get stiff and arthritic." Daisy twirled her bare feet in front of her.

Tilly watched Daisy's feet. They seemed anything but stiff.

"It's a wonder to have a life, really," Daisy continued.

"I've decided I want to study music."

"Exactly! And so you should. And when you travel you can switch from piano to violin." Daisy clapped her hands. "You know, Raff is in the city. I can give you his address. He's staying with his cousin."

It was what Tilly wanted, though she never would have asked for it.

Daisy sat up. "Come, let's play the piano now. We will channel Dollar Brand. African piano."

Having Raff's address was like holding a ticket out of town, far away from the disappearance of Mr. Layton and the creeping fear that she might know something about it.

Her life was ready to get going all on its own without her pleading with it to move. Soon her results would arrive, her future would be decided, but for a moment, everything had parted just enough for her to slip through. Tilly could go to the city without telling anyone. She left a note for her parents, saying she was staying with Alice.

She gave her backpack a little heave, patting the small weight fondly. It was just she and it.

She should have told Alice what she was doing. But she wasn't sure anymore where the feeling of having to leave had started and she began to doubt its integrity, because it had possibly started as a small idea, and it had grown inside her. It was shaped like a little arrow and it had flung her toward an elsewhere.

It was almost dusk by the time she got there. Shop interiors sang out as bright as beating hearts in the coming night. Cars swished by. People marched homeward. Tilly waited momentarily on a busy corner, leaning back against a lamppost. She would just watch what it was that rushed around her, steady herself in the evening's swell.

The lights changed, and Tilly crossed the road. She had a pencil-drawn map of where Raff lived. She planned to show him who she could be. When he had driven her home in the rain, he had said, "You're so shy, aren't you? It's like you're still a kid." And she had flushed. She should have risen up and shown her tiger teeth. She could have laughed, like he did, with that sort of submerged contempt. No wonder he hadn't tried to kiss her again.

Raff's cousin's house was in Carlton, a single-fronted terrace. A tall thin boy in a blue T-shirt answered the door. His arms hung by his sides. He seemed lank. Or long. Or in limbo, hovering.

"I'm looking for Raff?" she said.

"Cavallo?"

"Yeah."

"He's not here. Is he expecting you?" He shook his head, looped a thumb in his jean pocket.

She hadn't expected this.

"Oh, no. I just wanted to say hello."

"Who are you, then?"

"Tilly." She had nothing to add. She saw he expected more. And she remembered. "We were at school together."

"Well, I guess you can come in and wait a bit? I'm Steve. We're cousins." She didn't want to go in. But she wasn't sure what else to do.

"Okay. Thanks. I don't want to disturb you, though."

"No worries. I'm having a beer. Want one?"

"Okay."

She followed him down a dark hall into a small ugly room. There was little furniture: a couch, a small side table, a record player, milk crates full of records, a mantelpiece above an empty fireplace, and above that a poster of Bob Dylan, which read, "Don't look back." She stared at the one window, through which the evening light slanted in. She sat next to Steve on the couch.

He passed her the bottle of beer. "Should I get a glass?"

"I can drink it like this." She felt unsure about everything. She drank the beer. Steve watched her. He was waiting for her to talk, perhaps. She smiled at him.

He lunged forward, picking up her wrist, as if it were something of his that he had dropped. She took it back.

"So, how old are you?" He wasn't embarrassed. Maybe he was already drunk.

"Old enough." She laughed.

"I can take you to the nightclub where Raff will be if you want?" he said.

"Did Raff mention me?" She wished she hadn't asked.

"Nope. But Raff's got a lot of girls on the go." Steve smirked. Perhaps he knew it went in like a knife. She was nothing to Raff. That was what he meant. If she were alone, she could let this go in and beat around inside her head till she was nothing but sorrow. She wanted to leave. She wanted Ada. She wanted this all to be over. But she couldn't show this to Steve.

"Shall we go then?" she said.

Inside the nightclub he bought her a drink. The music was loud and the air shadowy. Everything was half hidden, half revealed. She was heavy and sinking, and she kept looking out as if Raff might appear, as if Steve might disappear and instead it would be Raff dancing in front of her. If he saw her, would he choose her? Nothing could be certain in there; nothing would hold. Even Tilly had disappeared from herself.

She took Steve's hand and led him toward the dance floor. If Raff could see her, he would see she wasn't such a child. She was taking the lead, unfolding to the bone. The mirror ball showered them with flickering light. Her hands wove through the spinning lights.

Later they stumbled home as if the world were still a whirling mirror ball. In bed he put his hands on the bones of her hips. Go ahead, she thought. She wanted every bit of her to break open, every tightly held fear to be unwound, every buried hope or rising whim to be set free. She wanted oblivion. She would surface, blank as an unwritten page, even if it hurt.

A sudden knocking on the door woke her early in the morning. Raff called out. He said his mother was on the phone. Tilly threw on her dress. The door opened, and Raff stared at her as if she were still a child, a dirty child.

"Your parents are worried about you," he said, ignoring Steve.

So she hadn't been rubbed out after all. Nothing had changed. She was still susceptible. Regrets gripped her. Raff turned back and said there was bad news too.

"What?" She squeezed the word out.

"They found Mr. Layton's body at the bottom of the well. Where we threw the fox."

39

Ada clamped her hands to her ears. Her mind had taken an axe blow. She could see everyone in the room; she could see her father crumpled over the stool and Martha fixing her eyes on him, and Ben, motionless, with a purple towel over his shoulder, bending his head.

Mr. Layton was dead.

Dead in the endless hole. In the hole that the old windmill stood over like the guard of all death. It had triumphed.

But Ada could not adjust to the reality of death, or death would not let her mind take hold of it. She tried, but everything hovered meaninglessly, as if nothing could find its weight.

Her father had not explained anything. Had they pulled Mr. Layton's body up from the hole? Was his body broken and wet? Was there blood? Were his eyes closed? Were there drops of rain on his eyelids?

Her eyes flicked wide open and clamped on her father. His hands twisted in his lap. The terror of summer was squished into the pressure between his thumbs. All her swirling thoughts came together and with one hard point, they pushed terribly at her heart.

"Where is Tilly?" she said.

40

It hadn't helped that Tilly had disappeared that night. But in a way Mike was relieved she wasn't there. How could he have faced her? It was bad enough the way Ada looked at him. And Martha wept against him in the bed. She had visited Susie and said Susie was "a wreck, of course." Toby had hardly spoken since they found out. Poor Toby, Martha said. And Alice.

Where had Tilly been? Why had she said she was at Alice's? If something had happened to Tilly he would feel responsible. What would they do now?

Mike had gone over and over it in his mind. He had worked it out. Joe must have sat by the mineshaft, drinking the whiskey, to numb his pain. Mike imagined it happening quickly: the fire had come, and Joe had climbed into the shaft to escape it and had fallen. That must have been the way it happened. He couldn't have gone to his death with this hatred of Mike foremost in his mind. But that meant Mike had to do it for him, and with his perfect aim, he pointed hatred at himself. He turned away from Martha and curled on his side, gut-punched and sober.

Joe had always been liked. Never had Mike heard a word against him. Because he was softhearted, he never got too drunk;

he was always emitting an affable sort of warmth. It came natu-rally to him. Mike knew what people would be saying: it was a tragedy for such a good bloke to die like that.

Mike had always liked Joe, but they had never been friends. But did Mike have any real friends? Ever since Arnold Buch, he had been afraid of any man who seemed to have any inclination for closeness. He kept his friends at a distance. Men he worked with, men he played tennis with—there was no one he would talk to, not properly, no one who would push him closer to him-self. Even with his defenses in place, Mike was susceptible. Joe Layton had caused the most unforeseeable violence to his soul. For the first time Mike felt he had a soul, and that night it lay down inside him and wept.

41

Tilly went straight to Alice's house from the station. The footpath was still wet and glistening from the rain.

Nothing looked the same. Alice's house was silent. Its tidiness seemed forced, like gritted teeth. Mr. Layton was never coming home. Tilly began to cry before the door opened as if she could feel the house's sorrow pressed up against that door. She didn't even know the woman who opened it.

Everything had swerved so sharply from one thing to another. Raff Cavallo would never love her. She had meant to impress him with her worldliness and instead she had turned him against her. She had done something terribly, irreversibly wrong. And her dad had done something terribly, irreversibly wrong, too.

The woman at the door guided Tilly inside. The woman knew nothing of her wrongs. There were already flowers. Alice sat at the kitchen table. She didn't smile. Her lip trembled. Alice, who usually bounced past all calamity, had fallen beneath it.

She and Tilly went into Alice's bedroom, sat on the bedspread of roses, and wept.

42

Ada saw Toby at the funeral. Alice Layton wore her hair in a bun at the back and was dressed like a grown-up in a dark-blue skirt with a white shirt tucked in and a butterfly brooch pinned on the side. But Toby held his mother's hand. The church was crowded; half the town was there, and they were all hushed and solemn, and the men in suits clasped their hands behind their backs and were grave as the night. Tilly said Ada should go and say she was sorry for Toby that his father had died.

The problem was that Ada didn't believe Tilly about accidents, about life just being like that. Ada believed that everything that happened was purposeful and that there was mystery so deep and full of intent that it could be sensed, not spoken. These were the signs the world offered up. Silence was always full of meaning. In the church she'd looked up at Tilly and wanted to ask her again. Did one thing happen because of another thing, because of the living room? But Tilly had frowned and leaned the weight of that frown on Ada's thoughts, pressing them till they were so limp and shapeless that Ada couldn't speak them. Tilly bent and whispered, "Just think how Toby feels. Let him know you care about him."

Ada wasn't sure if she did care about Toby. She knew she should, especially now. She broke free of Tilly and walked over to the people who surrounded Toby and his mother. She pushed through the dark clothes. Toby stood with his legs crossed over, leaning in to his mother and staring out, as if he was separated from everything. When Ada touched him, he jumped as if waking from a dream.

"Hi, Ada," he said. His face was as soft as a cloud.

"Hi," Ada said. She was so surprised to find Toby was still just a boy with a long face, apart from his hair, which was all brushed and parted on the side, that she forgot the words she had prepared to say. Her cheek itched. The light was muted and the air stuffy with the smell of musty suits. She stared inquiringly into Toby's face for a moment and felt her own face growing hot.

"There's a whole lot of people here," she whispered.

Toby nodded. He didn't look too terrible at all; he just looked like Toby—the aura of death had only touched his hair. But why hadn't Ada said the thing she was meant to say? She opened her mouth to say it, but Toby said something instead.

"I might not go back to school next week."

"Oh," said Ada. She nodded sympathetically. She wanted to tell him she was going to plant new trees where the old ones had died, but the words got stuck inside.

Toby wiped at his eye. Mrs. Layton clasped his head and pulled him into her hip as if to submerge him in a fresh torrent of tears that erupted with Mrs. Aldrich. Mrs. Aldrich hugged Mrs. Layton to her, and Toby was folded into a privacy that didn't include him. Ada backed away. She hadn't had the chance to say she was sorry.

Afterward, when she got home, Ada sat on her swing beneath the elm and drew long pendulum shapes in the dirt with her feet. How would life go on? What would happen to Alice and Toby now that their father had died in the hole with the fox? And where was the soul of Mr. Layton now that it had climbed out of his dead body? Ada sensed that the death of Mr. Layton had fallen like a shadow over the family and maybe over the town too. Soon summer would be over and the hush of autumn would make everything even more solemn.

Tilly came and sat on the bench under the tree. She had a toasted sandwich.

"What are you eating?" Ada knew what it was, she just wanted to hear it in case it made her want some too.

"Cheese toastie. What are you doing?"

"Being sad."

Tilly didn't answer. She never wanted to talk about Mr. Layton. It took ages for her to say anything. She said, "You can't count on life doing what you want it to do."

Ada didn't appreciate these sorts of explanations. They seemed to mean too much and the truths inside them were locked up and impenetrable. She dangled her feet in the dirt and didn't look at Tilly.

"Guess what I did last night?" Tilly said.

"What?" Ada had forgotten that Tilly had a secret that she hadn't yet shared.

"I had sex."

"Oh." Ada felt alarmed.

"I went to Melbourne to see Raff, but he wasn't there, so I went out with his cousin and we danced and then I stayed the night with him."

"Did it hurt?" Ada said.

"Did what hurt?"

"Sex."

Tilly shifted and frowned. "No, not really. I only did it to get it out of the way. It has to happen sooner or later." Tilly was sad too, Ada could tell.

"But I thought you loved Raff." Ada was hurt by this betrayal. She had given over her own secret admiration and let Tilly have it, but Tilly had ruined it by taking it in the wrong direction, and now it wasn't even a love story.

Tilly sighed.

"I did love him. But he wasn't there, and he didn't love me. And I wanted to not care about that. I wanted to stop caring about everything. I just wanted to forget myself. And to show Raff."

"You can't forget yourself, though, because when you wake up, there you are again."

"That's the problem," Tilly said.

There they were—back to where they started, with Tilly emptied of love and Ada swollen with secrets. It was just like the tides and it wouldn't stop. People were always filling themselves up and emptying themselves out again. It was the feeling she had been avoiding all summer. The feeling that life wouldn't stop taking away from her everything she wanted to hold near. And that then it would dump at her feet the life-worn remnants of another tide.

The day before, she had tried to jump on the trampoline with Louis and May but had soon tired of it, and she hadn't even wanted to play the elf game. Ada had never believed the elves were there in the garden, anyway; she had made it all up to entertain Louis and

May. Make-believe games were too little for her, now that William Blake had turned black. Now that the endless hole had triumphed. Now that Toby Layton had been drawn into his mother and taken away. These were big important events, events that would mark a life properly. Elves wouldn't do that.

Ada watched the leaves twirl. Tilly went quiet and watchful too, because the sun-lit elm leaves were a splendor that overtook them.

Tilly stood up and went back inside. She had finished her toastie. There were cockatoos on the apple tree already. Even though the apples weren't ripe. They bit at them, tossed them to the ground, and flew off, squawking, with the pips. They were the larrikins of the sky. Ada didn't run at them to scare them off. It was too late already.

43

Ben was already thinking about footy season. On the field, ducking and weaving through the other bodies like an atom, he felt untouchable. With the girls on the sidelines and the coach rocking back and forth on his feet, and the backslapping afterward in the change room. "Nice work, Bloomo," they'd say.

After the games, he always smoked a joint with Jimmy and walked home stoned. Plenty of girls would come to him just like the ball did. They'd let him undo the buttons on their shirts.

But he'd never wanted a girl for real. It annoyed him a bit. He wished he hadn't even thought of it. He feared there was something he was missing out on. Jimmy thought about one girl, and for her, for Laura Petty, he would do anything. He watched Laura Petty with a fretful sadness because she never showed any interest in him. Ben kissed her one night under the white cedar in the schoolground and she leaned back so willingly, he saw her eyes close. But she was no different to the others. He never told Jimmy; if Jimmy ever found out he would have gone mad with the agony of such a betrayal. He would have rushed at Ben, flailing, punching, yelling, even though he was scrawny. He had the passion of a wild cat. Ben envied him that. If life lacked grit, passion would give him a grip on something, the way he'd thought cheating death would.

That was the problem with the death of Mr. Layton. Everyone else had been so affected by it. Ada still moped. But that was because she took everything so personally. And Martha was full of sorrow too. It was hard to know if it was the fox or Mr. Layton, but she was worse after it all. More needy, more wronged.

But at least Martha bore the death with some dignity. Women could do this better. His father couldn't. He seemed to have lost his mind, rousing from stupefied silences to shout at Ada for nothing, or to leave a room and hide on his own somewhere else. He had even taken to walking with PJ.

And there was Tilly, who seemed focused on leaving. She was waiting for her exam results. The sudden effort she put in to get through those exams was the first time Ben had witnessed any aspiration in Tilly at all. If she had done well, it could set up an expectation. If Tilly could succeed at something, it might mean he should try.

But then again, it probably wouldn't.

44

Martha was bereft. There had been too many departures from her life. Susie had gone and Tilly had moved out, and she missed how it had been. She hadn't even realized she liked how it was until it wasn't anymore. Tilly's absence had unhinged them. The family was like a loose shutter, flapping about in the open air. Even worse was the sense that it would all keep going. Ben would leave next. Ada felt it too—Martha could see that something had seeped from her. She had lost her plump cheeks, her strident little moves, her Ada-shaped plans and intentions. She lay on her bed and read books. The house was quiet, motionless. It was Tilly's fault.

Something had ended for Martha when Tilly left. Her child had gone from her and from all that had grown inside her to accommodate that child, leaving Martha empty, like a seashell. She was obsolete in Tilly's life. Cast off. Her indignation rose. After all that she had given. Martha didn't even have the satisfaction of feeling the job was well done. She felt a secret sense of shame, so secret that, even to her, it had always manifested not as a secret but as an irritation. She was ashamed of the friction between her and Tilly—it always rose up, though she promised herself not to let it. She had failed at motherhood, just as she had failed in all those other ways.

Martha had behaved badly—she knew it. When Tilly's final-year results arrived, Martha had been out shopping. When she arrived home, Tilly was sitting at one end of the kitchen table. Ada was slouched next to her, but she stood up, grinning, and watched Martha dump the shopping on the kitchen bench.

"Guess what?" Ada said, beaming.

Martha began to unpack the groceries. No one offered to help, of course. "What?" she said, turning her back to put the rice in the cupboard.

"Tilly got her results today—in the post. Guess what she got?"

Martha tightened. She had forgotten that results were due. The jars of nuts weren't on the right shelf. No one ever put anything back where it was meant to go. She began to rearrange them.

"All A's," shouted Ada. "Straight A's. She's going to university."

Martha's heart twisted. She kept at her task in the cupboard. She couldn't bear to look at Tilly.

"That's good," she said firmly.

There was a silence. Ada began to move again. Her voice rose up a register. "Mum? Tilly got straight A's." Ada repeated it as if Martha hadn't understood.

But Martha had understood. All those lingering disappointments surged forward. That old pain. Tilly would get the life that Martha hadn't gotten. She turned slowly and bent her head over the shopping basket. "Is that what you want, Tilly? To go to university?" Her voice came out with a cool edge. Martha finally raised her eyes to meet Tilly's.

Tilly's face shone. She stared back at Martha inquisitively, and this angered Martha even more. Tilly could never understand what Martha felt.

"Yes, I'm going to move to Melbourne." She instantly looked at the table, as if this declaration had sapped her of all her courage.

"Well, don't expect your father and me to pay your rent. You'll have to make your own way."

"I know, Mum," Tilly said, laughing like she didn't care.

When Mike came home, Ada rushed up and told him too. Martha watched his reaction. He grinned instantly. He hugged Tilly.

"Well done, poppet," he said, calling her that baby name. He was proud. His face showed that plain, unaffected happiness that he was able to feel. Martha was relieved to see it. He had taken Joe Layton's death so badly. But here he was, grinning.

"Well, let's get out the champagne," he shouted, rubbing his hands together. Tilly leaned like a swan against the table, smiling. Mike did everything a parent was meant to do. It was easy for him. Martha felt the first pricking of shame, but she hurried away from it and found the champagne glasses instead. She wasn't going to be left out of this. She made sure to give the first glass to Tilly, and as Tilly stood there, overwhelmed, tears welling at her eyes, Martha caught a glimpse of the young girl who had been so much easier to love.

45

Ada had seen Raff. He was standing outside the theater with his bike. He came back sometimes to visit his mother. She wasn't going to even speak to him, but he saw her and said, "Hello, Ada." It was nice of him to say hello and to use her name too, because lots of the older kids just didn't bother saying hello. So Ada stopped. She said hello. She couldn't think what else to say and instead of speaking she pressed her finger into the steel ruts of the gate and wiped the dust. Eventually he asked her if she'd like a ride home.

Ada shook her head.

"Are you scared?"

"No." (Had he forgotten how she went down the hole already? She'd nearly died, and he didn't even remember.)

"Okay, then."

He swung his leg over his bike. She might never see him again. And there were things she didn't know that she wanted to know.

"Is your father a gypsy?" she said.

"Apparently my great-grandmother was a gypsy."

"Do you like Tilly?"

He grinned as if he thought it was a funny question. "Did she tell you to ask me that?"

"No. I just asked by myself, because she likes you."

"Does she? She didn't act like it." He didn't look at Ada when he said that.

Ada realized she shouldn't have told, and Tilly would kill her if she ever found out. She turned red and gave the smallest of nods. But she stepped forward and frowned. "I hope you won't give her heartbreak."

"Your sister gives out heartbreak too, you know."

Ada shook her head. She wasn't sure why.

"Here, you have this." He fumbled about in his jean pocket and pulled out a stone that looked like honey gone hard and gave it to her. He rode off before Ada could ask him why she should have the honey stone. As far as she knew, Raff didn't even know she collected stones.

That night she put it under her pillow along with her other special gifts from nature—the green feather, the dead Christmas beetle, and the river stone. But she still couldn't sleep. The window was open and bare. The curtain had fallen and no one had bothered to put it back up because it always fell again when you tried to pull it across. Ada was afraid that something bad was in the garden. The trees creaked. The night swam through the window and came into the room like a river. She got up and pulled the curtain off the floor and climbed on the desk and balanced it precariously across the top of the window. She rummaged in the drawer and found her diary and the torch and read:

After the fire I collected seeds for new trees in the bush. I have to wait for them to sprout and then I will plant them and make a new forest.

This is a promise to Ada, herself, and to William Blake, who is a tree.

She added: *I am awake in the night. The night is in the garden.* Ada read it over. Even though she didn't say everything, like Tilly did, all that was written was true and real and hers. When she read it, it made her feel that the things that happened couldn't be forgotten. If everything was forgotten, what were you? Weren't you all that had happened before? And if you didn't remember it, then you lost part of you too. And instead you would be patchwork pieces of you. Everything else behind her had blurred into floating impressions already. It was falling out of her, like stuffing falls out of an old pillow. She remembered when Tilly went to high school and stopped catching the bus with her, she had been so proud to get on the bus on her own. But she didn't feel like that.

Ada put her hands over her eyes. She was so tired but she couldn't sleep.

46

Ada was sick. Doctor Maise said it was a virus. But the virus never showed itself, not beyond lethargy, lack of appetite, pains. The vagueness of it frustrated Mike. Ada had rarely been sick and always had a healthy appetite, so it was disturbing to see her so limp and disinterested. She got up to watch *Ivan's Midday Movie* and lay silently on the beanbag, eyes fixed zombie-like on the television. Ada was no zombie. Ada was a sprite, a kid who sang songs while wandering barefoot in the garden.

Martha allowed her anything. Her anxiety had brought on a flurry of maternal devotion. She was cooking soups. She hovered about Ada's bedside and bought alternative remedies from the health-food shop. If Martha hadn't been so on edge, Mike would have told her it was a waste of money. But there was no point starting an argument.

The banishment of Tilly hung coldly over everything and, Mike suspected, over Ada especially. But what could Mike do against Martha's inflammable impulses? If he tried to reason with her, there would be an argument. And he did still have to tread carefully. He was a criminal who had, until now at least, gotten away with his crime. But the noose still hung there, waiting, should he trip up. His crime couldn't be erased and the tragedy it had provoked was still fresh. There wasn't a person who hadn't heard about it, who hadn't thought of it in one way or another. Even if they hadn't known Joe Layton, they knew a man had fallen in the mineshaft and it would be talked about long into the future. But Mike was the story's secret villain—he might have been able to push clear of this if his treachery hadn't been witnessed and held deeply yet perilously within his own family. It was reflected back at him daily out of the distant eyes of Ada. For some time, he had lived in fear of Susie returning, and it was an enormous relief to him to see the For Sale sign go up on the Layton house. Even though she, as much as he, wouldn't want their affair exposed, women talk. They tell each other everything. Things Martha revealed to him that had come to her through the river-mouths of other women made him uncomfortable. Once gossip about other people's private worlds had been vaguely titillating or sometimes intriguing; now it just reminded him of how thin the veneer of his own life was.

It was Glenda who had struck open the problem with Ada. Glenda had come to visit. They were having dinner, all of them except Ada, who was in bed.

"How is Tilly getting on?" Glenda asked.

Martha frowned, "We haven't heard from her," she said.

"That's because she's banished," Ben chimed in.

Glenda looked confused. "What? She can't be banished from her own home."

Ben smirked. "Yes, she can."

Martha sighed. "She was very rude to me when she was leaving. She's completely ungrateful for everything we've done for her."

It embarrassed him when Martha said things like that. They had done for Tilly what any parents were required to do. Mike never knew what Martha was referring to when she paraded this line "all they had done for her." Glenda glanced briefly at Mike. She was waiting for him to explain. He ignored the prompt. Glenda gathered her breath and dived in, leaning her large bosom forward.

"She may have been rude, but she's young. You didn't just cut her off, surely?"

"She was rude to me. Dismissive. Since she can't appreciate us, I told her not to come back." Martha was brittle. She seemed to have sucked herself inward.

"But aren't you concerned? She's in the city alone. Don't you want to know how she is? Does she know anyone there who could help her if she needed help? At least tell her to ring me."

Martha colored. She stopped eating. She looked blankly at Glenda and dropped her fork on her plate. "She can ring you if she likes. I don't care."

"She rang me the other day," Mike said casually.

"What did she say?" Glenda asked.

"She said she was lonely."

Martha glared at him. He had shamed her. He didn't care. He even issued a proud snort. It was a noble act, and in such contrast to how he had been feeling that he couldn't stop himself. He went even further. "Of course she can come home."

Ben was astonished. He leaned back on his chair and grinned. Mike would get a roasting.

But Martha had withdrawn. She said nothing.

Glenda took over. "Look, don't you think that Ada is simply grieving for Tilly. I mean you know how she is. Doesn't she still climb into Tilly's bed? It must be a shock to find herself alone."

"She's not alone," snapped Martha.

"She is a bit, Mum. She doesn't have anyone to talk to. She told Tilly everything," said Ben. It was odd for him to pipe up. Even he must have been worried about Ada. But what would Ben know? He hadn't even noticed Martha was on edge. If he had, it didn't affect him. Mike began to feel sorry for Martha. Everyone was against her. Even Ada's illness was against her. And now Ben. But she was so unforgiving. Once she steeled herself against something, her surface was so unflinching, so hard.

Glenda saw it too and quickly steered the attention off Martha. "Anyway, isn't it wonderful Tilly did so well at school. That's a testament to you both."

No one answered her.

Ben said, "Can I leave the table?"

47

Martha had almost drifted into a sort of light sleep, but an image had come to her mind and woken her. The stand of elm trees in the garden where the children played. It flashed in her mind for an instant. It wasn't a disturbing image—she saw those trees every day—yet it had disturbed her. What came before it, what led to it, she couldn't remember. The moon was up, and a pale light fell across the garden. She never slept well on a full moon. Perhaps it was just that. But she sensed a presence in the garden.

Something had stirred up her anxiety. She felt the uneasy feelings of the passing of time—for what she'd felt as soon as she'd seen the trees was the emptiness of them. Where was the little red swing? And where was the patch of dirt beneath it where no grass grew because of the children's feet dragging over it? And the slats of wood that made a platform in the branches and all the mess that kids made: the discarded socks, the emptied plates, cups, hats, Frisbees, tennis balls, PJ's gnawed bones? None of these were there, just the dark figures of the branches sweeping up against the pale sky. The children had gone.

Was it Ada's illness? Or was it Tilly? She didn't want to think about Tilly. Martha had failed her. Is this what the empty trees meant? They looked so much like a memory. Had she dreamed herself forward in time so she could see the poignancy of now, the feeling that there was nothing she could hold forever, that even the trees—with their hundred-year-old trunks, their deep roots, their heights, their solidity—had been passed through, no longer to be climbed over, swung from, lain under, nested in?

Martha wanted to hold her children close. They were what pulled time forward: their bodies charging ahead, their discovering hands digging through, their voices shouting out, their startled eyes growing accustomed to it all. But she couldn't hold them. Tilly was already gone from her and Ben was straining at the leash. It was only Ada who still played in the elms. And when Ada stopped, children would be gone from Martha's life. That would be the end of something vital and tender. There was nothing growing in her life anymore. Was Ada leaving her? Was that the dream's meaning? A family was nothing against the onslaught that life was. A family was too concentrated, too damp, too susceptible to rot.

She wriggled away from Mike in the bed and curled onto her side. He was sleeping well again. Martha had never known him not to sleep well, not until Joe's death. Sometimes she suspected she had been attracted to Mike because his lack of emotion would balance her excess. She had been touched by his distress; it had even restored something of her feeling toward him. He wasn't as mechanical or predictable as she had come to find him. It had been a strange surprise that Joe had meant that much to him. She had been relieved—this show of vulnerability was like a soft bruise that she could tend to. She had wanted to touch that softness, to feel it. And he had rushed away.

If he were awake, she would make love to him. Suddenly it seemed important. And she would take the lead, draw in the sweetness, the density of love, and from it, replenish the brittle aspects of their togetherness.

But she was too tired, too glum, too raw. She rotated as if on a spit, from side to front to other side to back, each time thinking the next position would bring her sleep. Mike's limbs, heavy with sleep, sought her out in the bed and rested heavily on her. This irritated her—she couldn't turn as she liked. No wonder she couldn't sleep. No wonder those elm trees had made her sad. Life rushed through her, with a buffeting force, while Mike's sleep-weighted body pinned her down. He wasn't the only weight; it was other people's opinions, expectations, and convictions, and institutions and history and men and all that greatness with its hidden lies and the accumulation of dust on her floors. Even that.

And there was the constant, unassailable claustrophobia of family. The airless juncture of the couple. They had flung their feelings at each other till they were battered; they had wrung the life out of the smallest coalescence of their emotion and lost any hope of magnificence.

Soon she would be worn away, like those skeletons of leaves you find at the end of autumn, half rotten in the wet ground. Joe Layton was in the ground, and Martha would die one day too. She would turn into a pale old lady with fluttering hands, the temerity in her blue blinking eyes faded into a slight bewilderment. One day she would be just a memory in her children's lives. One day she would not even be that.

48

Vince poked his head into her room, as if he were a cockatoo looking for a plum. Tilly had never had her own space before and this room was all hers and it cost her thirty-three bucks a week. She made a forbidding face. Vince said her mother was on the phone.

"Are you sure?" she said. "My mother?"

"Yes." He was sure.

They all knew about the terrible exile. It had earned her some jungle credibility. She'd had experiences. She wasn't just a freshly scrubbed country girl. She had told them in a careless fashion, so as to sound tough, even a little rebellious. None of them knew that it hurt her as much as it did.

Tilly went to where the phone sat on a stool by the front door. What would make her mother call? Someone must have died. Maybe PJ.

She took a deep breath before picking up the receiver. "Hello?"

"It's Mum. How are you?" Her mother's voice was as far away as a star she couldn't see anymore.

"I'm all right, thanks."

"That's good." A pause. "How is university?"

"It's okay," Tilly lied. She was skipping lectures. "How is PJ?"

"He's the same." Martha sounded sad. "How is your house?"

"Good." Why should she offer her new life for her mother to examine? Tilly held it all in like a child hiding an unfinished drawing.

"Well, who does the cooking?"

"No one cooks much. Sometimes Frank makes pasta. How is everyone at home?"

Another pause.

"Ada isn't well, actually. I mean it's nothing serious. But it just seems to be going on longer than it should."

"What's wrong with her?"

"Oh, she's just not herself. We thought it would cheer her up to see you."

So that was why she was calling. Ada needed her. They would see that she was a good person after all. "So do you want me to come?"

"Yes, would you?" Her mother's voice broke into a childish plaintiveness. Was she about to cry?

"When?"

"Just when you can." There was a long sigh.

"Wednesday?"

"Okay, let me know what train you'll be on. I'll pick you up."

Tilly padded back up the hall. No doubt Vince had been listening. She walked quickly past his room. She went out into the back garden. No one looked after it. The poor garden. There were crimson flowers with yellow-button centers, but you could hardly see them for all the long grass. Tilly began to tug at the weeds.

She thought of her mother's small voice, without its whip edge. She thought of Ada.

She caught the early train on Wednesday. She didn't phone to say which train. She wanted to surprise Ada. She had used the newspaper to wrap up a parcel of things: a bottle of bubble bath, a sea urchin shell, and some Hubba Bubba bubblegum. She had to work out how to tell it all to Ada, how to break it up into the sort of moments Ada would like to hear. It was exciting to tell Ada. Telling Ada was what she always did. She would say, "Guess what?"

Ada would say, "What?"

She would say, "At work I can eat as much spaghetti Bolognese as I want. They throw out buttered white bread rolls and leftover cakes. Straight in the bin."

Ada's eyes would pop with envy.

"And outside there are people asking for money to buy food. Really. This is the city."

Ada would be solemn.

"And in my share house, my room is half the size of ours."

Of ours? It was Ada's now.

"And my window looks onto a fence and I bought a blue cupboard and a secondhand dress with a ruffled collar like a clown. You'd like it. It makes me look like royalty. Don't tell Mum, she'd hate it. The park is full of people walking dogs. I miss PJ!"

It was true, the thought of PJ. His fat waddling form. His obliging face. His unerring love. If only people could love like that.

"I went to the Crystal Ballroom. I wore eyeliner. Everyone there wore black. There was a band. We drank a drink that looked like the sunset. Then I danced till morning. There is no one to tell you when to go home. Imagine."

Ada would grin.

"And I played table soccer in a pub."

"Who won?" Ada would ask.

"I did," Tilly would say.

Did it sound true? She couldn't lie to Ada. Ada would be excited to think of a boyfriend, especially if it was Raff. Raff was Ada's first false dream.

It was so early when she got there, the town was still sleeping; its wide streets were empty and there was only the dimly lit bakery and the smells of baking bread. The morning was hers. The town's bones were bare. She walked up the middle of the road just because she could. There was the church in golden sandstone, with clambering piles of shrub and winding paths, all leading upward.

Something had shifted for her in that church at Mr. Layton's funeral. Or perhaps it hadn't, perhaps it was just that the solemnity of the occasion made life so luminous and fleeting that she had wanted to align herself with its mystery, with its light pouring through the high windows and slanting across the bowed heads and the backs of the people, as if holding them in joint reverence.

The limits of her world crammed beneath that beam of light at the funeral of Mr. Layton. What had struck her was the way those lives were so entangled, so caught in the threads of other lives, so that they moved not by their own impulse but by imperceptible communal patterns. It was what steered everything forward. But it suffocated too. It pressed her into the shape the world wanted of her. Mr. Layton's body lay in the coffin—the whole effort of a life, all its labor and goodness thrown down a hole. Didn't it waste that sort of sanctity, that effort?

She had experienced a sudden social claustrophobia and had had to get clear of everyone. That was when she saw Daisy. She was stealing away. Tilly watched her. A solitary woman, pulling a sun hat over her face as she moved into the distance with an uneven, faltering step. It seemed to Tilly that Daisy was not walking musically but was stumbling, while the hat was failing to protect her. Even someone as spontaneous as Daisy wasn't inured to sadness.

And Alice had gone away. She missed Alice more than she could have realized. For her the town was just a place full of vanished hopes and hurts. All that had to stay behind her now.

There was the old house sitting on the hill, as if guarding her old life. PJ came toward her. His whole body wriggled. She knelt to him. "Oh, PJ," she said. "Old PJ." His silent, steady love, unquestioning as a worn old sock waiting in the drawer.

PJ had come from the pound, already with his name. No one knew what it stood for. Ben said it was short for Peter Jackson cigarettes. But Ada said it was short for pajamas, and Tilly believed her.

Tilly went to the kitchen door. She pushed it open. Everyone was still asleep. She crept quietly to her old room. Ada turned in the bed. A smile broke across her sleep-squished face and her eyes welled with tears. Tilly laughed, and she hopped on the bed and gave her a kiss.

"Don't cry, Snug. I'm home."

"But did Mum say you could come?" Ada sat up and wiped her eyes.

"Yes, she rang me. She said you were sick. What's wrong with you?"

"Did Mum say I might die?" Ada looked eagerly at Tilly.

"No, of course not. She said you hadn't gone back to school, though."

Ada caught Tilly's wrist and tugged it. "Well, I might die. You never know."

"Look what I got you." Tilly pulled the parcel out of her bag and pushed it into Ada's hands. Ada held it on her lap thoughtfully. Her lip trembled.

"I thought you were never coming back again."

Tilly took Ada's hands and began pulling the clench out of them.

"Well, even if Mum had said no, I still would have come back to see you." It was a paltry offering, she knew—had she even thought of visiting Ada? She had been too busy living her new life. Maybe Martha was right. She was selfish. She squeezed the soft little hands, urging her presence into them. Ada wasn't selfish.

"Why can't I live with you in Melbourne?" Ada said.

"Mum wouldn't let you. I can't even cook. And what about PJ? He would be so miserable without you—"

"You don't want me to come!" Ada drew her hands back.

"It's not your time yet, you're still a kid." Tilly groped for something reasonable. "Remember Evie and her little dog, the one that can't see?"

"Elmer," Ada said.

"I'm like Elmer. I'm just bumping along, trying to find a way. I need to find my way before I can show you anything."

Ada shook her head and whispered, "Evie already knows the way—she just lets Elmer think he is leading because it makes him feel important."

"That's what I mean. You have to let me feel important for a while and find my own way."

There was a moment of quiet. Tilly had lost something that Ada still had. Ada was still herself.

Ada eyed the parcel on her lap. Slowly she began to open it. She laid out the things one by one. She lifted the bubble bath to her nose and felt the prickly surface of the sea urchin shell. Her movements were deliberate, circumspect. It was unsettling. Where was the old Ada who rushed headlong into everything? She was like someone trying to create an answer by adding one thing to another. As if the substance of things could hold out against the falling away of beliefs. Poor Ada—too young and true to ignore the changes that upturned the long-lived silent direction of the heart.

Tilly wanted to hold her close, to be submerged again in the familiarity, the warm drowsy breath of childhood, of all that had passed and all that had stayed, still caught in the gaps between them. Right there between her and Ada and the large trees that leaned in the sky toward them.

Ada took all the presents and put them on the floor. She began to cry.

"Now, move over. Don't you want to hear about my new house? And how I went out dancing?"

"All right," Ada conceded solemnly and wriggled into the bed.

Tilly meant to sound strong and safe and tidying up everything, but she didn't sound like that at all. She curled up behind Ada and pulled her in close, breathing in their half-lived lives.

"You be little spoon," she whispered.

49

Ada and PJ went together to the burnt patch of bush. PJ plodded, and Ada didn't go too fast either, since she had a wheelbarrow and the seven seedlings she had grown from the seeds she salvaged there. It was time to plant them. She wanted to communicate this all to William Blake, who had survived the fire in part, which is why she stood for a moment there, showing off the seedlings. There were tiny smoke-blue shoots climbing his branches.

The canopy was gone. Ada could see the fullness of sky everywhere. She could see the hills behind and if she stood up she could even see the glint of a tin roof that was the Laytons' old house. She still thought of it as Toby and Alice's house, even though it belonged to people Ada didn't even know. No matter how Ada looked back at the summer, she couldn't help feeling that something had reared up, a sort of force that came right up out of the earth and flung everything off balance. She partly blamed the old windmill, since it had stood like a sentinel at the beginning and end of everything. It had jangled loudly with a satisfied sense of portent and gloom, and it was as silent as the air. What had come up must have come out of the old windmill's hole and gone back inside it too. It had dragged the truth so far inside that no one could see it anymore. Bones had filled the hole; the hushed, gone-away bones of the past. The withholding of things had gone against the telling of things, and the clash of telling and not telling unleashed a violence, as pressing and as mighty as the sun. Only Ada had the memory of it, a secret stamped on her.

Summer, when it went, took the hot whiff of sky and the stench of secrets with it, but something had sunk so deep within her that it had transformed itself, like faraway bones and burned trees, into the strange and careless agitation of her soul.

Ada stared up into the burgeoning new shoots of William Blake and began to sing him her traveling-along song: "Did you ever come to meet me, Farmer Joe, Farmer Joe." She stomped out a circle to help her decide where she would dig the holes. PJ lay in the shade and watched her with one eye. After a while she tired of her one line of song over and over again and wished she could remember how it went on. That was what she wanted to think about. Not the way the summer had gone.

There was no reason why time, instead of stopping, could not also go around in circles like she was. Like the sun did. And the moon. And PJ, when he was about to lie down. If time kept always marching away from you, you had to run after it and keep up or you would be left behind like that old deathly windmill, rotting over the hole. Ada didn't want to be nothing.

The way she saw it, the new Ada Bloom was beginning. Her trees were beginning too. William Blake was regrowing. There would be a new forest to go along in. Time would not run away from her there.

She straightened up and began to skip. What she needed most of all was a new traveling-along song. Soon she would be in double figures. All she had to do to keep going was what she had already done to get here. Tilly had sent her a card with a painting on the front that was just colors, like pools of water, bleeding into each other. Like time slipping from one moment to another. Ada would tell Tilly that was what it was on the telephone. In the meantime, she would look after her trees. She would pat them down in their holes and she would bring them water. And she would warn William Blake that she would now also be reading novels.

READER'S GUIDE:

1. Why do you think Martine Murray chose to open the book with the scene of Ada and the windmill? What does the windmill come to symbolize for Ada, and within the context of the book as a whole?

2. Sisterhood plays a big role in this novel. How does Ada's relationship with Tilly change over the course of the book, and what do these sisters learn from one another?

3. In what ways do the expectations for, and of, Tilly differ from the expectations the Bloom family has for Ben? How does this difference affect the relationship between these two siblings?

4. What does it mean in the context of this book to "grow up"? How do you see the various characters growing?

5. How are weather and the natural world used in the context of this novel? How do they connect with what the characters are experiencing and feeling?

6. What role does voice play in this book, and how does it feel particular to each character? Are there certain voices that stand out to you?

7. Which characters in this novel would you say are trustworthy? How do the secrets they keep drive the plot forward?

8. In chapter twelve, Tilly notes that "Martha's whole life was a performance, with men as the audience." Would you agree with this characterization of her mother? Are there moments in which Martha or other characters seem to be "performing" certain roles that might differ from who they actually are?

9. How does the small-town setting influence the goals and aspirations of the main characters? In what ways does this setting inform the plot of the book?

10. Do the books Ada reads shape the way she sees and approaches the world? Are there particular books you loved as a child that similarly impacted you?